THE TREE OF LIGHT AND FLOWERS

ALSO BY THOMAS PERRY

The Butcher's Boy

Metzger's Dog

Big Fish

Island

Sleeping Dogs

Vanishing Act

Dance for the Dead

Shadow Woman

The Face-Changers

Blood Money

Death Benefits

Pursuit

Dead Aim

Nightlife

Silence

Fidelity

Runner

Strip

The Informant

Poison Flower

The Boyfriend

A String of Beads

Forty Thieves

The Old Man

The Bomb Maker

The Burglar

A Small Town

Eddie's Boy

The Left-Handed Twin

Murder Book

Hero

Pro Bono

THE TREE OF LIGHT AND FLOWERS

A Jane Whitefield Novel

Thomas Perry

THE MYSTERIOUS PRESS
NEW YORK

THE TREE OF LIGHT AND FLOWERS

Mysterious Press
An Imprint of Penzler Publishers
58 Warren Street
New York, N.Y. 10007

First Mysterious Press edition

Interior design by Lia Kantrowitz

Library of Congress Control Number: 2025942840

ISBN: 978-1-61316-729-8
eBook ISBN: 978-1-61316-730-4

10 9 8 7 6 5 4 3 2 1

Printed in the United States of America
Distributed by Simon & Schuster

To Jo Perry, the brilliant writer I married 45 years ago.

THE TREE OF LIGHT AND FLOWERS

In the beginning before there was any earth, there was a world above, in the sky . . . There was no sun or moon or stars; instead, there was a great tree that shed light half the time and half the time kept dark, so that the sky-beings had a kind of night and day.

. . . The youngest of the four brothers took the tree down to the ground. Then the whole tree, roots, trunk, branches, and leaves, plunged through the hole . . . When they came to the place where the tree had stood, they saw only the hole in the plain. The man-being stood at the edge of the pit and looking down saw a light. He called to his wife, "Come and look. Sit down by me." So she did. Then he blessed the tree that had fallen through the earth for the new creation and he blessed the young tree that remained. While they sat there and gazed at the light below, an air came up through the hole in the earth, very tender, and they heard the sound of the south wind, which is the air of life. And from this air she conceived a child.

He said to her, "Do you see plainly the light below?" She answered, Yes."

"There shall be your new home, on a new-created earth below, and you shall be the mother of the earth-beings," he said. And he pushed her off the edge of the pit and she fell through the hole in the sky.

—*The Death and Rebirth of the Seneca*, by Anthony F. C. Wallace, Vintage Books, 1972

1

The early spring morning was perfect, still cool but with enough sun to show that the western New York winter had lost its bite. There were thin remnants of snow in the deeply shaded spots near buildings, but crocuses were already poking green unopened leaves like spears through some of them.

Jane drove along Sheridan Drive and turned into the vast parking lot of the Amherst Commons. She checked her mirrors to see what the next two cars to turn in looked like. Black Chevrolet sedan. Red Toyota SUV. She took a left turn up the third aisle and looked in her mirror again. Neither car had followed. The first one, the one she had paid most attention to because there were two young-looking men in it, had parked by the fitness place. The woman in the red SUV didn't appear to be much of a threat, but Jane didn't appear to be a threat either, so she watched the woman as she parked at the DSW shoe store and went inside.

Jane followed her ritual of scanning the rest of the parking lot to see who else was in it. Police cars were neutral or good. Civilian cars parked and containing more than one man were worth a second look. Vans with their business names on magnetic signs instead of painted were to be avoided, and any car that had its trunk lock punched out was probably stolen and might be there for a bad purpose. She saw none of those, and nobody who appeared to know her or be looking at her for too long. She parked in a row near the Wholesale Warehouse, got out of her car, took a shopping cart, and entered the store. She instantly resumed her scanning, but saw nobody who raised her suspicion.

Her days were all special days now, and she intended to make practical use of this one. This was a time to stock up. She liked the giant big-box store, which had a no-nonsense look, with wide aisles between the tall steel racks containing large-quantity versions of the staple foods and supplies that families needed. She started with the dense items she wanted on the bottom of her cart—detergents, trash bags, coffee—and finished with things like the soft fruits and eggs on the top.

She joined the checkout line, paid, and was out the door, wheeling her cart to her car. She loaded the trunk with her usual efficiency, making sure every item was in its ideal spot, with frozen food keeping the meat and fish cold, and the big heavy items from the bottom of her cart holding the other things hemmed in place.

Jane returned the cart, got into the driver's seat, and made her way to the Sheridan Drive exit. She pulled out into traffic and headed for home. As she did, she saw unexpected motion in the corner of her eye. She looked into her mirror. Another car was pulling out too, but it was out of turn, and someone behind it was offended, and leaned on his horn. She couldn't see which car had honked, but she could see the first car very well. It was the sedan she had seen before, with the two men in it. Could she have taken long enough for those two to have finished a workout?

She returned her attention to the road ahead. Sheridan was a busy thoroughfare, with businesses and major intersections. She slowed slightly to put some more space between her and the car ahead. She heard the sound of an engine accelerating behind her and saw the black car had pulled out of the left lane to straddle the double lines, coming from behind fast. Was the driver trying to evade somebody with a case of road rage, or was it something worse? Had those men committed a crime? Could they have been looking for her?

Jane looked for a chance to switch to the right lane and pull off Sheridan into a lot. She saw her opening and veered into the right lane, but so did the car in front of her, and then it stopped abruptly partway in the entrance to the lot. Jane stomped on her brake pedal and managed to screech to a stop, but the car behind her slammed into her, pounding her car into the right rear side of the other car, spinning her around and into the left lane, which was where she was when the black Chevrolet hit her. Her airbag burst open, pinning her in the seat.

Things had happened so fast that there had been only about three seconds of loud impact bangs and then trailing sounds of scraping metal and broken glass as the motion ended. There was a moment of curious silence so profound that Jane wondered if she had lost her hearing. She undid her seat belt, felt for her purse, opened it, found the pocketknife in the zippered pocket, opened it, and stabbed the airbag twice to deflate it. She saw the cubes of broken safety glass all over the interior of the car, reclined her seat as far as it would go, and crawled to what remained of the back seat, pushing the jagged remnants of the rear window's glass away with her purse. She climbed out over the bent and sprung trunk, and slid down the side of the car to the street.

She stared at the windshield of the black Chevrolet, and saw the milky impact marks in front of each seat that looked like pounded ice. There was blood in the centers of both, but the two men were not visible. She came closer.

She walked along the side of her car to the side of theirs. Jane realized she had been right. They were gone.

She stepped to the car that had stopped in front of her, and looked in. The woman in the driver's seat was sitting with her hands on the steering wheel, staring straight ahead. Jane leaned in, and said, "Are you hurt?"

"Me? No," the woman said.

"Her?" It was a male voice, behind her. She turned to look. He was a cop. "I think you're losing your water, ma'am."

Jane already knew the cop was right. He lifted a handheld radio. "One Zebra sixteen, we'll need one more ambulance at the Amherst Center."

There seemed to be only a minute or two before the pain arrived, and that worried her. Everything was happening too fast.

◆

While Jane was lying in the ambulance, she heard the doors slam, and felt the vibration of the engine, and then the movement. Thoughts flooded her consciousness.

She remembered that at first she had not really considered marrying Carey McKinnon, and a child was far from her mind. She had known Carey in college, and when he had shown up at her door years later, she had been glad to see him. By then he'd completed medical school and residency and had just accepted a new job at Buffalo General.

They resumed their friendship, and in time she had allowed herself to love him. She had been happy having an intimate relationship with him, perfectly willing to continue indefinitely, but refused to marry him. How could she? She wasn't the business consultant he thought she was. She was a guide who took people who knew they were about to be murdered and made them disappear.

Carey had asked her again and again. She had realized after a year of his pestering that she loved him enough to make one more person disappear. The guide Jane Whitefield would vanish. She would be Mrs. McKinnon, the loving wife of a surgeon in Amherst, New York.

Sometimes their life together would go quiet for a while. After one such quiet stretch, Jane and Carey had decided it was time to have a baby.

At first, they were confident that if they took no action to prevent a pregnancy, it would simply happen. That confidence eroded. Every month there was probability, then possibility, and then disappointment. Carey had turned them both over to the specialists for an explanation and a cure, but they all came up with the same result—no physical problems detected in either of them, and no explanation for the infertility.

She had thought long and deeply about babies each month. She had listened to the doctors, and then had begun reading the scientific papers published about various aspects of the problem. It was later, after Carey was asleep, that she thought with other parts of her brain.

Her ancestors, alive in her mind, would have said that there were men's things and women's things, and she had spent the years after college doing men's things. What she called being a guide was essentially leaving home to go into the forests to war. Had she triggered some unspeakably ancient bit of nature that made her less womanly, unable to conceive? The old people had believed the ideal state of the universe was Sken:nen, a Seneca word which meant both health and balance. Or maybe the years of using medicine to prevent conception had somehow changed her permanently. The universe was complex, and actions had costs— consequences and side effects that people didn't always understand.

Jane had chosen a room in the big old McKinnon house and furnished it for a baby, bought baby clothes, toys, and supplies, and hung an antique

Seneca cradleboard on the wall. It was an heirloom made of bent wood and covered with black cloth embroidered with a tree covered in bright yellow flowers. The design represented the great tree that brought light to the Sky World before there was an earth. When the tree was pushed over, a hole appeared where its roots had been and pregnant Sky Woman fell through, bringing with her the first human life to the world below.

One day, after years of trying and failing to become pregnant, Jane took the blankets and little socks and T-shirts and one-piece outfits, folded them into the drawers of the dresser, took the cradleboard down, wrapped it up again in acid-free archival paper, and stored it in the attic. After that, her old, dangerous life gradually drew her back.

In one particularly awful experience she was injured and left barely able to breathe. She was hospitalized for weeks. After Jane left the hospital, she spent months in mandatory rest and recovery in the McKinnon house. While summer ended, and the western New York fall turned the leaves fiery bright and the sky dark, and then winter winds battered the trees and left them bare as skeletons and froze the world solid, she was getting her health and strength back. But something else had happened. Jane had become pregnant.

The doctors were no more able to explain why it had happened now than why it hadn't before. For most of her pregnancy she still ran as she had since she'd learned to walk, still did tai chi, lifted weights, punched the heavy bag. In time, the runs became walks and swims. The martial arts became yoga, and she thrived. That was true until this morning, when she decided to make a trip to the big-box store.

◆

The ambulance was moving fast, and the siren was blaring. Every bump on the pavement seemed to be jarring her spine, and she was beginning to feel contractions. During her lifetime, Jane had learned to know pain. She had trained herself to study it and locate what was hurting and make herself tolerate it. As the ambulance zigzagged through the stopped cars, she began to understand this was going to be different. The contractions did not stop for long spaces of time and reappear. They were much more frequent than she had expected, and each one was stronger than the last. She worried about what that meant. Was she losing the baby?

She realized there was no way they were taking her to Buffalo General, the hospital where Carey worked. What was the closest to here? Probably Kenmore Mercy on Delaware, or even DeGraff Memorial in North Tonawanda. She could call him and let him know where to go.

In another couple of contractions, she could feel the ambulance making a right turn, slowing to bump-bump over a big obstruction and then swing to the left and back up. Strong hands pulled her gurney out of its berth, through the door of the ambulance so she was staring up at the sky, past doors that were automatically huffing open, and into the hospital.

The pain grew. It was everything other women had said it was. It made sweat appear on her forehead and made her feel as if she was being torn apart. People walking beside the gurney were fiddling with her, pulling back her sheets and talking to each other. "Take her right to Maternity. Room 5 is open."

This time there was no fighting back, nothing to do but accept what was happening and hope it would end with the baby she had loved unseen for months.

She had taught herself not to cry out when she was hurt, because when it had happened before, letting the pain out with her voice would have been speaking to an enemy, like shouting to him, "Here I am, too weak to save myself. Come finish me." This time there was no fighting back, nothing to do but accept what was happening. She heard a female voice say the word "Epidural?" but another replied "Not enough time."

The pain grew more intense and she strained to help the baby out, felt the release, and heard nurses murmuring and oohing to reassure her, and then the loud, screaming cries as the baby reached the world.

"Nya:weh-sgeh," she said in Nundawaono, the ancient language: "Welcome." "I've been waiting for you for so long."

◆

Jane Whitefield had been born and raised in a home that people called traditionalist, meaning that in these families, children were taught the stories Senecas had been telling each other forever, their ways of looking at the world, in the language they had always spoken. Their religion was the old one, last modified by the visionary Handsome Lake during the years following his prophetic dreams in 1799, and still repeated in each of the Seneca reservations in New York and Ontario on a rotating basis. If asked, as a modern woman she would have said she believed only in science, but advocated preserving the rich culture she'd inherited. At other times, maybe in one of the hard, dark, terrifying places where she'd been, she might have given a different answer.

Jane's family followed the custom of giving a baby an English name and a Seneca name, often called the "real name." For the English name, people tended to avoid the names of Christian saints. Jesuits had introduced Christianity to some of the northeastern nations in the 1600s, but they'd only lasted a short time with the Senecas before the Senecas killed them. Jane and Carey had talked about the English name, and decided on May Dawn McKinnon.

The Seneca name was always, ideally, the reuse of a name that belonged to the mother's clan, a name that had been passed down from someone who had died. The names belonged to the clan, so Jane could not simply take one. The proper way was to wait for her clan leaders to decide.

On the third day after May was home, Jane heard a knock on the front door. She went to the bedroom window to see who was at the door. She looked down at Ellen Dickerson, clan mother of the Agata:yonih, the Wolf clan. Jane's father had been Snipe clan, and when he had brought the blond, blue-eyed woman he had met in New York City back to his world and let it be known that they wanted to marry, the women of the Wolf clan, part of the opposite moiety of the nation, had adopted her, the traditional way to do things. When Jane was born, she was a member of her mother's clan.

From her upper window, Jane saw other people who were members of her clan, male and female, a dozen of them—not counting Ellen's husband, Ray Dickerson—Wallace Golden, the chief who represented the clan and attended the Haudenosaunee Six Nation events, and Jane's friends the Caines, and Jimmy Sanders and his mother Mattie. Jane made her way downstairs carrying May and opened the door. The singing began before Ellen took her first step inside. It was a song that the people had sung on occasions like this for hundreds of years, maybe thousands, to welcome a new baby. It was impossible not to hear and feel the joy, and not to see the assembled people as at once themselves and their most distant ancestors. Jane kept herself from crying when the time came to bestow May with her real name, the one the Creator would know her by. It was Dayeno onyo: k, which meant "people will be thankful." To Jane that sounded like an auspicious name, and she was thankful.

2

Magda Kaprovna lay in her prison bunk until it was her turn to go for a shower. She got up and walked to the showers, slipped the baby blue top and dark blue uniform pants off and hung them on an empty hook. She was slender, just under six feet. If she had been born somewhere other than Russia, she might have been a model. She wasn't a model. The pale skin of her body had bluish tattoos done for her by a woman in her first Russian prison, a forger and counterfeiter. There was a picture of Mary and baby Jesus on her back that was a good luck token among the vors. *Vor* meant "thief," the term professional criminals called themselves, regardless of their specialties.

There were two eight-pointed stars on the fronts of her shoulders, an emblem of the Bratva, or Brotherhood, she belonged to. And just below her hip bones, equidistant from her groin, were two American hundred-dollar bills, so perfectly done that they looked as though they could be peeled off and spent. Most of the California women who populated the prison had no idea what her tattoos meant. Many of them had tattoos of their own, mostly hearts, flowers, butterflies, or the names of the boyfriends who had gotten them in there by talking them into holding drugs, guns, or merchandise, or driving cars.

Magda stepped onto the wet tile and ducked under a showerhead, letting the warm water rain down on her, soak her long black hair, and stream down her spine. When a younger woman left one of the showers on the other wall, Magda spun, crouched, and had both fists up in an instant, although it was hard to know how she had even seen the woman behind her.

She saw the young woman's light brown hair, her body with a Madonna on her stomach holding the baby up as though to let it suck on her left breast, and two small eight-pointed stars on her shoulders. She relaxed and stepped back under the water. The young woman moved close, their faces almost touching, and said in Russian, "They sent me to find you."

Magda asked, "How did they get you to the right prison?"

"You had robbed a jewelry store in Modesto, so I robbed a jewelry store in Modesto."

"Thank you. You could have been shot."

"I wasn't, and they'll get me out—mistaken identity."

"What do they want?" Magda said.

"There was a house where all the people died of smoke inhalation except you. There was a woman you had captured."

"What about her? She died too."

"Members of the Bratva watched for a long time—a couple years—and there was never a funeral for her. Never an obituary. They told me she's not dead."

"They're sure?"

"They're sure." She took a step away and smiled. "Don't you trust them?"

◆

Magda was wearing the same uniform that she and all the other prisoners wore during the three years she had been locked up in the California Institute for Women in Chino—baby blue top and dark blue pants. This time she had a chain around her waist with handcuffs attached to it so she couldn't even bring her hand up to brush the hair out of her face. She had to flip her head to swing the hair behind her like a horse with a mane.

She wasn't dissatisfied. This place was a resort compared with the places where she'd been locked up in Russia. But time was not about how she felt while it was passing. It wasn't about feeling at all. Time was a thing, solid and unchanging as a row of bricks—something that governments measured in midnights. Magda had been sentenced to be deprived of 1,825 midnights. Someone in the system had placed her name on a list of inmates who were foreign nationals and had served enough of their sentences to be deported right away. She hoped that she was not really being sent back to Russia, but all she could do was what the Brotherhood wanted.

When the male guards had loaded her into the van to be driven to the airport, the short, bulky woman in a uniform she hadn't seen before looked at some papers and said Magda Kaprovna was going to board a United flight from Los Angeles to New York, then another to Istanbul, and then a Turkish Airlines flight from Istanbul to Sheremetyevo International Airport in Moscow.

Magda could tell that the woman considered this to be a routine deportation, because her face was expressionless as a welder's mask, so Magda remained silent and pretended to be unaffected too. She remembered that her first flight to this country had been over ten hours. This trip sounded much longer. She had spent most of her life as a thief, so she knew that a female thief could not succeed through aggression. She had to be patient and watch and listen, to perceive openings and use them, not try to force things open.

At the airport, she was escorted to a small, featureless room with no designation on the door, and given street clothes to wear—a white pullover shirt, a sweater, and black jeans—probably to avoid drawing the attention of other passengers. She was escorted to the plane by a pair of marshals, a man and a woman, and sat in the middle seat between them. They stayed with her for the layover at JFK, and then the second flight.

She flew to Istanbul Airport sitting between the two, except when she went to the airplane bathroom and the woman went with her and stood leaning on the little door so Magda had to knock to get out.

At Istanbul they handed her over to two Russians, a woman and a man. Those two walked her to a boarding gate where there were no airline people visible. They opened the door, walked her along the twisting Jetway tunnel, unlocked her handcuffs and removed them, took her through the hatch, then down the aisle to the tail of the airplane, where there was another open hatch. There was a staircase with wheels pushed up against the fuselage where workers were restocking the galley's supplies. The man and woman conducted her out through the hatch to the tarmac, walked her to a different plane parked three spaces farther, and up a similar set of steps to the rear hatch and into that plane.

The woman said to her in Russian, "The plane leaves in thirty-one minutes. The other passengers will begin boarding in one minute. This is your seat." She pointed to one on the aisle beside her. "Get in it and stay there." Magda obeyed, and the woman handed her an airline ticket and the purse she'd been carrying. Magda took them and waited. The woman said, "Have a safe trip," and then she and the man walked to the rear of the plane and out through the open hatch. In a moment a flight attendant walked from the nose of the airplane, past Magda to the tail hatch, swung it shut, sealed, and locked it.

No escort, no marshal, no police came onto the plane, only regular passengers—businessmen wearing suits, old women carrying cloth valises that were nearly bursting, younger women with children whose dark, shiny eyes viewed Magda with curiosity and suspicion. This was clearly the leg of the trip that would bring her back to the United States. She sat back and relaxed.

3

The girl's legal name was Clare Markham, and that was the name the law enforcement officers of the State of Oklahoma would use to look for her. She had the sense to get out of Oklahoma on the day she learned they were blaming her. She plugged in her phone charger and left her phone under her bed, and walked over to the house where her best friend, Allison Thompkins, lived and asked Allison to drive her east across the state line.

The Seneca-Cayuga Tribal Statistical Area was right up in the northeast corner of the state and was home to about five thousand people. If you were in Oklahoma and needed to go toward the original Seneca country, that was where you wanted to be to start. Some Senecas and some Cayugas had moved to what was going to be Ohio in the mid-1700s. Later, when history had shaken up most of the east and blown the people west into what was later called Indian Territory, this was where they ended up, with a random sampling of friendly tribes and enemy tribes and tribes that they had never known existed. It was not a bad place—not a vast forest like Ohio still was in those days, but green, with a big lake called Grand Lake O' the Cherokees.

Clare and Allison took turns driving eastward, and Allison kept going as far across the state line as she could, which was all the way to just south of Joplin, Missouri. She stopped there and called the restaurant where she worked, said she had a COVID infection, and kept going all the way to St. Louis on Route 44.

They slept in the car and then moved on when Allison's phone alarm went off at 5:30 A.M. They went to a diner to use the restroom and then shared a big plate of pancakes and sausage before they split up. Clare told Allison that she would always remember her, and anybody else who would ever become her best friend would only be a stand-in for Allison.

As Clare watched Allison drive off, she knew that she would never see her again. This reminded her of the deaths in her family. Once she lost sight of them, people weren't coming back, so it was best to turn your face forward as soon as you could manage.

Clare had not traveled alone long distances from Oklahoma before, but she'd heard that the best way was to take a bus. She took a city bus to the Greyhound station at South 15th Street, looked at the schedules, and went to the window to buy a ticket. It was before noon and nobody was in line so she asked the woman in the window her questions.

She learned that the bus trip to Buffalo was 660 miles, that it usually took a whole day and fifteen hours, and that it was going to cost her a hundred and nine dollars. Clare could hardly believe how cheap it was. She wanted to get on the bus right away before they raised their prices. The next bus was not going to leave until 1:15 A.M., and there would be five stops with changes of buses and drivers: Springfield Transit Center at 5:00, Memphis Bus Station at 4:00 P.M., Nashville at 5:10 P.M., Cleveland at 11:20 A.M., and Buffalo at 4:35 P.M.

She was going to have to wait a long time to even start. She sat on a bench in the station for a while, leaned on her backpack, fell asleep on it, and then woke up with a stiff neck and an angry woman staring down at her. The woman appeared to be about fifty, and she had the badly wrinkled skin of hard drinkers and heavy users. Her eyes had blue irises but whites that were jaundiced.

Clare sat up and said, “Hi.”

The woman said nothing, but sat down hard in the space that Clare had vacated when she’d sat up. The woman glared at her again, but then turned straight ahead. There were about twenty people in the station now, but at least ten other seats that were empty. After a couple of minutes, the woman said in a low voice, so only Clare could hear, “When I was young, a Black girl wouldn’t have taken her seat and mine too.”

Clare got it. This wasn’t the first time. Many Senecas had dark skin, and she was one who did. She said, “Too bad that Black girl couldn’t make it. I’m sure she would have been better company than you.”

Clare realized instantly that she had made a mistake. This awful woman would tell everybody she could corner about the dark-skinned girl who had been rude to her. There just might be somebody coming through here in a day or two asking about a young woman traveling by herself who had done something in Oklahoma and was in a hurry to go far and fast.

Clare knew the best thing she could do was to get away from the station and this woman before she made some kind of a scene that people might remember. She picked up her backpack and went straight out to the street. She walked about a half mile before she passed under the marquee of a movie theater. It had the name of a newish movie that had won some Oscars, showing at 7:00 and 9:30, but she’d seen it already with Allison.

Below that, a smaller line said “Classic Matinee Double Features.” She stopped to look at the antique posters for old movies in glass cases around the ticket booth, like a collection in a museum. Old posters had always struck Clare as odd—touched up so the lips were too red, the eyes too blue, the teeth too white. She saw the names of movies that she had heard of, but knew nothing about, except that they were made years and years ago. *Lawrence of Arabia. Blow-Up.*

She saw that a woman with long red hair was sitting on a tall stool in the ticket booth staring at her phone and typing furiously with her thumbs. Above her was a sign that said "Classic Matinee Double Feature, $8." She liked the price, and didn't feel like walking from then until 1:00 A.M. so she gave the woman the money. She guessed that the movies from a lifetime ago that people still watched might be pretty good, but if they were bad, she could sleep. When she was in the theater, she saw that the dozen other customers were mostly alone, spread out in all sides of the theater, and some were slouched low in their seats as though the idea of sleeping had occurred to them too.

She watched *Doctor Zhivago* with Omar Sharif, a handsome man, and Julie Christie, a pretty woman, but she had no idea what was going on. Then she watched *The Graduate*, which was a bit more comprehensible to her, and at least was set in America. When the matinee was over and the lights came on, she went to the restroom and then came back when the lights were off again, and slept. When she woke, she was alert and hungry, so she left the theater and hunted for food.

She found a place that sold pizza by the slice and had big plastic cups of cola. It was not a pretty restaurant, but it wasn't in a hurry to get customers to clear out, so she was able to stay for hours at a small table along the wall.

She had spent the past two days sitting in a car and then a theater, and sitting that long made her feel tired and stiff and unhealthy, so she stood up for a while, but wasn't eager to go out on the street again. A young girl alone on a big city street was vulnerable to creepy men. She really did not want to have to stab another one.

She walked back to the bus station at nearly 1:00 A.M., and the bus arrived only a few minutes later. The driver opened the door at the front and began to check people's tickets. She had ridden enough buses to know that it was not a good idea to sit in the back. The ride was bumpier there, and if there was a problem with ventilation, that was always where it was worst because the exhaust was back there. She chose a seat five rows from the front next to the window.

When the door whished shut and the bus began to move, her heart started to celebrate in her chest. She was going back to the place where her ancestors had come from, or at least the spot where their particular recipe for DNA had been mixed and formulated by the Creator. Her grandmother had shown her a picture of the place she had taken on some trip, but it was just trees and hills and a lake. That didn't matter now. She would be in Buffalo, New York, at 4:35 the day after tomorrow, and then she could start looking for Jane Whitefield.

4

Magda's flight landed at Pearson International Airport in Mississauga, Ontario. When she walked off the plane and down the Jetway into the terminal, she had the purse the Russian couple had given her at the Istanbul Airport. Inside were a wallet and a genuine-looking American passport in the name of Natalya Kuznetsov. She didn't know if the passport had been stolen from somebody with that name—Kuznetsov was a common name in Russia—or if they had started by putting her picture on a blank document and used Kuznetsov because it was so common. People who did these things didn't explain their methods. The photograph in the front was of Magda, and there were visa stamps in the pages, including a fresh one for Turkey. The passport said she was a naturalized U.S. citizen and her birthplace was Novgorod, Russia.

She walked to the baggage area and stood there waiting while the luggage from her flight began to slide down onto the carousel to be claimed by passengers. She expected someone to walk up to her and take charge, but instead the phone that was in the purse began to vibrate. She took it out and said, "Natalya."

The voice was male. It said in Russian, "There's a green bag on the carousel. Pick it up and take it with you to Canadian customs."

"I see it," she said. She stepped forward to time the approach of the green suitcase and snatch it off the moving carousel. When she had it, she said, "Got it," but realized the man had ended the call.

She went through this airport's version of the universal procedures. When she put the passport on the reader and stood in front of the screen, she was relieved to see that it had accepted her face as Natalya's, but didn't know how the Bratva had accomplished this. Maybe the Canadian database didn't include Americans, and so it didn't already have her face as Magda, and that was why she'd been put on a flight to Canada. So many difficult and time-consuming tasks had been performed to get her out of prison and deported, then diverted from the route to Russia and onto an arc that would take her back to North America.

Her phone vibrated again and told her that the Mobile Passport Control app had been downloaded from the Apple app store. Her name and passport number had been entered. Now she should look at the display, select Pearson International Airport, take a photo of herself, and answer the questions the app asked. She did what she was told, was sent a QR code, and was directed to processing lane 3 for her interview with a Customs and Border Patrol agent.

She knew roughly what the agent's questions would be and began inventing answers. She had been a buyer in a boutique in Boston, but had quit the job to take a trip to Turkey to visit some Kuznetsov relatives. She planned to go back to Boston within a week and begin another job in fashion. When the agent opened her green suitcase she showed no interest, and he shut the lid again, sent her on, and turned to size up the next person waiting in lane number 3.

As she walked into the large, open space of the terminal, she looked at her new phone again. She had decided that the people who had arranged her freedom and travel were almost sure to be the Boston group of the Bratva. They had been the ones to help the Los Angeles branch run by Oleg Porchen first find the woman three years ago. They had lent men to follow the woman to Maine and then down the Hundred Mile Wilderness section of the Appalachian Trail. Magda stepped out of the terminal, moved away from the door to the sidewalk, and waited.

Her phone vibrated again and a text appeared. It was a picture of a car—small and dark blue and very shiny. She looked to her left and in another minute, she could see the blue car coming along the drive toward her, so she stepped to the curb.

The car pulled up in front of her, and she got a good look at the driver while she put her green suitcase into the back seat. He was about thirty years old, fit looking, with a face that reminded her of a boxer—thick neck, nearly shaved head. He had eyes that seemed never to meet hers, but would stare as soon as she appeared not to be looking. She got into the seat beside him and fastened her seat belt while he pulled the car ahead and merged into traffic. She said in Russian, "Hello. Who are you?"

"I'm Vladimir. I'm driving you to your hotel. You will check in with the name Natalya Kuznetsov and stay for two nights. That will give you time to rest and recover and buy the things you'll need. When you check out, you'll take this car with you. It's registered and insured in the name of Natalya Kuznetsov. In the glove compartment you'll find the papers, a driver's license, three credit cards, and some cash."

"Is there a gun?"

"There's an address in Buffalo and a phone number. After you get across the bridge into Buffalo, you'll call the number and drive to the address. There's no reason for you to take the risk of crossing the border with a gun."

She was silent for a few minutes while she took the credit cards, driver's license, and cash he'd mentioned out of the glove compartment and put them in the appropriate places in her purse. Then she said, "Are you from here?"

"No, Boston. We're the ones who had been after her before. She was supposed to be dead, but we've noticed there were never any obituaries or announcements of her death. I don't know why the Pachans went to so much trouble to get you to find her."

"Because I found her the first time. The people who were with me are all dead, including my Pachan and the men he brought with us and the men he borrowed from Boston. When they didn't come back, did you think they went off to college?"

His face formed a skeptical smirk, but he was silent and still didn't look into her eyes. After a while he said, "The hotel isn't far now. It's right up there. You can see the sign."

"It looks like a nice hotel."

"I'll pull the car up at the entrance and wait so you can go and check in. And I know you've been locked in a women's prison for over a year. If you've been missing something, I can stay tonight and fly to Boston tomorrow, or even the next day."

She turned to face him. "You think I'm pretty?"

"Yes. Anyone would." A little smile appeared on his face, but he looked ahead as he turned the car into the driveway, drove toward the entrance, and stopped.

"Thank you," she said, "but you can just leave the car with the parking attendant and go. I can do much better than you."

5

Jane put May into a onesie suitable for the warm spring day, cradled her in her left arm and put the handles of the baby bag over her right, armed the security system, locked the kitchen door and pocketed the keys, then walked to her car and strapped May in the baby seat in the back.

Jane hadn't gotten used to everything about her new car yet, even though it was just a newer version of the one wrecked in the accident the day May was born. As she went to get into the driver's seat she said, "We're going to visit the house where I grew up." She kept up the cheerful tone. "Our oldest friend Jake called to tell me he'd noticed something there."

While Jane would never have taken May with her to the old house like this, she had nobody to leave her with, and what Jake had seen was a very young woman, maybe even a teenager, knocking on the door and then looking in a window. It was probably nothing to worry about—a kid selling candy for her class trip or something.

She started the car and backed out of the long driveway. "My grandfather built the house with the help of a bunch of his friends. He was very young. He was about twenty when he bought the lot, the piece of land. He had just married my grandmother, and he wanted to make them a place to live as soon as possible. In the old days, a husband would always go to live in the longhouse that belonged to the women of his wife's clan. But by then nobody had lived in longhouses for two hundred years. He and grandma were living in her parents' regular wooden house on the Tonawanda reservation. He had just gotten a job in a grinding wheel factory, and it was too far away from the reservation to go back and forth.

"He and his friends came to the lot with shovels and wheelbarrows and began to dig a huge hole for the cellar. It took weeks of very hard work just to dig a hole ten feet deep and thirty feet wide and fifty feet long with shovels." Jane drove along Brighton Road, past the cemetery. In the mirror on the sun visor, she could see May was looking out her window at the acres of green grass and the rows of gray stones. May saw only the beauty of this place. Jane waited at the traffic light at the corner, crossed Delaware Avenue and kept going onto Knoche Road, then turned right onto Military Road, which would change names where it reached the town border to be called Main Street.

"In those days Haudenosaunee boys didn't have enough money to buy all the building materials the way we would now, so he had to do it other ways. He traded his work to the stores and construction companies for things he couldn't make, and did everything he could himself or with his friends. He might go to a building site and work for a certain time in exchange for a keg of nails or some cans of paint." She made it to Main, and turned left on Wheeler Street. When she reached the street where her old house was, she turned onto it and took her foot off the gas pedal.

"Oh, look at that beautiful red bird! It's called a cardinal. They like to come and eat the seeds that Mrs. Ronkowski puts in her feeder. I'll just pull the car over to the curb so we can watch him for a minute or two."

The drive from the McKinnon house in Amherst where Carey had grown up to the Whitefield house where Jane had grown up was about twenty minutes for a person who only wanted to get from one to the other. May's world was not like that yet. May was just seeing things for the first time, and Jane didn't want her to miss any part of it. Jane had memories of the town—every part of it and her father and mother showing her things. She wanted her child to have as many memories as she could give her.

The cardinal flew up into a tall oak tree at the corner of the block, leaving the bird feeder swinging above Mrs. Ronkowski's lawn. A moment later, several dark, short-tailed starlings landed on the lawn below the feeder, where many seeds had been spilled by the birds that had visited. The starlings strutted around down there eating up the spilled seeds. "Those are starlings," Jane said. "Ready to go now?"

She got out of the car and opened the curbside rear door to release May from her car seat. She kept her in her arms and carried her past the old Whitefield house. The house was one of four old two-story houses on the block, all of them narrow, with front porches. The one to the right of hers belonged to Jake Reinert. He had been a close friend of her father, Henry Whitefield, and after her father had died, Jake had assumed a role like an uncle for Jane—not ever prying or telling her what to do, but always saying hello and asking her how she and her mother were and doing things for them. When his trees' peaches or apples ripened, there would be a full basket on the Whitefield porch. Jake's wife, Norma, had baked pies and left one of those sometimes, and Jake's daughters were friends of Jane's. She rang Jake's doorbell, but didn't hear Jake coming, so she looked to see if he seemed to be at home. He didn't.

Jane was frustrated. She had been planning to leave May with him for a few minutes—just as long as it took to check her house—so if there was a problem, May would be safe. She went down Jake's front steps carrying May, and walked across his lawn to her old house, and around the back.

Jane was holding May up close. While Jane had immediately immersed herself in May's world, she didn't inhabit that world. Her mind was still the same, the mind of a woman who had stayed alive for years of taking endangered people away from the enemies who wanted them dead. Death had been near many times. She was alive because she had been alert, and that could never change.

She walked around the house looking for broken windows or doors that had been tampered with. As she walked, she kept talking so quietly that only May could hear. "I wanted you to see this place. It will belong to you some day, because I can't get rid of it. The buyers would go to sleep one night and wake up with some poor scared person at their door looking for the kind of help I used to give before I was your mother, or some bad person. But maybe that's already over and I'm just being overly careful to worry."

When they reached the back steps, she climbed up, looked at the motion sensor light above the door to be sure the bulb was intact and turned on when approached. It did. She had never had an alarm system in this house, for many reasons. One was that if the police were summoned by the alarm service, they would probably find either a runner Jane was hiding or some of the unregistered weapons, traveling money, or forged documents Jane kept hidden there.

She glanced at the big dog bowl near the back steps. Jake had been good about keeping the water in the bowl full and fresh. She had never had a dog here—she had not lived here since she'd married—but she'd made it look as though she had. There were even a few dog toys at random places in the backyard. They were secondhand, ones that had been chewed by a friend's Doberman before he'd died of old age—a couple of tennis balls and a big rubber bone with his teeth marks.

Since she had moved into Carey's family house, she had returned here regularly, staying aware of the state of the place, cleaning it, making sure the timers were turning the lights on and off at the right times, and examining the markers she always left—single hairs on the tops of interior doors for an intruder to dislodge, holding a layer of flour in the palm of her hand and blowing it into the air to form a film on the floor of a dark hallway that would show a footprint, vacuuming the living room carpet to leave a particular pattern.

She unlocked the kitchen door, but didn't step inside. She inhaled. The air had the reassuring stale smell that indicated the house had been closed up since her last visit. There was no movement of the air, probably because she had set the thermostat for her new heating system at fifty. That had made it only turn on during cold weather to keep the water in the pipes from freezing. She stepped into the kitchen and closed the door. She walked past the dining room door and saw the thin layer of flour on the hardwood floor had not been disturbed. Then she noticed that during all the walking, May had fallen asleep. She spread her blanket in the middle of the soft carpet in the living room, set her down on it, and went to see whether the hair she had left on the top of the door between the kitchen and dining room had been dislodged.

She heard something. It was faint and high-pitched, from behind her. She turned to bring her ears into that direction. It sounded like May, but it also didn't sound like May. She felt the hairs on her arms standing up.

Jane took long, fast steps to get to her baby. As she crossed the hall into the living room she saw a standing figure with long hair, a woman facing away, holding May in her arms. The woman started to walk. In an instant Jane's left arm was around the woman's neck. She whispered in her ear, "Turn around and carefully give me the baby. It would take a second to kill you."

The woman said in Nundawaono, "She opened her eyes and was worried because she couldn't see you."

Jane turned her around. She was young—very young—and she had the dark skin that many Senecas had.

The girl was frightened. "I said—"

Jane answered in Nundawaono, "I know what you said." Jane lifted May from her and took a step back, holding her close. Jane could feel her own heart pounding, but May was looking serene.

The girl said, "I would never hurt a baby. I love babies."

"What's your name?"

"Clare Markham. From Oklahoma."

"What do you want here?"

"I was looking for Jane Whitefield."

"You were?"

"Not now. I found you."

Jane stared at her. She could feel her new contentment and feelings of security and freedom crumbling. "What makes you think that's who I am?"

"This is your house and I knew this is how you would be."

"Who told you this address?"

"My grandmother. She met you in Oklahoma. My mother died in a car crash a few years ago, and my grandmother raised me the rest of the way. Her name was Dorothy Woods."

"I remember her. Is she still alive?"

"Not for two years."

"I'm very sorry about that. I liked her. Who takes care of you now?"

"My aunt moved into the house. She pays for everything, and we all split up the work."

"What are you running from?"

"I stabbed a man. He had friends."

"Had. So he's dead."

"Yes. Not before they got him to say who stabbed him. I read somewhere that when somebody says something while he's dying, they always believe it. I wouldn't have denied it anyway. He had dragged me off the sidewalk and wrestled most of my clothes off me and was prying my legs apart, and he'd opened his own jeans and pulled them down a ways. I could see the handle of a knife sticking out of his pocket so I grabbed it. The knife had a spring-assist blade so I opened it with one hand and stuck him in the leg. I just wanted to get away, but it hit some artery and he started bleeding like crazy."

"I'm pretty sure that's self-defense."

"The cops who were in the hospital room when he died wrote down that he said I'd accepted money from him, but really just wanted to lure him into the park to stab and rob him. I didn't even know him. He was a grown man—somebody said he was, like, twenty-six—but they came after me just the same."

Jane said, "Are you smart or are you stupid?"

"I guess I'm not smart about some things, but I'm getting smarter as fast as I can."

"How about getting followed?" Jane asked. "Would you know if anybody could have followed you here?"

"I knew I couldn't get on a plane. I left my cell phone plugged in at home, and got a ride from my best friend, who took me all the way from Oklahoma to St. Louis. I wore my baseball cap and looked down so the camera wouldn't get me and I bought bus fare from St. Louis to Buffalo with cash and gave the name Marcy Hall. My bus didn't leave until 1:30 at night so I stayed away from the station until then. There were five stops, and each one was a new ticket and new bus and driver. It took almost two full days and nights. I think they would have caught me by now if they could."

"You're smart enough."

"Enough for what?"

"Living." Jane pointed. "Sit down there."

Clare sat down on the couch and waited. May had fallen asleep again, so Jane set her down on the blanket and stood in front of Clare.

Jane said, "Before anything else happens you need to know some things. I know you think that because you found me, you're safe. But being here might actually be the most dangerous thing you've done. I've taken a lot of people away from their troubles. Dozens. For each of them, there's somebody out there still searching. After the first few years I've always told my runners that. But as years came and went, there were more runners, more people who wanted to kill them and kill me too, if that was what it took to get to them. It's also gotten harder to keep from getting found. And the world has become a more warlike and dangerous place in general. It makes the things I did for years—getting false identifications and documents and making false histories for people to help them start new lives—nearly impossible."

"You're saying you can't help me?"

"I'm not saying that. I'm making sure that I'm not asking you to tell me the truth without first telling you the truth. Your chances—our chances—are worse than they would have been even three or four years ago. If you know of any other way to go somewhere and be safe, take it. You said you had a public defender. What's his or her name?"

"Monica Fawcett."

"What did she tell you?"

"That the district attorney would charge me as an adult. That they almost always do in a case like mine, where the man was twenty-six and

I was sixteen, because otherwise they would be saying the victim—that's Gerry Fenton, not me—was a child molester. That's something prosecutors wouldn't do. There were other details in the police report that she thought were made up, like if I took money for sex, it would make me seem older to a jury. She said that they would probably start out saying I should get the death penalty, but that would probably just be to make me want to take a deal to plead guilty."

"Did you?"

"I didn't get to court yet. Not real court. My lawyer said I was going to plead not guilty, so they just set bail and a few hours later I was out."

Suddenly May was awake and screaming. Both Jane and Clare lunged forward to reach her, but Jane was there first and scooped her up. She said, "You felt that, didn't you?"

Clare said, "That cry, it's like it grabs your heart."

"She's just hungry," Jane said. "My job." She raised her sweater and her bra and held May to her breast. "Were you the oldest?"

"Yeah. I helped out with the others. Then babysitting and stuff. That cry, it's designed so you can't ignore it."

"How did you get in here?" Jane asked. "I didn't see any broken windows or anything."

"I found this address about five thirty yesterday. Nobody was home, so I walked, found a house about half a mile from here behind a chain-link fence. The fence had a notice on it that said it was a permit for demolition. There was nobody around, so I climbed over, and went in. The furniture was gone, but there were some cardboard boxes, so I slept on a pile of them. I came back here a couple of times to check your house through the windows. This time you were here, and the back door was unlocked."

"How did the rest of the house look to you?"

"Look?"

"Yes. Is anything broken—a window? Does it look like somebody has been living here?"

"It looks like a normal house. Nothing is broken or anything. I was afraid you'd gone on vacation, because your dog wasn't here. Everything else looked like you'd be back any minute."

"Good. Then we can get going as soon as May is finished eating."

"Where are we going?"

"Home."

6

Jane drove along Erie Street toward Wheeler Street, then took that to Delaware Avenue so she could get back to Amherst without taking the expressway. She said, "I'm doing something that I've never done before. May and I live in a big old house that my husband—her father—inherited from his family. His name is Carey McKinnon and he's a doctor, a thoracic surgeon who goes to work every day at Buffalo General Hospital. I trust him absolutely, but you and I are not going to tell him your legal name. Nobody accidentally blurts anything out if they've never heard it. Do you have a name you'd like to use temporarily?"

"I like Kate."

"Kate is not a close friend or a relative or something?"

"No. I think I must have heard it, liked it, and it stuck with me."

"Then it's good. There are popular names that are popular for people, and other ones that are popular for television characters. Kate is both, but mostly a people name. You also need a last name. That should sound familiar but not too popular, and not a name of an Indian family. We want anybody who hears it to think anything but Indian."

"I don't know. Johnson, Jenson, Jackson, Moore? Barnes."

"Moore is good, and Barnes. The others might be too common."

"Kate Barnes. Maybe Katie Barnes sometimes. It sounds more like my age."

"Good choice."

Jane drove for a few minutes, then said, "I should make it clear that I don't usually lie to my husband. I made sure he knew what I was doing before I married him, and he's never told anybody anything. But there are big reasons why I never want him to know anything that would help anyone find someone like you. I want him to be safe, and I want you to be safe."

Jane thought about what she wasn't telling her. Carey strongly disapproved of her life as a guide, and never wanted her to do it again. She said, "I've taken people away from their troubles since I was twenty and in college. Now I have May, and I never intend to leave her."

"Nobody would want you to leave your baby."

Jane looked at her. "Most people who need to disappear would. They're going on a dangerous trip that I've already taken. I know the way. I can do most of the things that have kept runners safe. Even if I can't go, I can help. I can invent a past for you. I can get you set up somewhere that you want to live, get you to look the right way with the right clothes and things. I can teach you."

"I haven't got a way to pay you back for any of that."

"Forget money."

"How can I?"

"We don't have to be like that. We'll be like the old people. They didn't pay each other for things, they gave gifts. What I give you starting today will be a present. Years from now, a day is probably going to come when you're feeling good about life. You're going to remember how scared you were for the past few days, and how vulnerable and lost, and how happy you are on that day. Then, if you feel like it, send me a present."

"That's it? A present?"

"Yes."

"What kind of present?"

"People are different, so their gifts are too. The gifts tell me that they're okay, and that they're still living their new lives, making the most of their second chance. If you're ever in that mood, you'll know what you want to send."

May began to cry again, and Clare spoke gently. "May, May, everybody loves you. Do you think your mother will let me go back and sit with you?"

"Let me pull over," Jane said. She coasted to stop on the shoulder.

Clare got into the seat next to May. She said, "I can tell what's wrong. Here, let me open the baby bag. We'll get you a new diaper and put you back in your seat and then we'll talk." A minute later Jane heard Clare singing in Nundawaono, very softly. Jane pulled the car back onto the road and kept going.

Jane recognized the song. It was music for the dance in the green corn ceremony, one of the annual feasts that the women of the nation traditionally hosted. May was quiet, and she seemed fascinated. A few minutes later Jane turned and drove slowly up the long driveway past the big stone house. She pressed the remote control and the doors of the garage opened. She pulled inside. "Carey isn't home yet, so we have time to prepare. You're going to have to stay with us for a while. Don't forget that your name is Katie Barnes."

"What are you going to tell him I'm doing in your house?"

"He's been after me to hire a babysitter to help me with May. You're the first person I've met lately that I'd trust to do it."

7

Magda walked along the street in front of the building that her boss and mentor Oleg Porchen had built. It was four stories of black glass that reflected the near-constant Los Angeles sunshine. Behind the glass were walls that stretched from the floor to a height of five feet on each level. Inside the wall was a layer of steel plating that Mr. Porchen said was thick enough to stop an anti-tank round. She had known it was probably a lie, but it was good for morale.

New signs on the outside of the building indicated it was now owned by a real estate development company. She wondered why these signs were almost always printed in bright red in America. It made them look so cheap and gaudy, making a brave and visionary thief's stronghold seem clownish.

Oleg Porchen had suffered for this building. It took years to build to his specifications. The contractors were always finding that the materials—first the steel and glass—were not available to exactly match the order. Then it was the light fixtures, and then the faucets. Midway in the installation of the heating and air-conditioning units, there were faulty parts. They couldn't be replaced because those models were about to be discontinued and made obsolete by newly designed and superior models, which would not actually be available for a few months. Mr. Porchen had been in a rage about some aspect of the construction project every day for years. The worst parts had been the basic electrical system, which would go dead, and the pipes, and anything else that had water running through it or condensing in it, would leak. There had been two times when he had changed suppliers or subcontractors, and the old contractor had simply vanished somewhere in the hills, the ocean, or the desert.

One contractor had been in charge of the parking system. Cars driven to the building were supposed to be parked in the two-level lot under the building. The elevators that a driver then took to the floors of the building never worked right, and at times, people had been stranded inside them. This bothered Mr. Porchen because it tarnished his reputation as a host to important visitors, and compromised the security of the building. If he needed to, he wanted to be able to call his people in, like the knights of a medieval castle. He used to ask Magda, "Making an elevator that works. Is that so hard?"

It was. It was also difficult to make the six-screen ultrahigh-definition television system in his office operate. The installers would come and work for a day assembling a new sophisticated system for showing five sets of computer-fed images and a sixth for security zones. Later, when Mr. Porchen would pick up the remote control handset and press a button, it might as well have been a brick. It was dangerous to look foolish in front of his vors, the word that meant thieves, but in most cases implied much more, so after each failure he ordered a larger set of screens. That made it appear that he had simply learned bigger ones were available. He had improved the situation, as great leaders tended to do. The last ones he ordered before his death were eighty-five inches.

Magda stood at the tinted glass entrance of the building, shaded her eyes, and stared into the lobby and the hallway beyond. They were empty. The building had the look of a place that might never be occupied again. She had never quite understood how American businesspeople made the calculation that it was better to tear down a building and replace it rather than make a few modifications. She assumed that, as in Russia, there were so many aspects of a business deal that could put somebody in prison that the simple arithmetic was a thing to be hidden.

She considered trying to find out who owned the company that owned this building now. She had hoped to come here and find some remnant of Mr. Porchen's group operating his businesses. She needed men, and only a few of the people who had worked for Mr. Porchen had been killed in that last failed job. Where were the others?

Had they been killed, imprisoned, or deported, either in one terrible screwup, or one at a time? Had they simply been unable to find methods of monetizing their criminal behavior the way Mr. Porchen had, gone broke, and drifted apart? It was a mystery.

Magda walked away from the building. The Bratva in Boston would be expecting her to work quickly to earn back their investment in her. She had been hoping to bring back men she already knew and could trust. She would just have to catch the first flight to Boston and find some there.

8

"Who's that kid on the porch with May?" Carey said.

"Her name is Katie Barnes, the girl I'm thinking of hiring to help me with May. I'm paying her for two days so May and I can get to know her better."

Carey looked out the window at the girl. She was in the rocking chair holding May in a sling and talking to her, apparently about a rubber ring toy she held up. Their faces were about eighteen inches apart and they appeared to be both talking at once, although May was far too young for that to be true. "How old is she?" he said.

"Old enough. She was the eldest daughter in a big family, so she got years of meaningful experience at baby care. Much more than I had when May was born."

"When I asked, I was thinking about a numerical age. You know, a number of candles on a birthday cake. Something between one and say, sixteen."

"Sixteen," Jane said. "Good eye."

"I do take patients of all ages. Is it even legal to employ a sixteen-year-old?" Carey said.

"Yes. I looked it up. The New York State Department of Labor says no more than six days a week, eight hours a day, between 6:00 A.M. and midnight. We would never come close to having a kid do anything like that. Oh yeah, and we're required to post her schedule where she can read it."

"When I suggested you hire a helper, I was thinking of somebody more like a wise grandma, not a teenager."

"Okay. Got one? Me either. Also, no PhDs in child development, no registered nurses, or retired teachers." Jane faced him. "You know, maybe we should just skip this. I'm fine with raising our child by ourselves. We can save the money for later, to pay for orthodontists, driver training, martial arts, piano lessons."

"And med school, yes. I'm just trying to get used to the idea," Carey said.

Jane went to the refrigerator, took a sheet of paper that was held there by a magnet, and handed it to Carey. He looked it over. "Be available from four P.M. to six P.M."

"That's when I shop and cook dinner."

"How did you arrive at fifteen dollars an hour?"

"I didn't. That's the minimum wage in this part of New York State. We'll pay her more, but we have to look as though we know what we're doing, or the authorities will feel like they have to explain everything. We'll also provide meals and a bedroom."

He put the sheet back on the refrigerator. "If she's okay with you she's fine with me, but I don't need to tell you that if you start to feel any doubt about the decision, I want to know about it right away."

"Of course."

"What about school?" Carey looked out the window and saw Katie playing peekaboo with May on a blanket. "Doesn't she go to school?"

"She's enrolled in a mostly online GED program to finish high school, but I'll be trying to persuade her to enroll in the regular in-person version, at least. That takes us until about the time when May will be ready for preschool. By then Katie will be ready for a new start herself. Maybe college."

"What about her family?"

"A dismal story followed by a few failed placements in foster care. I promised I'd respect her privacy about the specifics." She leaned close to Carey and whispered, "I don't know how much is accurate, but I sense the truth is worse rather than better."

"Okay," he said. "Let me know what I should do."

"You'll figure out the right thing, as you always do. Come on out and get introduced."

They went out the kitchen door, and Jane said, "How are you two doing, Katie?"

"May and I are playing," she said. "She seems to like it."

"This is my husband, Dr. McKinnon."

"Carey," he said to her. "Pleased to meet you, Katie. Welcome to our home."

That night Jane spent an hour at her computer checking details of Clare's story—the bus schedules and fare from St. Louis to Buffalo, the obituary of Dorothy Woods, the name Clare Markham on the list of enrolled members of the Seneca tribe in Oklahoma. When she found the Google map showing the bus station in St. Louis, she traced her way along the street until she found a movie theater.

◆

The next morning, Jane began constructing a new person. She started with a blank birth certificate which she filled in with the name Katherine Marie Barnes, and called to report the name to one of the two women she knew who worked in the Cook County, Illinois, records office. Years ago, they had given her the present of fifty blank certificates and the promise that they would insert corresponding certificates into the official record for her as long as they worked there. The certificate listed Katherine's place of birth as Chicago.

Then she moved to school records. Jane had a list of accredited private schools all over the country that had gone bankrupt or been combined with others to make larger schools. Jane picked one that had gone under when Katherine Barnes would have been about ten, and began to fill in her grades on printed forms. There were registration records, certificates for making the honor roll, belonging to clubs, taking part in plays, choruses, teams. Jane was able to use the computer to alter some genuine group photographs to include Katie Barnes. There were health forms in which she was certified as having had annual physical exams and immunizations. Jane had a good supply of forms and folders and envelopes. She had performed this process before for other runners. There were early childhood addresses that corresponded with the school's locations, three of them from her list of addresses that used to be residential but weren't anything now because of things like highway widening and a new stadium.

The information gathering had been made much easier by the computer-flooded information banks now available, and printing forms with the computer on thick, high rag content paper made them all look more professional and legitimate. Much of the value was not only that anyone would see it, but the runner could look at it and memorize it, and have a detailed false history.

The project took about a week. Katie Barnes's history had to resemble Clare's more and more closely as the records purported to be more recent. She had to be certified as good at mathematics, because that was

Clare's biggest academic strength, and she would probably get chances to prove it later. Her math might also get her admitted to more selective science classes. Clare was very good at Spanish, so Katie was good at Spanish. Everything had to fit, and each item had to provide Katie with an advantage. The grades were all good—mostly A's—because what high grades signified in real-life schools was that the student was not troublesome and had regular attendance.

During the days when Jane and Clare were working on building Katie and talking about what she should be like, they went out walking with May and made her part of the conversation.

There was much knowledge that Jane had to pass on to Katie Barnes about constructing a new life and living as a new person. She knew how tricky and frightening it could be to a sixteen-year-old. She was afraid that Katie would get caught in a mistake, and the mistake would be something that Jane had known and hadn't had the time to teach her.

Jane was helping assemble the information that formed the basis of a new identity. The identification documents had to start with the sort of information that Jane had prepared, so that all the names, dates, addresses, parents' names, and so on agreed. But nobody except a pro could move on to the next step, obtaining or producing the government-controlled certifications—driver's license, social security card, and ultimately, passport. She let the time pass, observing Clare every day, and making no quick decisions.

After a few more days, Jane had a new conversation with Clare. She said, "I've been watching you, and I think you've figured out what the hardest part of this is. When Katie is completed and you make her come to life, Clare is supposed to disappear. That doesn't have to happen. If you decide to go back and face the legal jeopardy and the risk, I'll do what I can to help. I'll hire you the best lawyers, and that sometimes is enough to win. Sometimes a jurisdiction that has been sloppy about evaluating potential cases will mysteriously change their minds as soon as they hear who the other side is going to be. Good lawyers also win on appeal more often.

"If you believe that your last, best hope is to step out of the life of Clare and become Katie, then I'll help you do that instead. If you do that, you will pay a different terrible price. It will never be safe to go back or to communicate with any member of your family again, or any old friend. The police will be watching them, very closely at first, then less closely, but they will never give up. A murder case is never closed. By now they know that your best friend disappeared for a couple of days about the time you left, so she's already under suspicion and being watched and maybe interrogated. All the people you love and the places you know are off limits. You are good, brave, and smart. You have what it takes to do this. But you have to want to."

"What do you think I should do?"

"For now, you should let the things that have happened sink in. Allow your mind to wander over your past life and the life you would like to have. Take your time. You're safe and you can stay here with us as long as it takes. If you want to talk, I'll listen. I'll answer any question I can. Right now, I'm going to go out for a while to get us some groceries. If you feel up to it, I'll leave May with you."

"Sure," Clare said. "We'll get along fine, won't we, May?"

May knew she was being addressed and seemed to like it.

Jane said, "I pumped a while ago, and there's a fresh bottle in the fridge." She walked into the kitchen, picked up her purse, and kept going out the door to prevent May from thinking about it too much. She went down the path to the garage and drove her car down the driveway and along the road to the Fosters' house. The Fosters both worked and their boys were both away in college, so she knew they wouldn't be at home on a normal weekday. She parked far back in their driveway and used her cell phone to look at the images from the security cameras in the McKinnon house.

Jane watched Clare and May behaving as they usually did. Clare picked May up and carried her around the house showing her things that were kept at adult height and talking about them. May cried and Clare changed her, and then carried her around some more. She had a conversation with May that seemed to keep her amused. Jane waited for them to be on the other side of the house, and started her car. Clare was smart enough to know that the best time to make a private phone call was when Jane had just left, so she wouldn't come back and catch her at it. Clare had never gone near the telephones. All that it proved, really, was that the girl wasn't stupid. Jane had already known that much, but it was also comforting to see how good Clare was with May. After a few minutes Jane admitted to herself that maybe she wasn't quite as pleased that May liked someone else too.

Jane did the family's grocery shopping and added several treats and snacks that she guessed Clare would like.

9

Magda's phone had received a text message telling her to come to a bar in Boston, so this afternoon she was at a small round table in the bar having tea. She had already had her lunch in her hotel. It had been a treat not to have the plain sameness of prison food, and she was still thinking about the nice hotel meal. Everything had been so fresh and perfect and carefully prepared that she had hated to have it end. The tea she was drinking now was the real thing. It reminded her of winter afternoons in her grandmother's kitchen. It was Russian Caravan tea, steeped with orange juice, lemon juice, cloves, cinnamon, and allspice, served very hot in a glass set in a metal holder with a handle.

She looked at the display on the telephone she'd been given at the Toronto airport. The man she was waiting for was late. She set the phone back down on the small round table.

Of course he was late. He was Pavel Obolonsky, the Pachan of the Bratva of Boston. He really was more than a boss. Leaders didn't control or run cities, they lived off them. A major city was a hunting ground. She understood that he had to behave in ways that reminded people that they were not his equals, especially people who were not members of his inner circle, and certainly not a woman.

She had been introduced to him over three years ago when she had been in Boston with Oleg Porchen, her Pachan. When she'd met Obolonsky that time, she and the other California vors had been here to try to catch the woman who made people disappear. Magda had attracted some attention, partly because she always did in gatherings of men. Bratva meant "brotherhood," and it was an organization that seldom included women. It employed women. Obolonsky had taken her hand too hard. She had acquiesced, as one did with a man of his importance, let him shake her hand, then backed away, and went up the sidewalk to the rented van and waited for the others from Los Angeles. Her Pachan was not jealous, because thin women didn't interest him, but he was a suspicious man, and if he'd seen her having a long conversation with Obolonsky, it could have brought on a suspicion of disloyalty.

Magda looked down and sipped her tea. She had just seen the first man come in the front door of the bar. Her waiting time was nearly over. The man wasn't big, but he was about six feet and had thick arms and shoulders, like a professional soldier. He wore a gray suit and shiny brown shoes. He didn't look at anything he didn't need to—her, for instance. He had expected to see her. He was looking for something he wasn't supposed to see. He walked straight to the end of the bar, so he could see if anyone was hiding behind it, sat at the last seat at the end of the bar, watched the street in the giant mirror behind the bartender, and ordered a drink, but didn't touch it.

The second man came in. He looked a lot like the first one, trim and athletic with a body that she guessed had been built in some martial art.

He sat at a little round table like hers by the front wall where he could cover the sidewalk, the center of the room, and the opposite side.

After a minute, Pavel Obolonsky stepped inside, smiled at Magda, walked up, and sat at her little table. It occurred to her that he was a lot like his two bodyguards—physically fit, with movements that were direct and aggressive—only twenty years older. "Hello, Magda," he said. "I'm glad to see you got here. You took the long way."

"I went to Los Angeles to see who was available from the last time. I knew everybody and I thought I would pick the best ones and bring them back for the job. They weren't there anymore."

"No," he said. "They aren't. Do you know why I chose to find you and bring you here?"

She said, "I wouldn't presume to imagine I know what you're thinking."

He smiled again. "I'll bet you thought Oleg was bragging to me about you."

"Did he say good things to you about me?"

"No. Not one. That was how I know he valued you and wanted to keep you."

She said, "Well, I'm here now. I hope bringing me here turns out to be worth the trouble."

"Don't worry about that. I won't hold you responsible for anything but the parts that only you can do. We'll do the rest."

"I know where we caught her," she said. "I would have told you the address if you had asked, without getting me out of prison."

"That isn't why I want you. There were five vors and her in that house that night. Now we learn that she's still alive. Who else? Only you. I don't give people tests to find out who is the smartest. The universe is a test of who's smartest. The one who is alive. How many men will you need?"

"Four. Five of us will be the most who will fit in a car." She stared hard at his two bodyguards. "I don't want men who look like them."

"Why not?"

"If men like them come to your door, you think either they're cops or they've been sent to kill you. I need men who wear glasses or look like they play the cello. If the woman we were hunting is alive, then we made her even better than she was at scanning the people around her. If she sees men like these, she'll be gone before they ever come close."

"All right," he said. "You'll meet some and pick the ones you want."

"What's my time limit? How long do I have?"

"Until you find her." He got up. "Or she finds you. Come again tomorrow at this time and you can meet some men who might be right for this."

10

The past few days at the McKinnon house had proceeded much as they had before the arrival of Clare from Oklahoma. Jane took time out when the baby was sleeping or playing with her new friend to make progress on Clare's safety.

Jane searched the internet again for recent news from Oklahoma, particularly for anything about violent crimes, or people whom the police considered suspects or persons of interest in crimes. She also tried obituaries, funerals, burial notices. She glanced at Clare. "What's the name of the man you stabbed?"

"Gerry. Gerard Fenton."

"And you're sure he died?"

"That's what the police said."

"The police are allowed to lie when they're questioning a suspect. What did your lawyer say?'

"She said he was dead too."

Jane had searched the newspapers: the *Tulsa World*, *Oklahoma City Oklahoman*, and then anything out of Norman, but the story had not attracted much interest with the press, since it had nothing to do with those cities.

When Carey came home from the hospital, he came in the kitchen door, kissed Jane, and took May into his arms and lifted her up and carried her around the room. He talked to her in the soft, cheerful voice he used with her. "Hello, May. What was your day like? Did you learn anything about the world? Hear any funny new words?" He looked at Jane, and saw that her welcoming smile had faded. His eyebrows went up.

Jane responded. "I've got to go out of town for a day or two."

"Why?" he said.

"It's about one of my runners, as you probably expected. It's not dangerous, and I'm not going to be with the runner. I'm going alone to check on some facts. What I expect to find is that the problem has gone away or even never existed."

"What about May?"

"If I do it right it'll be one day, and Katie will be here for all of it. I'll take a red-eye flight, get in early, and catch an early flight home."

His eyes settled on Jane and stayed there.

She shrugged. "I'm sorry, Carey."

"I guess I just wasn't ready for this now. I guess when it seems like everything changes, not everything does. When are you going?"

She stepped close and hugged him. "I'm sorry, I'm sorry. You know I don't want to do this, even for an hour."

"It's all right, Jane. The baby has two parents. Just make sure there's enough milk."

She touched his shoulder, began to massage it, and then moved her hand down his back. "Come on, Carey. You feel like you're made of iron."

He consciously relaxed the muscles of his upper body. "You know I love you. I had just assumed . . ." He paused. "Something that wasn't true. Maybe it couldn't be true. When do you have to go?"

"I checked your schedule. You're going to be in surgery every day this week until Friday, when you see patients in your office. I know there could be emergencies, but Friday looks like the best. So I thought I'd go for a flight Thursday evening after your last one and any follow-ups or walk-ins. Then I have a hope of getting home Friday, probably late evening."

"That sounds well planned."

"Don't do that," she said.

"Do what?"

"Think that because I bothered to consider your schedule, I must be a master schemer, and not just your wife who loves you."

He gently pulled her to him and held her for a few seconds, and then a few more seconds. She popped up and kissed him, then turned away and walked across the kitchen.

As she walked out and across the living room toward the den she used as an office, the voice in her head was saying, *I do love you, and I'm sorry.* She heard Carey go to the playroom with May.

While she heard him talking to Katie and then to May, she made the reservation on the computer, but it was to Springfield, Missouri, and it was for Nora Jean Gibbs, whose home address was in Los Angeles. This was one of Jane's oldest and deepest identities, one that she took the time and effort to keep fresh and viable. She had gone in to the DMV in Van Nuys, California, only about two years ago to renew Nora Jean's driver's license and upgrade it to an official Real ID to conform to the change in the law that had been postponed about eight times before being implemented in that state. She bought a ticket for Thursday evening from Buffalo to Chicago, another an hour later from Chicago to Springfield,

Missouri, a third for Springfield back to Chicago with an open date. She charged them to Nora Jean Gibbs's Visa card.

As she printed her itineraries, she thought about how much more difficult what she was doing had become over the years. It was already nearly impossible to build an identity as strong and old as Nora Jean Gibbs was. She hoped that she could find a way to do it again for Clare. What she was hoping for most was that she would find that Clare wouldn't need it.

On Wednesday night Jane followed a policy that her mother had told her when she was in college. The way to preserve a marriage was to remember always that she was in love and act that way. When Jane and Carey were going to be apart, even for a day or two, she made sure that the night before she left didn't go by without being together so each had fresh memories of the other.

The flight from Buffalo to Chicago was an hour and a half. There was an hour between flights, and the one from Chicago to Missouri was an hour and twenty minutes, but there was a delay of a half hour taking off. She reached Springfield-Branson Airport at nearly midnight, checked into the nearby Best Western, and slept for six hours. She put on the outfit she had chosen—black pantsuit, hat that hid her hair, big sunglasses to hide her eyes and change her profile, loose raincoat for the late spring weather and to hide her body. Then she went back to the airport to pick up Nora Gibbs's rental car and got on the road.

She drove south to Interstate 44, then west. She made it into Oklahoma before it was fully light out, and was in Stanton before eight. As she drove, she thought about the things she'd read about homicide laws in Oklahoma during the days before this trip. With a population of four million, it was the state that had held the second most executions since they'd been allowed again in 1976, exceeded only by Texas, which had a population of thirty million. The methods were lethal injection, nitrogen hypoxia, electrocution, and firing squad, to be tried in that order, in case the first one didn't work. There were provisions in the law for "excusable homicide" and "justifiable homicide," but she didn't have enough information to be confident in whether they would be applied in Clare's case. The idea that a sixteen-year-old had even been charged in such a clear instance of self-defense didn't make Jane want to know.

She parked the rental car in a municipal lot that only had a few cars in it at this hour, paid the machine for a full day at the pedestrian exit, took her receipt, and left. She had been in this northeastern corner of Oklahoma once, about fifteen years ago, with a runner. The few Seneca people she had met were elderly even then. She remembered Clare's grandmother, Dorothy Woods. Jane wished she could talk to her now to get a sense of things, but she was dead.

Jane was almost alone on the street this morning. There was a remnant of spring fog in the still, early morning air, and sounds carried better than sight. She dimly remembered that there was a popular diner in the middle of town. She didn't see it, but while she walked, she passed the office of the local newspaper, which was called the *Clarion*. The masthead said it was published twice a week, on Tuesdays and Fridays. The office was still dark, but they had covered the big storefront windows with the last few issues. She had read some of the major stories online at home. The pages in the window were mostly local-interest stories.

There was a lot of news about children's events, a surprising number of obituaries of people with dates of birth in the 1920s and '30s, but no police blotter, which was what Jane had been hoping for. The only crimes she could find were a middle-aged woman arrested for bad checks and a marijuana grower who had been raided, but it wasn't clear from the story what the crime was. The high school senior class had 180 graduates at commencement. The Cherokee nation had donated a large sum for the development of the new fairgrounds.

When Jane continued down Main Street, she found a restaurant that was not the diner she remembered, but looked larger and as busy as that diner had been. She went to the front entrance and saw a "Please seat yourself" sign, so she sat down in the third booth along the side and faced the back wall, where she could see most of the room, but not have newcomers see her face as soon as they came in the door.

After a few minutes the lone waitress—a middle-aged woman with short, blond hair and sinewy muscles in her forearms—came with her order pad. Jane smiled and ordered fried eggs, wheat toast, orange juice, and coffee. Then she looked down at the prepaid burner phone she had bought for cash a few months ago while she was refreshing the bugout kits she had always kept for Carey and herself.

When the waitress saw the phone appear she went away, and Jane returned the phone to her coat pocket. For the moment she had not put the battery in, because she had no need to make a call or use the internet, and no reason to have it pinging off any cell towers and creating a record of where she had been.

She had counted only eleven people in the diner when she'd entered. Most were men dressed like farmers or tradespeople. There were a couple of women friends dressed like schoolteachers—attractive but modest. School was already out for summer, but it was possible they were signed up for summer school duty. Eight o'clock approached, and they made no move to leave, so Jane decided they probably sold real estate or cars. Today was Friday, and that was a work day, so either way, they'd be on their way before long.

Jane listened to the voices she could hear from the booths, the tables, and the counter. People were talking, but their talk was what it always was—the early arrival of warm weather, which was sticky and made the mosquitoes thrive, but was also a damned good thing after the flooding they got this spring; the politicians turning every tax into a fee so people didn't notice it. They didn't remember that an ordinary family that didn't have a pot to piss in had to pay just as much for a quart of milk as a billionaire. And where does all that money go anyway?

The mid-morning waitress, much younger than the early one, came in so there would be two for the rush, took off a thin raincoat like Jane's, and disappeared through a door to the left of the counter. She came back a minute later with Jane's food, a small shiny carafe of coffee, and a small silvery cream pitcher. Jane kept listening while she ate. Each time the street door opened she used her ears to get a sense of who it was—male/ female, old/young, big/small. She would look at the shiny carafe to pick up the person's reflection.

This one was big and male. After a moment she saw the khaki uniform had a badge. Cop. Someone said, "Davy," and the cop stopped walking. He turned to the side and looked at the group at the first table from the door. He said, "Good morning." His voice was strong and yet appealing, a smooth and polite cop voice, the one they used when they called you "ma'am."

A woman said, "We're so sorry for your loss."

His voice warmed a bit. "I appreciate that. It's one of those times that every family dreads. No matter how many times you see it happen, you never think the next time it's going to be your family."

Jane had noticed that the chatter quieted when the cop came in.

The cop said, "We were grateful to see you all at the funeral."

"Well, we wish you and your family the best."

"Thank you." Jane heard a slight change in his voice that indicated he was shaking somebody's hand. Jane heard him walking toward her booth, and then past, and she raised her eyes. He was about six feet two inches, two hundred and ten or two twenty. The buzz-cut hair was reddish. He had the familiar cop swagger and a pair of aviator sunglasses were propped above his forehead.

He walked up to the counter and the early waitress came around from behind the cash register and hugged him. When she let him go and returned behind the counter, she took her pad out of her apron pocket and seemed ready to take his order.

He leaned toward her to tell her what it was, but she didn't write it down on her pad. She just unfolded a cardboard carry tray, poured two cups of coffee, capped them with tops, tossed in packets of sugar and pods of cream, handed him the tray, and then watched him walk back out to the front door.

Jane could still hear the people in the front booth. A man said, "Have they found the girl yet? I didn't want to ask him."

"I think we'd have heard if they had," one of the others said.

"They could be keeping it to themselves," a woman said.

"Why?"

"She's a minor. Aren't there special rules about releasing their names?"

"I don't think they apply in a murder," the first man said. "She should be grateful if she gets a trial."

"You think so? I mean Gerry, he was always a kind of wild guy, and he was twice as old as her, nearly," she said. "I'm not so sure she wasn't in the right. Maybe he did just what she said."

"I don't know. Even if he did, you think that gave her a right to stab him to death? And why was she carrying a great big knife? A killing knife?"

"How do you know how big it was?"

"I just assumed it was, because a sixteen-year-old girl killed somebody with it."

Jane paid at the cash register and went to the back of the diner to the restroom, then left through the back door.

She walked to the main street and she could see the old white Greek-inspired city hall a distance away. The closer she came to it the more convinced she was that they had put all the local gravestone carvers to work on the engraved letters and embellishments of the building. As she drew nearer, she began to see the offices of legal firms, a couple of bail bond businesses. She found the office of the public defenders, entered, saw the sign-in book sitting open on the counter, and filled in two lines in the page. She wrote that she was Dora Bull, from the Legal Equality Committee of the National Congress of American Indians. The National Congress was well-known, but the committee was Jane's invention. In the space for the name of the person she was there to see, Jane wrote Monica Fawcett.

After about twenty-five minutes a door across the room opened and a woman wearing a light gray jacket and a charcoal skirt came out. She went to the counter to look at the sign-in book, turned around, and looked at Jane. "Ms. Bull?"

Jane stood and smiled, then followed her through the door into a room that didn't look like an office but like a converted storeroom. There was a large cafeteria table with a computer on it with its cord trailing across the open floor like a snake to a wall socket. There was a cheap bookcase that held a mixed set of law books and a few notebooks that Jane guessed held updates. The one thing this office didn't lack was filing cabinets. Three walls were dominated by a two-tiered collection of olive drab filing cabinets. On top of those were cardboard file boxes. The woman said, "I'm Monica Fawcett. Please take a seat. I apologize for the wait. Everything seems to get busier on Fridays, when people are trying to get bail approved before the weekend."

"I'm glad that you could fit me in at all," Jane said. "Thank you. I'm here for the Committee to see if we can assist in the case of Clare Markham."

Monica Fawcett took a deep breath and blew it out, and Jane could see she was anxious. "I can't discuss anything that's confidential between attorney and client."

"Of course," Jane said. "I'll supply the information we have, and we can talk about that only. Clare is sixteen. She was subjected to a forced physical encounter by a man named Gerard Fenton, age twenty-six. He got most of her clothes off and was attempting to rape her. She pulled a knife out of his jeans pocket and stabbed him in the leg. He died. She was arrested and charged with murder. Is that all correct?"

"Substantially," Monica Fawcett said.

"You must have convinced a judge that she was not a threat or a flight risk, because she released her on little or no bail."

"Yes."

"Now I have to ask you a couple of questions that you may decline to answer, and I will respect your decision. They're only asked for her benefit and any answers you give will never be repeated. Is there any chance she is guilty of murder?"

"She committed a homicide. I don't believe it was murder. She's a victim who defended herself. Also, you mentioned the ages of her and her attacker. The age of consent in Oklahoma is sixteen. The Senate passed a bill last year which would raise it to eighteen and add a provision that sex between two consenting persons age fourteen to eighteen will not be statutory rape. Whether or not that bill becomes law doesn't matter. Under present law, Clare was of the age to give consent, but she didn't. Gerard Fenton's age is legally irrelevant, but his conduct isn't."

"I assume you know that Fenton has a family that people admire, and one of them is a police officer."

"Yes."

"What are Clare's chances of being treated and tried fairly in local court?"

"I wish I could stick out my chin and say that everyone gets a fair trial here. I don't believe the record is flawless. Maybe it isn't anywhere. And Clare is exactly the kind of person who is most at risk from the justice system."

"Because she's Native?"

"She might have a jury with a bigot or two in it, or somebody who thinks every woman who is raped is asking for it. These people still exist, but everybody is watching for it. I'm more worried about her age. Kids don't have any extra rights or protections that are worth much. They can be tried as adults without having any of the control adults have over their own defense. They can be held for indefinite periods before they even get to trial on the grounds that they need treatment for mental illness, including drugs, repeated evaluations, and so on."

"But her case, specifically. What are you recommending?"

"I've given it a lot of thought. A rape is validated by physical evidence. She prevented hers, so there's no DNA evidence, and no bodily damage to her. The prosecution will argue she could have made up that part of it. The man she stabbed was a member of a family that's respected and loved. He was always wild as a young man, and was picked up by the police a number of times. But I've been told that, as of the night he died, he had a clean record. I suspect that there were infractions that somehow never made it to the record and some juvenile offenses that have been sealed. He made a deathbed statement that she had offered sex for money, and as they were about to begin, she stabbed him to take his wallet."

"Where does that leave her?"

"I think she won't get the death penalty, but I think she may get stuck in the system for years, maybe forever, charged with offenses that seem minor but can add decades to a sentence—not just manslaughter, but robbery with a deadly weapon, even prostitution, since deathbed statements are given a lot of weight and are often treated as proven. And since she was arrested at home after the encounter, the fact that she had no money on her probably won't help in court."

"Where does that leave her?"

"I don't know, really. You came to see if your committee can help. What I believe is the best we can do is to negotiate a plea for a lesser charge. She's so young. If she accepted a twenty-year manslaughter sentence, she could get out at thirty-six. For violent crimes you can be considered for parole after eighty-five percent of your sentence, so she might be out after seventeen years and only be thirty-three."

"Pretty bleak."

"It is. Or she could roll the dice and hope to get off. But I think the best we can hope for is a hung jury, based on a principled holdout or two. But the DA could keep filing the charge as many times as it took, and the judges here would probably allow it."

"Well, thank you, Ms. Fawcett. I may check in with you again as the process goes on."

"Thank you for coming, and for your concern."

The two stood, and both went out into the waiting room, Monica Fawcett to look at the next name on the sign-in list, and Jane to leave the building and become Nora Gibbs again.

Jane started back across the business section of the town toward the lot where she'd left her rental car, walking slowly and scanning to find a place where she might be able to overhear answers to some more of the questions on her mind. She had learned a bit about the legal threats Clare was likely to face in this jurisdiction, and now she wanted to get a broader impression of the way the people who were likely to be on a jury felt about the case. She began to scan the streets around her for a manicure shop or a hairdresser, or another restaurant that was likely to cater to a lunch crowd.

She noticed two sights. The first one was a police officer walking to the office she had just left. She tried to imagine why a uniformed officer would be entering the public defenders' office alone. She wondered if the cop might be giving an official statement about a crime. But wouldn't he have been on the same appointment schedule she had signed?

It was the fresh, quiet part of the morning, when the day was still getting started. There had been few sounds of car engines and no lawn machinery yet, and most of the stores still had Closed signs on their doors. There hadn't seemed to be anything out of the ordinary to attract police to that office. Yes, there had. A tall, thin woman with black hair, a stranger, had gone in, stayed for a while, and then left. As the cop reached for the doorknob with his right hand, his left hand pushed his sunglasses up on his forehead, and she was sure he was Davy, the brother of Gerry Fenton. The only thing that was visible in the outer office had been the sign-in book. Jane thought about it. So what if he found out that Ms. Bull from a national Indian organization had come to talk to Monica Fawcett? It meant nothing and led nowhere. If there was a problem, she would see something more ominous.

The second sight was another police officer, three hundred feet ahead of her in the parking lot where she had parked this morning. She judged from the angle of his head what he must be looking at. It was her rental car. As he approached the car, he took the handheld radio off his belt and raised it to his face to speak into it. The sight of the first cop had not seemed threatening. Two cops, both interested in her, was something else.

Jane knew that she had to move quickly. The next step was going to be to ask her some questions. That was not something she could allow. She turned left at the first intersection and headed toward the place where she had exited Highway 59 and entered town. As she walked, she took off her raincoat, folded it into her bag, put her hat in with it, shook out her hair, and ran her brush through it. When she reached Highway 59, she stationed herself a few feet before the northbound entrance, stuck out her hand with her thumb up, and began to hitchhike.

Jane was of the opinion that she was not as eye-catching as she had been at twenty-two, but she was still likely to get someone to stop for her.

After about a dozen cars passed her without stopping, she moved back from the entrance about fifty feet to give the drivers time to notice her, evaluate what they saw, and pull over to stop safely before they committed themselves to the entrance ramp. The third vehicle was a green pickup. She saw the front end dipping as the driver applied the brakes.

Jane ran to the right side of the truck, heard the door lock click, and climbed in. The driver was a man with Indian features—hair, eyes, skin. He said, "Where would you like to go?"

Jane was acutely conscious of the cars flashing past and swerving onto the entrance ramp. "If you're going as far as Joplin, that would be good."

He saw a break in the traffic, pulled forward, and accelerated up the ramp. "I didn't ask what would be good. Anyplace is better than standing beside the road. Where would you *like* to go?"

"The Springfield-Branson Airport."

"That makes me feel better," he said. "It's an intentional destination, not just a place you'll get stuck in, like you were stuck here. I'll take you to the airport. I'm going there to pick up my daughter anyway. And her luggage." He gestured toward the covered truck bed behind him. "It'll only be a couple hours."

"Thank you," she said. She liked him, and had an urge to say who she was, but she couldn't. "I'm Nora Gibbs, by the way."

"Tyler Shelford."

"Cherokee?"

"Wyandotte. You?"

"Shawnee," she lied. "Thank you for giving me a ride. I'd like to pay for your gas. If we stop for it where we can get some food, I'd like to buy that too."

"That's nice of you. I'll take it. You don't travel this way much, do you?"

"No," she said. "This is a special circumstance."

"You know it's dangerous, right?"

"Yep," she said. "And I don't do risky things unless it's to avoid something that's riskier. There were two men who seemed to have more than a healthy curiosity about me, and I saw one of them going to check out my rental car when he didn't know I was behind him. I decided to get to the airport another way, and pay the rental company to pick it up."

"Sometimes it's not an easy world," he said.

When they reached Joplin they stopped for gas and bought hamburgers for lunch. Then they got onto Interstate 44 for the rest of the trip.

When they approached the Springfield-Branson Airport, Shelford got a text message and went to the curb outside the baggage area and waited. Jane opened the door. "Thank you, Tyler. You've been a friend. I hope that if you ever have a problem there's someone as good as you to help you." She got out of the truck, hurried inside the terminal, and took the elevator up to the ticketing level.

Nora Gibbs flew to Chicago O'Hare, and bought a ticket on American Airlines for a flight ten days away for Los Angeles, Nora's home city. She took a cab to Midway Airport and used her Emily Whittaker ID to ask for the earliest flight on United to Buffalo. There was a flight that was undersold, almost ready to board. She got ticketed and ran for the gate. The flight took only a bit over an hour and a half.

At ten fifteen she was walking out to the parking lot of the Buffalo Niagara International Airport toward her car. She knew there were many people who didn't like being in a parking lot alone at night, but dark spaces anywhere could conceal an enemy, and Jane Whitefield knew how to use the advantages of the dark. It was easy to keep her face half turned away from the overhead lights so the movement and shadows made her face a series of impressions that kept changing as anyone watching her saw parts of it and his imagination kept filling in the rest. She was used to staying alert, and her body kept itself ready to run or fight.

She used her key fob to turn on her car's interior lights while she was still twenty feet away to be sure the car was empty, then turn them off. She didn't unlock the car until she was five feet from the door, and relocked it as soon as she was in. She tossed her bag on the passenger seat and drove.

She had spent too much of her life traveling not to see her home airport with eyes and memory at once. This was still the place where she felt sad going away and happy to return. After one day, she felt as though she had been away from Carey and May for weeks.

She headed out to Genesee Street. No Seneca could hear the word *Genesee* without thinking "pleasant banks," the Nundawaono name for the river at the center of Seneca country. She opened the window an inch so she could still feel the warm air. In minutes she was on the New York State Thruway, then the Youngmann Expressway, and then home to Amherst.

She turned the car into the long driveway and into the garage beside Carey's car. She got out and he was already outside and walking toward her. He put his arms around her and they kissed.

"You okay?" he said.

"Yeah," she said. "You?"

"Now I am."

"Did May miss me too?"

"Come on, let's go in and you can ask her."

Jane walked to the big old stone house regretting that what she'd said was a lie. She was not okay. She hoped he had been telling the truth.

11

Magda walked into the bar and sat down at the same little table where she had sat the day before. The bartender was at his station behind the bar. He spoke into his telephone, put it back into his pocket, and came to her table. "Would you like the same kind of tea today?"

She said, "Yes, please. I'm surprised that you remembered."

"You're special."

"Then I'll try to come back to see you."

"No, you won't," he said, and laughed.

"No," she said. "But whenever I want real tea, I'll remember you, and that's something."

He made her tea in exactly the same way as before and brought it to her table. She took a tiny sip to confirm that it tasted the same.

Magda was a suspicious person. If she had been walking alone into a random bar in Boston or anywhere else in the daytime when there were no other people, she would have been certain to order something in a sealed bottle, to be safe from being drugged. Here things were different. This was a bar controlled by the Pachan of the local Bratva, Pavel Obolonsky, who had just rescued her from a women's prison. For the moment that meant she was under his protection, and he had the power here. She also knew another thing about power. If Obolonsky wanted her to be drugged she would be.

It took a long time for the two bodyguards to appear. This time they appeared from the hall leading from the back of the building, separated, and took new positions in opposite corners of the room. She was not surprised, because they and their boss would be smart enough to vary the things they did. A few minutes later, there were car doors slamming and other men came in and sat at various tables. Among them, just one in a group of nine, was Pavel Obolonsky. If she had not been studying each man as he came in, she might not have noticed him. He came to her table and sat.

"These men are all members of the brotherhood. All of them are good earners and are loyal to me."

"Of course they are," she said. "But will they be loyal to me?"

"They'll be loyal to me. They'll show it by doing what you say."

"Have you asked them?"

"Yes. I told them who you were before they came here."

"Thank you," she said. "Are there any favorites you recommend?" If he pointed out any favorites, she would know who was his spy.

"They're all reliable. If they weren't, I would have been ashamed to bring them. I've put too much into this to throw it away. Look at them. Talk to them. Do whatever you need to find the ones you want."

Magda stood up and walked up to the nearest table. She said in English, "Tell me why you want to be part of this crew."

The first man was young and had an earnest expression. He said in Russian, "Because I want to do things that are important."

"I spoke to you in English. I know you speak Russian. How is your American?"

He said, "It's very good." It wasn't, so she excused him.

As Magda moved from man to man and talked to them, there were some who spoke English that sounded to her more like the pronunciation and cadence that she had been listening to since she'd arrived in Los Angeles ten years ago. She asked a blond one wearing a Red Sox hat to describe the last baseball game he'd seen the Red Sox play, and asked the one after that for directions to the Museum of Fine Arts, and the one after that to tell her what those buildings were on the other side of the bridge over the Charles River. She rejected one because his authentic American accent was pure Boston, and might be memorable anywhere else.

When she had talked to all eight, she said to Obolonsky, "Any of these men could do the job. But the ones I choose are that one, who looks like a young doctor, the one like a pianist over here, that one who looks like a lawyer, and the teacher beside him."

Obolonsky laughed. He stood and pointed. "You, Mr. Teacher, you, Doctor, you Mr. Lawyer, and your friend the piano player, come over here. The rest of you, stand by."

The four she had chosen were all men who didn't look especially menacing. They were fit and in their prime but weren't big or heavily muscled. They also didn't look very much like each other. They could speak English with American idioms and slang with comfort and authority.

Obolonsky sat down beside Magda again. "I'll make sure the credit card in your purse has plenty of money available, so you can buy a car or two and travel, and we'll give you some cash too, but remember when you're deciding what to use, a bill can hold a fingerprint or DNA."

"Thank you," she said.

"What else can I do?"

"I need to talk to them some more. I may find I need to change some of them, so will you please have the others stay here for a time—maybe an hour?"

"Yes."

"And I don't mean any disrespect to you, but I'll learn the most if I speak to them alone."

His eyes showed he was amused at her boldness. She didn't take her eyes off his or smile, and she was sure he realized she was right. He stood and said loudly, "Vlad and Ivan and I have to leave. Everyone else stay. Magda will tell you when to go."

Magda got up too and walked over to the space between the two large round tables where her choices were sitting. She sat down on one of the empty chairs. "I picked you because you look and sound the most like Americans, and you don't look like thieves." She smiled. "At least on the surface. But none of us is going to wear a bathing suit, eh?"

Two of them lifted their shirts to provide a fleeting glimpse of their tattooed torsos.

"Tell me your names."

"Maxim." "Dmitri." "Mikhail." "Daniil."

"Did the Pachan tell you what we're going to do?"

"He said you would tell us," Maxim said.

"We're going to find a woman, capture her alive, and bring her back here. She looks like she's in her mid-to-late thirties, black hair like mine, blue eyes, tall, and thin. A few years ago, I was one of a group from Los Angeles who came here to capture her. It sounds easy, doesn't it?"

The four all looked as though they agreed that it did. Daniil said, "I've helped do the same thing five times, twice in this country."

"It sounds the same, but it's not the same," Magda said. "She isn't like the ones you kidnapped. When we traced her here, your group helped us. Four vors, all of them former soldiers who liked to spend their spare time hunting and fishing together, followed this woman onto the north end of the Appalachian Trail into the Hundred Mile Wilderness. She let them follow her far from civilization, nearly catch up with her, and then she began to kill them one at a time. She left booby traps on trails, poisoned their food, ambushed them, whatever they were vulnerable to. She came out of the woods after a few days. None of them ever did."

Maxim said, "Are you sure she did all that alone?"

"Yes," she said. "I was one of the five who caught up with her later. We ambushed her and overpowered her. She fought, and we had to hurt her to control her, and then we tortured her to teach her that we would. Night came and we needed to sleep. We took her down to the windowless stone cellar of the house, chained her to the pipes so she couldn't escape, then climbed the wooden stairs. The men cut off the top of the wooden stairs with a chain saw so she had no way up. We locked the door, and left her in the dark. Then we went upstairs to sleep in the bedrooms. During the night she found a way to start a fire, fill the house with smoke, and get it to float up through old heating ducts to kill us with carbon monoxide. The important thing to know is that she knew the carbon monoxide would kill her too."

"How many of the Bratva was that?" Dmitri said.

"The Pachan and three men who were in the upstairs bedrooms all died first. The one besides me who was sleeping on the first floor woke up and ran away without even trying to wake the rest of us, so I had to pay him a visit later to kill him. With the ones in the forest, that makes eight. I always thought she had died too, but she didn't. Your boss had people watching for her obituary, or a local news report of her death, or any recognition. But they never found one."

Dmitri said, "Why are we going after her—revenge?"

She laughed. "Nothing sentimental like that. There's no money in revenge. She has helped dozens of people who were being hunted to disappear. My Pachan was sure that for each of them there were people who would love to pay him millions of dollars to find out where one of those people is now, and what name they're using."

"I don't understand," said Daniil. "You want to get the fugitive to pay you not to tell their enemies where they are?"

"No. We make the woman tell us where they are, then we go get them, and sell them to the people who hate them. What I think will work is to hurt her, make her feel the kind of pain that is also sorrow because you know that during those seconds, you're losing the use of something—a hand, a limb, an eye. Once we force her to give us one of those fugitives, it will get easier. She won't be trying to save her self-respect, because it will be gone. Each time we ask for another person, it will be harder for her to keep from telling us."

Magda could see that these men were paying close attention. She said, "Questions?"

"How do we find her?"

"Right now, I only know where she was when we found her the first time. If she's gone, there will be paths that lead on from there."

"When you caught her before, did you get her to tell you about any of her clients?"

"Very smart. No. She didn't tell us anything. But this time she will. When we catch her this time we can hold on to her as long as we want—maybe years. Other questions?"

None of the men spoke.

"Then get ready to leave in three days. One small suitcase, all clothes good quality. One sport coat and dress pants, nice shoes, nice watch. An informal outfit with jeans, walking shoes, that kind of thing. Before we go, it's okay to back out. But once the job starts, there's no quitting, only desertion." She studied them for another moment. "Last questions? No? Then I'll tell the others they can go. I'll see you on Monday morning."

12

Jane woke up in the morning to the sound of May's first movements in the crib and the audible quickening of her breathing. Jane turned off the baby monitor, slid out of the big bed silently so she wouldn't wake Carey, padded on bare feet to the nursery, lifted May up, wrapped her in a soft blanket, and closed the door.

May kicked and murmured, and Jane changed her and then sat in the rocking chair and fed her, singing a soft, simple song she had made up about a girl named May. She heard nothing from the master bedroom, which meant that she and May had succeeded again. The clock on the wall said 4:45. Pretty good.

As she rocked and felt the touch and warmth of May's little body, she thought about all the years she had spent wishing she could be doing what she was doing now. When May had been fed, Jane burped her, set her down on the changing table, and dressed her in a fresh onesie, then dressed herself in a pair of the jeans and one of the sweatshirts she kept in this room's closet for early awakenings, and carried May to the stairs and down to the ground floor.

The McKinnon house was not the only eighteenth-century house in this part of the state, but it was certainly one of the earliest, built well before the Revolution. Carey's ancestor had come through here after the French and Indian War to establish a business trading with the Senecas. This living room and the floor above it were the whole place at first—a stone fireplace and a rectangle made of straight tree trunks over a foot thick, the logs on the second floor drilled at intervals for gun ports. The building had been augmented and revised many times, generation after generation. The big kitchen had probably started as a detached cook-house, and the staircases to the second floor had been added later, after sawmills had been introduced to the area and boards were available. Jane walked across the living room and then saw Clare coming out of the kitchen to join them.

Jane said, "Clare. It's not even five. There's still plenty of time to go back to bed."

"I woke up and couldn't get back to sleep," Clare said. "I wanted to hear what you found out."

"I can give you the short version now. After talking with your lawyer, I think that nothing has improved. If you go back to Stanton, the very best you can hope for is a plea deal that gets you something like a ten- or twenty-year sentence. If they don't offer a deal or you don't take one, they might go through with it—try you as an adult and sentence you the same way. It's also possible that afterward a higher court will throw the whole case out because it's so outrageous, but I don't like the chances of that, and when it happens, it can take years."

"That's what I thought," Clare said.

"I also sat in that diner downtown, and the supposed victim's brother, who is a cop, stopped in to get some coffee. He got a lot of condolences and support. The people in there were not a cross section. They're older than the town's average resident, and they were sitting in a diner during the first part of a Friday morning, which means they're more on the boss side of things than the low-wage worker end. The problem is, that's who is most likely to be on a jury. Obviously, nobody your age is on any jury anywhere."

"Thank you for going," Clare said. "It was risky for you to go to Oklahoma to poke around."

They both heard the sound of Carey McKinnon's footsteps coming down the stairs, and fell silent.

Jane said, "Here, May. Let Katie take you while I make your daddy's breakfast." She handed May to Clare and led the way into the kitchen.

She plugged in the coffee maker and laid out the pan, spatula, eggs, olive oil, and butter, and put bread in the toaster. "Okay, what are we making today, Doc? Eggs, sausage, pancakes, smoked salmon, dinosaur, woolly mammoth?"

"Two eggs, sunny-side up, whole wheat toast would be nice," he said. I've got my first surgery at seven, two more after that, and then I'll have time for lunch so I don't think I'll have to worry about being hungry. Hi, Katie," he said. "I hope we didn't wake you up."

"No," she said. "I'm used to getting up when the sun does, but some days I just sleep enough before then, wake up, and feel fine."

"I'm like that too," he said. He walked up to her and held his arms out to take May from her, and walked around the kitchen carrying the baby, collecting his keys, wallet, and sunglasses while telling May what he was doing, and explaining to her that he was staying far from the stove because sometimes a little grease could splatter when somebody was cooking food, and right now Mommy was making him a nice breakfast.

He told May that pretty soon—not soon by her standards, but soon—she would be able to eat regular food, and then they would all be able to eat together at the same time. "Then, you'll be ready to go to your job as an airline pilot or a movie star or a diamond cutter and have a lot of energy." A few minutes later he said, "Oh, it looks as though Mommy is putting my breakfast on the table, so I guess you go back to Katie." He raised her high in the air and then brought her back down, kissed her cheek, and handed her to Katie, then ate while Jane sat with him and had a cup of caffeine-free herb tea.

In a few minutes they hugged and he was out the kitchen door on his way to the garage to drive to the hospital.

Katie said, "Do you do that every morning?"

"Cook his breakfast? Whenever I can. You know something about my life. There have been far too many days when I really wished that I could have been here to do that." She took Carey's plate and silverware to the sink. "What would you like for breakfast?"

"I can cook," she said.

"So can he," Jane said. "And I can do most of the things he does for me. It's not about capability, it's about giving to each other."

"I can make what you made for him," Clare said.

"Okay. Make it for me too. I'll take May."

When the food was ready, they ate, with Jane holding May on her lap. "The eggs are just right," she said. "I don't usually have breakfast until later, but this is nice." She watched Clare for a moment. "You're wondering what's going to happen to you."

"Yes," Clare said.

"So far you and I have been discussing two options. One was to go back and stand trial. Your public defender struck me as a competent attorney, and she thinks the chance you'll be tried as an adult is serious. Since you did stab a man who bled to death, the result would be bad."

"You think the best thing to do is to ask you to help me disappear and start a new life?"

"I think that would probably be the narrow winner for some people. I don't think it will work for you. You're smart and brave and self-reliant, but you're sixteen years old. Not many good things happen to girls on their own who are sixteen, no matter who they are."

"You said before that I'm smart enough."

"You are, but being smart is only one advantage, and you'll need a few more. We can do a lot to change your appearance, and maybe add a year or two to the way you look, but nothing we do is going to make you look twenty-one. Or even nineteen. A lot of the secrets of disappearing are about what totally random strangers think when they look at you. Right now, if most of those people saw you on your own, they would wonder what such a young girl is doing here alone. They would start asking each other, and then maybe the authorities. I'm talking about normal people who would only be concerned about you and want to help and protect you."

"I can handle myself," Clare said. "I found my way here, didn't I?"

"The best way to hide is to not stand out. Not standing out means you've got an identity, a role in society. What you do is a big part of who you seem to be. That usually means a job. But you just started high school, so you can't get the kind of job that will support you, or make people stop wondering and forget asking questions."

Clare said, "I'll start by doing the jobs I can get now, and work my way up from there."

"People do that. It takes a lot—work, patience, toughness, and luck."

"You make everything sound hard. Then what can I do?" Clare said.

"We talked about going back and we talked about disappearing. There's a third choice. What I'm thinking right now is that you need time. I'm guessing three years would do it. Three years from now you could graduate from high school in June and join the freshman class of a good college in September."

"I'll never have the money for that."

"I've got it. College gives you another four years of being a person with a certified identity and an obvious purpose, four more years of a fixed name and address. At the end of it you'll be twenty-two and you'll be qualified for good jobs."

"I can't believe this," Clare said. "First you make everything sound awful, and now you make it sound so good. What's after that?"

"By then you'll know. You'll settle somewhere. Maybe around here, maybe not. You'll make a good life for yourself. Then you'll live it."

"What do I have to do?"

"We'll start by enrolling you in a high school. It's barely summer. We can do it carefully, without being in a panic, and pick the right one."

13

"The lady's name is Nora Gibbs, officer," the rental car manager said. "She showed a California driver's license and paid with a Visa card. She called that day to have the rental car picked up because she didn't feel well enough to drive. We had a few of those during the pandemic, and sometimes when something is going around, we still do. The Visa was good, and the car was in perfect shape, so as far as we're concerned, she remains a good customer. Believe me, we'd much rather pick up a car than have a customer get in an accident or something."

"Well, thanks," said Officer Fenton. "I'm glad. We had this lady park an out-of-state car in the center of our business district, and it was still there twelve hours later. We thought we'd better find out if something happened to her, you know?"

"Oh, I understand," the manager said. "It's pretty busy around here, and we didn't have anybody to send to get it for a while. Uh, if that's all you needed, I've got a few people lining up for a car."

"Sure," said Officer Fenton. "Thanks for your help." He barely got the words out before the phone went dead. Fenton said to his partner, Campbell, "Interesting. Her name is Nora Gibbs, but she used a different name to sign in at the public defenders' office, and she showed a California license to rent the car."

"That's odd," Campbell said. "But a lot of women use their maiden name at work and their husband's name the rest of the time. She also might have been on a job for her boss, and signed in with the boss's name to identify what her business was."

"I don't know," Fenton said. "Those things are possible, sure. But sometimes you just get a feeling. You know, she walked around to a couple of places, and there aren't any pictures on the security cameras that really show what she looks like. Every single one is a big pair of sunglasses and a hat. She only took it off for a little while, when she was facing away from the camera, then put it back on."

Campbell stared out the window at the street. "I'm starting to wonder if we could be developing some federal troubles."

"What kind of federal troubles?"

"I don't know. But this is the kind of thing that happens just before a hundred FBI agents show up and start loading your filing cabinets and computers into trucks. Strangers show up in your town looking like they're lost and in no hurry to be found."

Fenton shrugged. "It could happen, I suppose. But let them come. We're honest, the DA is honest, and as far as I know, even the mayor and city council haven't taken any bribes. In order to get bribed, I think they'd have to do something, and they barely breathe."

"Sure we're honest, but the feds have got thousands of investigators on their payroll, so they've got to find stuff for them to investigate, and it's got to be as far from Washington as possible."

"I only hope this doesn't have something to do with my brother's murder."

"Amen," Campbell said, but he thought, how the hell can it not? A teenage Indian who claimed she was fighting off a rape by a twenty-six-year-old, and then a woman from a national Indian organization just happens to show up at the public defenders' office? Well, he had brought it up. That was about all he could do without destroying an eighteen-year friendship with his partner. Either it would give Dave Fenton's mind the little jolt it needed to realize there was something wrong with the whole theory of what had happened, or it wouldn't.

14

Jane took Clare through more steps to build a record for Katie Barnes. There were doctors for exams and shots, a dentist to have her teeth cleaned and examined. The purpose was to broaden and deepen the records, while also making Katie eligible to enter a school in New York State. Jane said Katie Barnes was a niece of hers who had come for the summer and would be staying for the next school year while her parents were working out of the country. She had notes that appeared to be signed by them giving her full authorization for medical and other decisions.

Jane arranged a visit to the Stanhope Country Day School, a private prep school in Buffalo. It was old, the main building a landmark made of slabs of Lockport limestone, with stained glass windows and high slate roofs. It had been in existence for well over a hundred years. Because it was expensive, it had remained small, and had a somewhat less obsessive view of the rules and procedures that practicality and the state education department imposed on public schools with thousands of students. Stanhope was able to offer personal attention from teachers. In spite of its age, the school had a liberal and forward-looking attitude, and had been one of the first to admit girls, about the same time the feeder schools for Harvard and Yale did in the 1960s.

Jane had a long, probing conversation with the admissions officer while she held May in her sling on her lap, skillfully using May's pretty face to keep the admissions officer charmed and distracted. Katie used the time to fill out the first few pages of the application devoted to who she was, where she was from, her current address and phone numbers, and what had drawn her to look into the Stanhope School. The admissions officer, Mona Stark, arranged an interview for Katie with the headmaster.

Katie's interview with the headmaster was scheduled for two days later, but then the headmaster, whose name was Dr. Simons, drifted into the admissions office, introduced herself as Judy Simons, said she'd had an appointment unexpectedly canceled, and initiated a friendly conversation with Katie Barnes.

At the end of it, Katie Barnes was admitted to the school as a special student for the fall semester, a status that Dr. Simons assured Katie and Jane would be regularized as soon as her records and essay could be properly evaluated, probably as early as mid-September.

Afterward, as they were walking across the parking lot toward Jane's car, Clare said, "I'm afraid."

"Sure you are," Jane said. "You'd be a fool not to be. But you obviously aced the interview with Dr. Simons. That's a beautiful start."

That reaction seemed to stagger Clare, but then she recovered a bit. "I won't know anybody, and I certainly won't have any friends. I'll eat lunch alone, and—"

"Yes. For a while you will. But Katie Barnes will be smart enough to pretend she's extremely confident, the kind of person other people want to meet. Above all, she will be receptive to anybody's attempt to connect with her. Receptive, not eager. If they say hi, you smile and say hi. The smile is not optional. If you do this right, your face will be tired at the end of the day. Some of those people will become friends. Others will not. But until the day they forget you entirely, they will think of you as a good person, who wasn't mean to anyone."

"You make it sound like a party, but I could be risking my life."

"That's right. Everything you do from now on can either increase your risk or make you temporarily safer than the average person. But you should be used to that by now. It's been true since you got attacked. And here you are: Katie Barnes, the newest student in the tenth grade of a respected private school, about five states away from Clare's troubles. Nobody is going to look for you there."

Jane turned on the car's interior lights and unlocked the car doors with the key fob from a distance, and then opened the back door to put May in her car seat. Clare got in beside May in the back seat, and Jane drove away from the school.

As the days passed May was growing, learning, and noticing more of her environment. She could hold her head up, reach for things, and had facial expressions of happiness when Jane, Carey, or Clare came near. Jane was watching the phenomena that mothers had been discovering for themselves for forever. Babies and young children learned more quickly than seemed to be possible. During her pregnancy Jane read that the average five-year-old knew ten thousand words. That meant learning at least five and a half new words every single day. May wasn't using words yet, but she was making cooing sounds and was already showing signs of responding to the voices of the people around her.

Clare was making progress at becoming Katie. She memorized all the details that she and Jane had put into her history. It wasn't enough to have all the addresses where Katie had lived on paper, Katie also had to know them. The names, personalities, and life stories of Katie's grandparents, parents, siblings, and friends, the names of her teachers, the stores where her parents had shopped, the schools that not only Katie, but also her parents, had attended all had to be ready in her mind. The parts of her lived experience that were necessary to make her stories seem real had to be studied closely in order to be sure that they didn't lead to the real place where she had lived.

Studying these things gave her the chance to revise and add details that worked. Every few days she would tell Jane and May the new parts, and Jane would listen for false notes or contradictions. Clare devised her own methods for calming her nerves about the new school. She and Jane ordered copies of the standard New York State school textbooks for the ninth and tenth grade curricula, and she studied them and took the practice exams. She also read some of the supplemental books recommended for discussion in English and history classes.

Jane was pleased that this was Clare's reaction to her predicament. She was preparing for every challenge she could anticipate, and if there was a way to increase her chance of fitting in by work and preparation, she embraced it.

Every day, Clare accompanied Jane on her long walk with May. Much of the time they spoke English, but when they were on a trail, in a park, or along the river where strangers were too far away to hear, they spoke Nundawaono, partly so that May would keep hearing it and begin to learn. There were many days when life seemed so simple and familiar to Jane that it felt as though she had two children, one less than a year old, and the other a teenager, the sort of sixteen-year-old who sometimes seemed like a vulnerable kid, and sometimes seemed like an adult who had already seen too much.

One night Jane heard an unfamiliar sound. When she got up to investigate, she realized the sound was Clare downstairs crying. Jane went to the staircase, then ventured as far as the foot of the stairs. Jane had the baby monitor in her hand, and the sound was the slow, measured breathing of May. Clare stood up, quickly ran her hands down her face to wipe the tears away, stood up, and hurried through the kitchen, then out the door into the night.

Jane walked outside. "It's me," she said to the night air. "I only want to help." She listened for an answer, but heard only May's slow, quiet breaths. After a long time, she said, "All right. I'm sorry I intruded on your privacy. If you ever want to talk to me, I'm always available. Good night." She turned and went inside, climbed the stairs, returned the baby monitor to the nightstand, and slid into bed beside Carey.

15

On Monday morning Magda drove a new olive green Subaru Outback to pick up Mikhail at his apartment. She had chosen him because he had struck her as capable and had a serious demeanor. When Mikhail had put his suitcase in the cargo bay, she said, "You drive. Take us to pick up one of the others." He drove to pick up Maxim, whose tone had made her worry that he might be overconfident. He drove to pick up Dmitri, the youngest and most cheerful, and parked the car at the bar. She got into another car, a new blue Ford Explorer, and had Dmitri drive her to pick up Daniil.

She was gaining a sense of which of these men were closer friends, which of them were the best drivers, as well as learning bits of random information about them from listening to their talk and looking at their apartments and the surrounding neighborhoods.

When all of them were back at the bar, she brought the men inside and told them to order what they wanted to drink. She was pleased that none of them ordered alcoholic drinks. They were at least self-disciplined to that extent. She said, "When we finish our drinks, we'll piss and then drive. We're going to get on the Massachusetts Turnpike and drive to

New York State, then get on the New York Thruway, which is also Route 90, and drive to the other end of New York State to the area around Buffalo. That's the last place where I saw her. There's an E-ZPass in each car, so forget tolls."

"We're going in two cars?" Maxim asked.

"Yes. We'll be in contact by phone. I bought two SUVs because it's the best way to do this kind of job. If one of them gets noticed by the wrong person, we will still have another car that nobody noticed or connects with the first one. If we're following somebody for too long, I'll have the lead car fall back and send the other one up. If one breaks down, we can all fit in the other. There will be two of you in one car and two in the other. Everybody will take a two-hour turn as driver, and a two-hour turn as passenger. When you've been a driver and a passenger with one person, move to be with a man you haven't driven with. If there's time left, then share a car with the third man. I'll sometimes move too. The trip is 454 miles, or about eight hours, but probably nine or ten with stops every two hours. Everybody understand?"

They all nodded or mumbled affirmatively.

"Anybody who doesn't feel fit to drive right now?"

Nobody spoke up. They all finished their drinks, visited the restrooms, and went outside to the cars and headed for the Massachusetts Turnpike. The drive started with an hour of slow traffic caused by several stretches where crews had closed down lanes to repair the pavement.

She talked to the men while they were trapped in the car. "Who is the best marksman? What if we needed to take out someone at a distance? Who should do it?"

"Daniil," Maxim said. "He was an army sniper."

"Before they threw him out," said Dmitri.

Magda said, "How about with a pistol? Who is the best?"

Maxim said, "I am."

"No," Dmitri said. "I'm better than you."

"Why?" said Magda. "What makes you better?"

"Ten bullets in the center circle."

"And you?" she asked Maxim.

"Two bullets in the enemy's head."

"Who is an enemy?"

"Whoever I kill."

"Good. Just remember what we're doing. Don't shoot the wrong person," she said. "If you kill the woman we're after, aim the next round through your own head and save Mr. Obolonsky the trouble."

The method of travel that Magda had adopted worked well. It allowed her to mix up the occupants of each car, including herself, so she spent half the day with each of her men, getting used to them and learning more about them with each hour. As the cars sped across the two states, she became satisfied that she had made good choices. They were genuine vors, men who had done little in their lives that was legal. They talked enough like Americans to be Americans. Each of them looked like a man who was on his way home from some dull low-paying job to face a complaining wife and a couple of smart-mouthed kids. She felt better as the day passed.

With the rest stops and driver replacements, the trip took nearly ten hours. It was after 1:00 A.M. when they left the New York State Thruway on Exit 50, outside Buffalo. She sent a map from her phone to her men's phones showing the way to a park along the Niagara River where there was an entrance road that led through a grove of old trees, turned and skirted some low, gentle hills, and led to a picnic area that was not visible from the main road.

They pulled onto the narrow drive into the park and turned off their lights, stopped at the picnic grove, and got out of the cars. Magda opened the back of the Subaru. "We're going to want to be hard to see in the dark. Maxim and Dmitri, put on darker shirts." She pushed aside a couple of suitcases, and then opened a carrying case. She used the light of her phone screen to show the men what was in it. "There's a Glock 17 pistol and three loaded magazines for each of you."

She opened the back of the Ford so the other two could reach their pistols and ammunition. She said, "There are New York license plates under the back rug. Now that we're off the toll roads it's time to take the Massachusetts plates off and put those on. Then get back in the cars. I'll drive this one to the house where we caught her last time. Daniil, drive the other car. Follow me, but stay at least two hundred feet behind."

As she was driving, she kept the phone line open on speaker. "Remember, we want her alive. If she's there, we take her now. Don't kill her, but beyond that, there are no rules."

Magda drove into the small town farther north along the Niagara River. Inland beyond the park they passed a complex of grassy athletic fields, then parking lots and a high school. She remembered this stretch of the trip. It had been about this time of the night when she had come to this house before. She remembered checking out of the hotel near the airport at midnight and getting into the big SUV. She and Mr. Porchen and Albert McKeith and the two vors had driven to this town, come down this street, three or four blocks in from the river, and stopped near the house.

Albert was a very young man who didn't know anything at all about the Bratva, or speak any Russian. Magda had become comfortable with American men because she had spent a year sleeping with them to repay the cost of her immigration to America. Albert had turned up because he had killed his girlfriend's lover in front of the girlfriend. She had testified against him, but he had been acquitted for some reason. Through an intermediary Albert had asked Mr. Porchen to help find the girlfriend so he could kill her. When Mr. Porchen had heard that the girlfriend had been helped to disappear by a tall, thin woman with black hair, Mr. Porchen had realized that he might be talking about the woman who had made people vanish.

Albert was weak-minded, he was lazy, he could not be trusted, but he was beautiful—young, with long, thin arms and legs, a flat stomach, and big, liquid blue eyes. She had taken him as a temporary companion for that trip. What made her nervous was that this had put her in the position of having to control him, explain him to the others, and be accountable to Mr. Porchen for him. That night as they came to this very spot, passing under the blinking red light by the elementary school, Albert had guided the group to this valuable woman's house. Magda had kept wondering, would he turn out to only think he knew the address? He had never been there. He had directions from a friend of his who had. If Albert had lied, or appeared to have lied, would Mr. Porchen only kill him, or kill her too? But Albert had not lied that time.

She said into her phone to the men in the car behind, "We're only two of these short blocks from the house now. I'll show you the place, and then I'm going to park a block away. You turn at the corner after the house and park on a cross street." She opened the windows in the SUV.

As she drove, she let the car idle, coasting down the very gradual incline. It was a warm, still night, and she would pause at each intersection, and then drift into the center of it and look up and down the cross streets to see if there were any headlights or any silhouettes of parked cars with gear on the roofs or any faint glow from instruments on a dashboard. In small American towns like this one, most of the traffic late at night was on the big highways. The narrow residential streets were dark and empty after midnight.

She pulled the car up along the curb, pointed across the street, and said, "That's it, the third house from the corner with the two big trees in front."

Maxim and Dmitri looked at it. "She picked a good place to hide," Maxim said. "Not new, not big, not fancy, one of about twenty right around here nearly the same style."

"There are more like this all over town," Magda said. "She's good at not standing out. Mr. Porchen said what she does isn't just to pretend she's not the woman you're hunting for. She makes up a whole new person, and becomes her. Do you understand?"

"I'll have to think about it."

Dmitri said, "Not looking like you're a thief isn't enough. You have to seem to be an electrical contractor or something."

They saw the other two men, Daniil and Mikhail, approaching on the sidewalk. Magda said, "Here come the others. Time to get started."

They got out, closed the car doors as quietly as they could, and walked across the street to the house. Magda stepped back and let her four men circle the building.

Outside the house she saw a dog bowl with water in it, a couple of tennis balls, and a rubber bone that had been chewed on. She looked around the section of the back lawn. There had been no dog here the last time. She saw the garbage bins—green, blue, black—at the back of the house. She opened the green, and could smell the cut grass inside. She closed it and opened the black can, and tapped her phone's screen for light. There were a few little green bags that Americans used to pick up and throw away dog feces, all of them tied with the same simple knot. But there was no smell. There was also a big black garbage bag with the top knotted, but that didn't smell rotten, like garbage, either.

She whispered to Mikhail, "There's no dog here. Get started."

Mikhail knelt at the back door and fiddled with his pick and tension wrench in the lock and then turned the knob. Magda nodded at Daniil and he drew his pistol and stepped into the kitchen.

The others followed. There were no gunshots, no sounds of fighting. They had made it inside without waking anyone or setting off an alarm. Magda had noticed on her other visit that the woman who owned this house was like most people who did things they didn't want the police to know. The security company stickers on windows and the alarm panels attached to walls were for show, connected to nothing and meaning nothing. Nobody wanted police responding to an alarm. But now there were cheap alarm systems a person could install herself and receive the alarm on her cell phone with a recorded video image of the intruders. This woman should certainly be smart enough to know those were available. But Magda didn't have time to think about that now.

Magda had her pistol in her right hand. She used her left to point silently at each of her four men, and then in a direction to search. She sent Daniil and Dmitri toward the stairs to the bedrooms, Mikhail and Maxim through the dining room and living room to the front of the house. Magda searched the pantry and closets, standing aside and flinging each door open with the gun pointed at belly height, and then going to clear the small office off the living room.

After about ten minutes, Daniil came to her and said, "She's not here, but the place seems occupied. We haven't found any cameras or silent alarms."

Magda patted his cheek to signal that was enough, and walked out into the living room as the others came and joined her there. She said, "Okay. You four take the bedrooms. Get some sleep while you can. I'm going to look around a bit, and then sleep down here to wait for her."

The men obeyed her order. She wondered what they thought of it. Like all men, they would be sure to think it would be wiser if they were down here on the ground floor ready to overpower the woman. But being here in this house had made Magda remember that other night she had spent here. The only reason she had lived through it was that she had been sleeping on the ground floor with Albert McKeith when the woman had killed the ones sleeping upstairs with smoke and carbon monoxide.

The woman wasn't here right now, and if she had been here, she couldn't fight back the same way twice, but she would do something. Magda waited until the four men were upstairs, and then she got up and walked from room to room. She passed familiar things she had seen years ago—the office, the living room, the little area off the kitchen with the benches and the rubber mats and coat hooks. What was the term? Mudroom. But all the time she had a destination and she was moving toward it.

Magda opened the door beside the pantry and saw the long, straight series of steps leading down into the dark of the basement. After she and Mr. Porchen and the others had ambushed, swarmed, and beaten the woman, they had wanted to be sure she couldn't escape while they slept. They had taken her down into the basement, chained her to pipes along the wall, gone back upstairs, run a power saw through the top of the steps so the whole length of them crashed to the floor, and then closed the door at the top so the whole basement was in total darkness. She remembered the loud clap of the wooden stairs hitting the floor, and the feeling she had as she walked away that there was no possibility of the woman escaping.

Magda had thought about this place many times in the three years since then. She remembered feeling uncomfortable that the woman had taken so many blows without crying out, weakening, or telling Mr. Porchen even the tiniest bit of information about anything. Seeing her left in this terrible captivity in the dark had made Magda smile in relief. Magda knew, positively knew, that now the woman would weaken, give in and reveal what she knew, and Mr. Porchen would get lots of money. Mr. Porchen was a boss who shared, and this would be enough to make them all rich.

Magda remembered seeing the others go upstairs, leaving her alone with Albert. The night started full of joy. Albert was a treat to look at, and he was a manipulator, and over the weeks while they had searched for this woman, he had studied Magda and learned exactly what she liked, and how to make her happy. That night was their last and the best. It had never occurred to Magda that if given the slightest chance, this woman would kill everyone in the house.

Magda listened for any sounds of movement from her new crew upstairs but heard nothing. She knelt on the kitchen floor above the stairs, turned on her phone, held it beside the pair of thick vertical boards that held the steps, and examined them closely. The stairs were made the same, but the whole structure was new. She saw that what held it in place were a set of six quarter-inch bolts, and the bolts were silvery and clean and new. The wood had been painted, but she could see a spot where the paint on the back of one of the steps had been brushed on too thin, and the wood beneath it was new. She stood and walked down the steps. The basement was cool, because the walls were made of big stones joined with mortar.

There were no windows, so she knew it was safe to turn on the flashlight app on her phone and throw the bright white beam on it. The space was as she had remembered it. There were a couple of old workbenches on the far end, with a vise and sharpening stones that must not have been used in a generation, and some paint cans, brushes, rollers, and pans. She walked past them and then moved along the stone wall with her light, as though she had just unearthed this new place. It almost was a new place to her. The last time she had seen it, this cellar had not yet been used to kill her Pachan and crew. It had been a neutral place until they had used it as a cage for the woman they'd captured.

She passed the second pipe that the woman had been chained to that night, and there was the old furnace, and beside it the outline of a coal bin, many years after the coal furnace had been decommissioned and replaced by an oil furnace. In the light of her phone, it looked like a giant octopus, the coal-burning part with a door in its belly, and above it, the several rounded heating ducts stretching up like tentacles toward the upper floors where the brass registers let the hot air pour into the rooms of the house. That night, the woman had burned something in the furnace that filled the ducts with carbon monoxide that killed the men on the second floor and nearly killed her and Albert on the first floor, and probably half-killed the woman chained down here. Magda had observed enough about the woman to know she had expected to die too.

Magda opened the old iron furnace's door and looked in, but there was nothing to see anymore, nothing to learn. Whatever the woman had burned had turned to ashes, and the ashes removed by a cleaning crew, or maybe by the workmen who had replaced the stairs. She climbed them carefully, up to the small landing, and into the kitchen. She closed the door and gave it a second push to be sure it couldn't swing open again.

Magda walked back along the hall from the kitchen toward the front of the house. She was going to sleep in the small room off the living room that the woman used as an office, because it had an oversize leather couch to sleep on, and a door with a lock on it.

She reached the living room, and she was conscious that it seemed lighter than she had expected. There was a faint glow from the street lamp about a hundred feet away that fell across the front curtains. Then she noticed a shadow she didn't remember across the curtain. Her hand went to the back of her waistband and gripped the pistol. She studied the shadow for a moment. What was throwing that shadow? The shadow moved and she brought the pistol around her body and held it against her right leg as the figure's arm rose and the fist knocked on the door.

The woman wouldn't knock on her own door. Magda said in English, "Who's that?"

The man's voice was quiet, but there was an urgency to it. "Miss Whitefield, please don't be startled. My name is Brian Finlay and I'm in trouble. Karen Alvarez sent me."

Magda held onto the pistol. This was something unexpected, but there was so much to take in and understand, and it had to be done quickly. Miss Whitefield must be the woman who lived here. He obviously thought that Magda was her. Was this a threat or an opportunity? She struggled to think ahead.

Magda hid the pistol back in her waistband and opened the door. "Come in and sit on the floor over there." She pointed at a spot in front of the couch.

He kept talking nervously. "I was very careful coming here, and I'm sure nobody could have followed me. I looked in your garage the night I got here and saw it was empty, so I put my car in it and slept there for a few days while I waited for you to come back."

"What did she tell you was going to happen when you got here?"

"That once you knew the trouble I was in, you would want to help me."

"With what? How can I help you?"

"She said you knew how to make people disappear."

Magda said, "I would need to know more. What are you running from?"

"My old boss. He's trying to have me killed."

"Tell me about it."

"It's a long story."

"It's a long night," she said.

"I was living in Chicago," he said. "For about the last ten years. I was working as an executive assistant." Even in the dim light he sensed from the way she tilted her head that she wasn't sure what that meant in his case.

She said, "What did you actually do?"

"A rich man named Barton Stillivant hired me to be around and do a lot of the things that maybe a rich guy doesn't have time to do, and sometimes the things he just doesn't want to do. I arranged his travel and went with him. I made sure his suitcases got picked up and toted to customs and loaded into the cab and taken to his hotel suite. I set up dinner parties for him. I maintained the list of people he gave presents to, picked out the gifts, sent or delivered them or whatever. Sometimes I would drive a woman friend of his home from a date so he could drink as much as he wanted without getting in trouble. After a couple years I was representing him at meetings with his brokers and accountants and so on. The job was whatever he wanted done."

Magda listened and waited. She knew that this was a delicate conversation. She had to learn as much as she could, and the way to do that was to let this man talk about his problems, no matter how impatient she was to learn about the woman he called Miss Whitefield.

"This went on for nearly ten years. He paid me well, and after a while he didn't want to bother with paying bills, so part of my job was paying myself. He seemed to trust me, but there were boundaries. Secrets. I never really knew what he was making money on, or how he got so rich. He would just say 'I buy bulk commodities cheap in one place and sell them in other places for more.'"

"You haven't said why he wants you dead."

"It was true that he bought and sold things in bulk, so he could pay less for a unit, and then sell them for more. But when I saw the bookkeeping, it was all order numbers, sometimes addresses and sometimes just a city, or a shipping company, but it was never a person's name or a clear product name. They were 'units' like 'two hundred thousand units' or just pages and pages of model numbers or serial numbers. If he went to examine the merchandise, I never went with him or saw him do it."

"What changed?"

"One day I saw a television news report of a big arrest in Mexico, and I recognized three of the people they were dragging off to jail. They had been in our Chicago living room a week before. When I realized that they were caught selling military weapons in Mexico, I knew that the man they'd bought them from was my boss, Bart Stillivant. I waited two weeks and then went to him and quit. I told him I had a sister in Phoenix who had a degenerative disease and needed my help. I was going to go take care of her. He acted as though he believed me."

"Did you actually expect him to? Who would believe a healthy man would quit a good job to go hold a relative's hand while she waited to die?"

"I did think he would. The truth was that I already had done that, about twelve years earlier. It was my mother, but it was the same story. And I really did go to Phoenix. If he had any doubts, he could call me."

"How did you learn that you were in danger?"

"Men came for me in the middle of the night in Phoenix. They tied my hands, pulled a bag over my head, and dragged me out to a van and drove into the desert. They went off-road some distance, and I knew they were taking me out there to kill me and bury my body. But at one point, they hit a rock. I couldn't see anything, but I heard it and I felt it. I could smell the leaking gasoline, and one of the men had hit his head when the van jerked to the side, and he was half-conscious and bleeding. When they dragged him out, I could hear them talking about how bad it was. I had been working on freeing my hands, and I knew this was my last chance, I was desperate, and finally succeeded. I pulled off the hood, went out the back door of the van, and ran into the darkness. I ran for a couple of miles, and then walked, looking for lights that would show me where the road was."

"You were lucky they didn't just walk in and kill you in your apartment," Magda said. "The only thing your boss could possibly think was that you were making a deal with the authorities to sell him out so you wouldn't be blamed for any of the things he was doing."

"Yes."

She thought for a moment. "You can sleep in this room tonight, and we'll talk again in the morning."

She climbed the stairs to the second floor and stepped into the bedroom where Daniil and Mikhail were in bed. She closed the door and whispered, "Are you awake?"

"Yes." They both started to get up.

"Don't get up now," she said. "Just listen. A man came to the door. Someone sent him here looking for the woman we want. He thinks I'm her. We're going to use him, so I don't want one of you to stumble across him and kill him. I'll tell the others." She went to the other bedroom and repeated the warning to Maxim and Dmitri. Then she went to the linen closet in the upstairs hallway, found a pillow and a blanket, and brought them downstairs, but found Brian Finlay was already asleep, so she left them by the couch. She went out the kitchen door, walked to the garage, and entered.

By the light of her phone, she saw that the car he had parked there was a modest-looking black Honda sedan with Illinois license plates. He had a laundry bag and a blanket in the back seat. She tried the driver's side door so the interior lights would go on. It opened. She got in and began her search with the glove compartment. The car registration confirmed his name was Brian Finlay and showed an address in Chicago. She kept looking in the glove compartment and found a vinyl pouch with the car manual and three smaller booklets about the car in it. She took them out, flipped through them, and noticed a yellow sheet that had the name of a car dealer in Chicago printed on the top, and had been used as a bookmark for a page about the car's lighting system.

She opened the other door and looked in the back seat. She lay on her side and reached under each of the front seats. She tugged on each section of the upholstery, feeling for any part that might move. She felt the laundry bag he seemed to have been using as a pillow to sleep in the back seat, found the outer parts soft, then reached down into the middle and found the gun.

Magda felt more relieved than anything else. It made her think Finlay genuinely thought he was in danger of being killed. He had been sleeping in his car in this garage, and he'd made sure that at any moment he could put his hand on a gun. She considered the implications. The first was that if he was thinking that way, he'd probably left the car keys somewhere close to the driver's seat. She sat in the front again. She turned down the two sunshades, then stuck her fingers under the mirrors attached to them.

Then she realized that she had not had to think of the key as a key. It was probably a fob. She looked beside the steering wheel and saw that there was a starter button, not a key slot. All that was necessary was that the fob be somewhere inside the car, and it would start. She looked in the drink holders, then under the seat, then felt around beneath the dash for tape. Then she sat in the back seat and reached into the pocket behind the driver's seat, and then the one behind the passenger seat, and there it was. It was there because it was an easy place to reach from the driver's seat. She took the gun and the key fob, closed the car quietly, and went back to the house. She hid the gun in a covered pan in one of the lower kitchen cupboards and the fob in a cracker box, and then went deeper into the house.

Magda used her phone to find the telephone number and address of Bart Stillivant and copied them in her phone's address book. Then she lay down on the couch in the den and went to sleep.

16

Memorial Day week was a time for conferences in the world of medicine. This year Carey McKinnon, MD, was leaving for the airport at 5:00 A.M. to catch his flight to Las Vegas for a trauma surgeons' convention. He lingered in the kitchen and kissed Jane one more time. She said, "Have a good trip. Learn all the latest ways of getting home earlier every night to be with your wife, and then fly home. We'll be waiting for you."

"Right," he said.

"Go catch your plane."

Carey picked up his suitcase and went out to the garage. She watched his strong back as he lifted the suitcase into the car trunk and got into the driver's seat, and began to miss him. She tended to think about all her time with him at once, because it was all one story, from the time they met at college, both eighteen and two of a group of a dozen friends, to their first real hug ever on graduation day when they thought they'd never see each other again, to the day eight years later when he simply showed up on her porch, already a surgeon, and knocked on the door as though the friendship had never been interrupted, and then nearly ten years of marriage. From this moment's perspective, it could have been one day. She watched him drive his car past the kitchen window and out to the street, and then she let go of the curtain.

Jane heard Katie above her, walking toward the stairs. It was too early for May to wake up, and she hadn't yet heard any of her stirring sounds from the baby monitor yet. Katie came into the kitchen. "I heard Carey's car. Is he heading for the airport?"

"Yes," Jane said. "Since he's up early for surgery most days anyway, he picked the first flight out. You gain three hours flying to Nevada because it's the only landlocked state on Pacific time. If the plane isn't delayed, he arrives in time for a late breakfast with friends. It also gives us more time."

"For what? What are we going to do?"

"Carey's conference is our chance to go on a long drive to see some friends of mine who can help with your identity."

"I thought we already did that," Katie said.

"We got a good start, but there's more to do. And this will give you a chance to learn some things. Pack for an overnight trip. We'll give May a bath and take her out for a walk and then get started this afternoon."

By mid-afternoon they were a hundred miles southwest and approaching the southern tip of Canandaigua Lake. "Do you see that big hill?"

"I see a bunch of them," Katie said.

Jane pointed. "That big green one there. People around here call it South Hill. Our real name is Onondowaga, the People of the Great Hill, right? Well, that's it—the great hill we're supposed to have come from. There was a village on that lower hill beside it. In the old days before the peace, when the first five nations joined to be the Haudenosaunee, villages were elevated and fortified. You can still see signs to show you where that one was."

Katie said, "So that's it? My relatives—mostly my grandma—told me the stories, but it was all so far away, and so old, that I never thought of any of the places as real spots that you could pull your car up to and walk around on."

"This part of the state is full of them. And the rest of the state is full of places where Cayuga, Onondaga, Oneida, and Mohawk villages were. Most of the big roads started out as trails between them, including this one."

◆

It was after nightfall when they reached the small central New York town. On the outskirts there was a sign that said "Welcome to Cantrell Falls" and then beyond it a John Deere farm equipment lot. Jane drove into town slowly, looking to both sides whenever they reached a cross street. She drove up and down a few streets, cutting back on her path every few minutes.

"Are we looking for something?" Katie said.

"Not exactly. What we're doing is fishing. We're the bait, trying to see if anyone is watching, or has followed us here. This is the place I was heading from the beginning. When you're trying to disappear and become somebody else, you need the help of experts. What the experts are doing, and what you're doing, is against the law. That means each of you is dealing with a criminal. A few people who break laws do it for good reasons, but not many. Others will take what you have and leave you dead. The people we've come to visit are ones I've learned I can trust. There's nothing more valuable than that."

"But you have to do all of this to protect us from them?"

"No. We're protecting them. They're a couple. The man, the one who started doing this in the first place, is named Stewart." She drove onto a circular street that went around a park with tall, wide old trees surrounding an antique bandstand. "He bought that big brick house across the park about twenty years ago, moved into it, and made sure the local people liked him, thought of him as a quiet, decent person, and then largely forgot to wonder about him anymore. Even then, he was one of the most skillful forgers anywhere.

"The woman is named Molly. She was young and being hunted, and she found her way to Stewart looking for some identification. He took her in to keep her out of sight and safe while he made a new identity for her. Stewart's work takes time. She was here for a week, two weeks, five weeks. After a while they realized that she was still here because neither of them wanted her to leave. Once they both knew that, she just moved from the room he'd given her to his room and stayed forever."

"That's kind of romantic."

"They still have to be practical. There are rules to coming here. You can't call and make an appointment, because if the authorities knew about him, or knew about any of his customers like me, they'd be listening in, and would round us all up. We have to park a distance away and walk to the front door, so they have time to see us, see if anybody is following or watching us, and decide if it's safe to let us in." She pulled the car over to the curb and turned off the engine.

"What would their other choice be?" Katie asked.

"I don't know," Jane said. "They probably have a car hidden somewhere nearby. But they've never told me, or probably anybody else. I wouldn't even be surprised if there was a tunnel to it." She lifted the sleeping May out of her car seat, put her in the modern version of a cradleboard, and slipped the straps over her shoulders. "Okay," she said. "I'm sure they're aware of us by now. Time to walk."

Jane took the first steps, and Katie joined her. They walked across the small circular park on the walkway made of fine-ground gravel, which led to the steps of the antique bandstand, then curved around it and continued to the far side. They crossed the street and went up the steps of the large redbrick house to the front porch.

As soon as they were on the porch, the polished wooden front door swung open and as she followed Jane inside, Katie's attention was drawn by two things at once. The door was about three inches thick, and the inner side was black steel. The second was the sight of the woman who pushed it shut. She was pretty, seemed to be in her mid-thirties, shorter than Seneca women like Jane and even Katie, with long reddish-blond hair. The woman stepped aside, into what looked like an open coat closet to put a rifle with a long magazine into a recessed vertical space that seemed to have been built to hold it. The woman closed the door on the closet, then turned to Jane. "Jane, Jane, Jane," she said. "Whenever you leave us, I'm afraid I'll never see you again. It's been a couple of years." Jane turned to the side and Molly saw May. "Oh my God, Jane. Is she yours?"

"Yes," Jane said.

"No wonder you disappeared. She's beautiful."

"It's wonderful to see you, Molly. But that's another long story I won't be able to tell you," Jane said. "Here's someone else I want you to meet. Her name is going to be Katie. It's the one we use already."

Molly said to her, "It's a good name. You look like you could be a Katie. Or a Kate. I assume the paperwork will say Katherine."

"I guess so," Katie said. "I'm new to this, so I'll do what Jane says."

"Come on. I'll take you up to see Stewart. He's in the studio. He'll be so pleased to see you, Jane. All three of you, in fact."

They all climbed the old-style curving staircase to the second-floor landing. Stewart came out of the large open room at the top of the stairs. "Jane! I thought that sounded like your voice," he said. "It's great to see you."

His eyes widened in surprise, and he stepped closer. "Yours?"

"It finally happened," she said. "We've been trying for years. Her name is May."

"I never knew there was a 'we' to try with. Congratulations. And who is this? Are you still taking on runners?"

"Her name is going to be Katherine with a *K* Marie Barnes."

"I'm pleased to meet you, Miss Barnes," he said. "I'm Stewart, and I guess Molly and I will be working on your identities."

"Identities? More than one?"

Stewart turned and looked at Jane.

Jane said, "I should have explained this ahead of time. No matter how good your identity is, and how closely you guard it, things can happen. Ten years from now you're in an airport in Chicago and someone who knows you bumps into you. So I ask Stewart to make not just the identity you live with, but also two others. They're not as elaborate, but they're good and they include the main things—a driver's license, a social security card, and a birth certificate. I'll add a credit card in each name later, so every time the bill gets paid, the identity is older and deeper."

"I get it," Katie said. She turned to Stewart. "I'm sorry. I don't mean to be stupid. It's just all so new."

Jane said to Stewart, "I'm afraid we only have another day to do this part, but the rest can take a month or two."

"We'd better get started on what we have to do right away."

Molly said, "Katie and I can get started on the photographs now. Maybe you and Jane can talk about the rest."

"Thanks, Molly."

Katie followed her down the hall into another room that seemed to have once been a bedroom. Now it was only furnished with a white screen, a digital camera on a tripod, a monitor, four long clothing racks on wheels, crowded with clothes on hangers, and a chair. She closed the door and said, "How old are you?"

"I'm sixteen."

"All right. We're going to take pictures of you in some different kinds of clothes, different hair, and so on. Some will be summer clothes, some winter, and some in between. They're for identification cards and so on. But in your case, we'll also take some that will still work when you're quite a bit older, and maybe a couple that make you younger, so you have a past. I've done this about a hundred times, so trust me. I work fast, and so will you. We'll start with the school picture, the kind that ends up in a school yearbook."

"Okay."

"Put these on." She gave her a pullover cashmere sweater and a thin white gold necklace chain with a tiny diamond on it. When Katie was ready, Molly seated her on the chair in front of the screen, brushed her hair, and posed her, then went to the camera. "Now smile."

She looked through the viewfinder. "Really smile. Not like you. Smile like that dumb-ass girl that always gets the male attention. Think cheerleader." She took the picture, turned her slightly, and took another. "Here. Take a look."

Molly hurried off to pick another outfit while Katie got up and looked at the monitor's screen. She hated the expression of the girl in the picture, but she recognized what Molly had done. She saw a completely different person who had her features.

Next there was an outfit Molly called "passport." The main thing she was concerned with was the size of the image of her face. With slight adjustments, they took the picture for "driver's license."

Then there was one she called "class president." That was followed by several she said were "work ID card." Some were simple blouses or jackets from suits, and others were more like the clothes she'd worn to school in Oklahoma.

Next Molly said, "Now I'm going to age you as much as I can, but gradually. First, 'senior prom.'" She went to work first on Katie's hair, pulling it into a tight ponytail, and making it into a French twist and then working on her makeup. Katie felt like she had when she was seven and tried her mother's makeup in front of a mirror. It felt thick, overdone. But she was not displeased with the picture.

"Now let's try a graduation picture. I'll pick out a cap and gown that'll fit you."

◆

In the studio, Jane and Stewart were talking about the identification. Jane paced back and forth carrying May while Stewart sat at his work table and took notes.

"She's sixteen. I wanted her to have a different birth date, so I registered her at school as a sixteen-year-old sophomore with a birthday of August 19. I would like the works for her—birth certificate, social security card, driver's license, passport, as much of it as possible real. I also want two other identities—let's say Martha Wilkes and Megan Phelan—in case she has to bail out. Those are names I've got credit cards for. What matters is some government-issued ID to make it all stick. Is that still possible?"

"The methods are different now, but the results are the same," Stewart said. "It's more expensive. I seem to say that every time I see you, but it's true. I got into this at the beginning because I was good at the art. The eye is still necessary but the hand is useless now. The first name will run fifty thousand, the others twenty."

"It's about what I expected," she said. "I can give you part in cash, and write you a few checks on different accounts for the rest. All right?"

"If you want to, but I know you're good for it," Stewart said. "I don't know much more than that about you, and I haven't ever tried to find out anything. But I see you have this beautiful baby now, and I wonder. I don't think you're going to leave her with a babysitter and go off with a sixteen-year-old to set her up as a freestanding adult somewhere. You said you registered her for school. I think that means you're going to hide her yourself."

Jane said, "There's no other choice. I want her to be safe. I think that will take somebody who knows how it's done to give her the years she needs to grow up."

He looked at her for a second, and then turned his attention to the paper on his desk. "I'll get to work on this later tonight. Is the old PO box number still good?"

"The one in Chicago? Yes."

Molly and Katie appeared in the doorway. Molly said, "We're done. Come and see what we've got."

They went into the photography studio and looked at the pictures on the monitor. Stewart said, "That's good. That one too. Love that. We can use either of these. This one might be stretching the age a little, but it looks professional. This one's a little safer, I think. Pretty can be dangerous, if it tends toward the sexy. We don't want a picture that sticks out among four hundred. These are all good. Great work, Molly. Can you make a set of proofs so I can remember what the options are while I'm working on this?"

"Sure."

"I think that's all we need," Stewart said. "You can stay the night or take the kids home now, if you want."

"I'll do that," she said. "But I want to pay you first."

"You don't have to," he said. "I trust you."

Jane intentionally didn't look at Katie. "I want to. These days I don't find it easy to travel."

They went back to the studio. Jane opened the larger baby bag she had brought, pushed aside a blanket and some tiny clothes, and took out three ten-thousand-dollar stacks of banded hundreds, and four checkbooks. The checks had different women's names and addresses printed on them, but they were all accounts in different banks where she stored money. She wrote checks for odd numbers, none of them the same. There were four for about five thousand, four for about four thousand, three for about eight thousand. When she finished, May began to cry. Jane said, "Trifecta. Wet, hungry, and poopy. As soon as I take care of her, we'll head for home."

◆

Jane drove patiently and with strict attention to speed limits and traffic regulations. She had always been aware that anything that made her car stand out could trigger a traffic stop and bring on the police curiosity that might end her runner's life. The only time that was different was when she was being chased. This night there were two extremely precious lives in her hands, and she was aware of it every second. "Talk to me," she said. "It keeps me from getting bored and falling asleep."

"Is there anything else you haven't told me we have to do?" Katie said.

"There will be something. I just don't know which problems are going to come up and need to be solved, and which ones are going to pass us by. We've got the obvious ones. I knew we were going to need to find you a protected place to be until you got a little older, and we've settled that. You've gotten yourself admitted to a nice school for fall, and it's the kind a runaway sixteen-year-old wouldn't be able to get into. We just made a start on the hardest and most risky part. I knew that before too long you were going to need masterpiece-grade fake identity documents and a couple of substitute sets in case one name got burned."

"That was dangerous?" Katie said. "They seemed so chill about it."

"Stewart and Molly are successful. That means they're in more danger every day of being destroyed by their success. If you're the best, people will love you or hate you. Either way they're likely to talk about you. If the authorities hear the talk, they'll arrest them. If competitors find them, they may try to sabotage, rob, or kill them. We're lucky to know them, and lucky we've got them started on your identification."

"But now it's done, right? Nothing else is going to happen?"

Jane hesitated for a second. In the next few weeks, Stewart and Molly would be doing the riskiest part, trying to insert Katie Barnes into governmental records. The process began logically with a birth certificate, then a Social Security number, and then a driver's license. At each step there were sophisticated and changing methods of catching someone doing exactly what Stewart and Molly would be doing. Someday Katie would have to know all of it, but not tonight.

She said, "Everything we had to do now is finished and you've done perfectly so far. Starting tomorrow, just concentrate on what you can do to help yourself. Get ahead on your studies, practice your backstory, and give me a hand with May a couple hours a day when Carey is home so he takes you seriously. During the next week or so I'd like to take you shopping and get you more clothes and things other girls are likely to have—a phone, a watch, some simple, tasteful jewelry, a purse. That kind of thing."

"That doesn't sound serious. It sounds like fun."

"It's both. Life isn't simple. I met your grandmother, so I know you were raised, as I was, to know that setting your heart on 'having nice things' is stupid. But in this situation, you're being smart. You're building a disguise that will help you fade into a crowd of conformists. It's always safer to be indistinguishable from the herd."

"I've been thinking about the herd since we started looking for schools. At home I had friends—real friends, and we'd do anything for each other. My best friend drove me halfway across the country to get to you, even though she knew it would mean driving back alone, and might get her fired and in trouble."

"Part of what that tells me is that you were a good friend to her," Jane said. "You'll make good friends here, too. You just have to be careful. People love to tell their friends everything and listen to all of their thoughts and stories. You can still do most of that. You just have to stick with the story about your past that you and I made up, and tell it the same way always. There can't be one special friend you tell the other story, or even parts of it. I'm afraid that's always going to be true."

"It's funny. I used to try to keep from telling lies. Now I'm afraid I won't be good enough at it."

"You'll get better and better at it. You can talk about things that are universally true. I don't know—the river is beautiful, but it looks best when the sun is out and the blue sky can reflect off it. You can say things about your parents, whom they're never going to expect to meet because we'll probably keep them working in a foreign country as long as possible. Nothing exciting, though, or too specific. Maybe they work for the government maintaining trade agreements in various countries. You'll have to mention your aunt Jane. But the best strategy is to talk to them about them. Ask questions, be interested in their lives."

"I guess I can do that," she said.

"The main thing is to keep your secrets while appearing to have no secrets. You're afraid. Fear isn't always a weakness. It can keep you safe. I guarantee that if any of the people you meet knew the full story, the rest would know it in a day, and within a week or so, you would be in a cell in Oklahoma. If you ever make a mistake, don't ignore it. Tell me about it that day. I'll figure out what has to be done, and if I need to, I'll get you far away fast."

"There's so much to remember, and so many chances to do the wrong thing."

"Yes. Remember you're brave. You were the victim who fought back. It's true that now you have to make an effort to be invisible and stay safe. It's not fair and it's not easy, but I've seen a lot of people do it. What they had to learn at the start was that they couldn't be the person they'd always been. The next thing they learned was that it also gave them a new opportunity."

"What kind of opportunity?"

"The reason a lot of them had to come to me was that they had made a mess of their lives. Having to start over gave them the chance to erase all that and become a new person—the one they would have wanted to be if they'd known more at the beginning. That's not you, but you have an even better chance to become exactly the adult you want to be, and you have a lot more years to think about it and prepare yourself for it."

The night drive home was faster than the trip to Stewart and Molly's house. The speed limits hadn't changed, but the Thruway traffic was thin, and there were no delays. They stopped once to buy gas and snacks and use the restroom, and then were off again. By 3:00 A.M. they were on the last stretch of road to the McKinnon house. Jane drove slowly to look at every one of the properties along the road, every spot where a vehicle could park, making sure that nothing had appeared since they had left in the afternoon. When she was satisfied that it was safe, she turned into the long driveway, around the house, and up into the garage.

17

The sky was beginning to lighten to a shade of gray that had the promise of morning behind it, and Magda opened her eyes. When it was the smartest thing to do, she could sleep twelve hours, but this morning she had to be awake before her prospective client, or prisoner, or whatever she decided he was. She stood up, picked up her purse, went into the bathroom in the hallway that led to the rear of the house, fixed her hair, and then brushed her teeth.

Magda didn't yet know how far to trust the deception skills of her four men, so she had already decided to talk to the newcomer alone. She went into the room where he was sleeping and said very quietly, "Brian."

His eyes opened and he saw her, and sat up from the couch.

"Good morning. I'm sorry to wake you," she said.

"Please don't worry about that. I think I just slept better because it's the first night I wasn't afraid."

"I don't blame you for being afraid," Magda said. "He didn't threaten you or yell at you. He just sent people to kill you. He's obviously serious, and he's not a fool. So here we are. We've got to find you a new life. I don't think being a billionaire's assistant has any future for you. Am I wrong?"

"No," Brian said. "They don't all know each other, and the ones who do certainly don't like each other, but Bart Stillivant is one of the ones who's addicted to luxury. Those people find themselves in the same places a lot—the same hotels in the European capitals, islands—they all love islands—a few spots in California and New York—and the same small, special sections of airports for private planes. I wouldn't be able to show up in those places anymore."

"I suppose not. While you're here, I want you to spend some time thinking about what you will be able to do, and where you would like to live. Then we'll find ways to help you do it. The sooner you start, the better your chances will be."

"You don't always find a way to make the people who come to you safe?"

"No. Unfortunately, I don't. But the ones who got caught and killed were all ones who didn't do exactly what I told them to."

Brian stared at her, silent for a moment. "I'll do what you tell me to."

She studied him. "I believe you will. Think about who you can realistically hope to become, and we'll talk some more later." She turned and began to climb the stairs to the second floor. She went into the room where Maxim and Dmitri were both dressed and sitting on their military-tight freshly made beds.

"I've talked to the man downstairs. I took his gun and the keys for his car last night. I also got the name of his old boss, who has been sending people out to look for him. We want to keep him in storage until we have the woman who owns this house. His boss will be willing to pay a lot for him. Even if we don't make the sale, his boss will help get the bidding up, because he's rich and he's vulnerable. I want you two to keep an eye on this man today. His name is Brian Finlay. Do not kill him. Let me repeat. Do not kill him. If he's dead, his old boss will have no reason to pay us. Understood?"

"Yes," Dmitri said. Maxim nodded.

"I haven't told him anything about you. Tell him you're people I'm helping to get new identities. You could tell him that you're peaceful immigrants being hunted by ICE agents trying to send you to Russia. It's something you know all about, but he doesn't. It also makes you seem harmless. Say what you like, just don't lose him. And if today is the day that the woman we want shows up, one of you keep him quiet until we have her."

She went into the bedroom that Mikhail and Daniil were sharing, to retrieve the suitcase she had left in their closet, told them the same things, and then took her suitcase into the upstairs bathroom, locked the door, showered, and dressed.

Downstairs, Brian Finlay was in the other bathroom getting washed and dressed. Jane Whitefield was not the way he had imagined her. She was a tall, thin woman in her late thirties with black hair, and she was very sure of herself and physically comfortable, as though she was at rest while standing, as athletes were. To that extent, she fit the description that Karen had given him.

There were things that he wondered about. There was something about the way she spoke. She didn't have an accent, and her command of slang and idioms was like everyone else's. Was it a regional tone or cadence from this part of upstate New York? Maybe it was. He supposed that his feeling was a normal by-product of having a person he'd never met occupy his imagination for several days. There were differences between what he'd imagined and the actual person. He wished there could have been a photograph of her, but of course it was too dangerous so there hadn't been. It occurred to him that he was letting his weeks of fear make him stupid. He was a drowning man looking at the only lifeboat, and questioning whether it was acceptable.

When he came out, the four men he had seen entering the house were in the kitchen eating breakfast. They stood up when he entered. He said, "Hi. I guess we're all here for Ms. Whitefield's help."

The four men smiled and nodded, and one of them said, "Yes. I guess the four of us will be moving on in a few days, when our IDs are ready. You may be here longer, but who knows?"

"It depends," another one said.

"Being able to stop in one place for a day feels like a rest," Brian said.

"Come, sit," said another one. "Eat. We scrambled some eggs and made pancakes."

Brian accepted their invitation, pulled over a fifth chair from along the far wall, and watched a plate and silverware appear in front of him. He did a lot of smiling and nodding as he listened to their talk and ate some of the food. A couple of times he heard the men at the table make quiet comments to each other in Russian. He decided that it wasn't because they were trying to hide anything from him, but out of a feeling of mild frustration because the speaker had forgotten an English equivalent. They seemed to be friendly and trying hard to be nice to him.

After a time, his impression that they had accepted him as a friend began to weaken. He had sensed that it was wrong to ask other fugitives any questions, because giving honest answers could put them in danger. Obviously, this group knew each other, and obviously they were all Russians, so he wondered who or what they were hiding from. Were they political resisters who were running from Russian operatives sent here to murder them? That had happened a few times in recent years, but the victims had always seemed to be famous or important. These men didn't appear to fit either description. As the day went on, he noticed that some of them were always near windows and looking out at the surrounding neighborhood as though they were standing guard, but there was always one man engaged with him, talking just to kill time, the way two strangers might on a long flight.

Eventually, the time came when the latest one, Maxim, ran low on talk about the best cars, and Brian excused himself to go to the bathroom. He stepped into the room, closed and locked the door, took his phone out of his pocket and reinserted the battery, and then pressed the number for Karen Alvarez in California. It took a very long minute to get his call transferred to Karen. When she came on, he said, "Karen, I don't have much time to talk. I'm at her house, but it doesn't feel right."

"What doesn't?"

"Her. She looks sort of the way you said, tall with black hair, late thirties. She talks differently."

"How?

"Just off, like a tiny difference in certain vowel tones, maybe, and sometimes an emphasis on one syllable or another. There are four Russian guys here, with accents. I'm beginning to think she sounds a little like them."

"She and I were in college together. She sounds like any woman born around Buffalo. If she doesn't sound like that, it's not her. Get out. Don't hesitate. Do it now."

"I'll have to wait for a chance, but I'll do it. I'd better end this call." He ended it and turned off the phone in case she tried to call back.

He took the battery out of his phone again while he flushed the toilet and ran the water in the sink. He had taken a big chance to call Karen. Not only was it potentially dangerous to risk making the four Russians distrust him, but he knew Bart Stillivant would be more desperate than ever to find him, and Bart might be capable of having Brian's new phone traced because it had called a number or two that he had also called with his old phone. He'd had it turned on for only a minute or two, but any time a call connection was made, the signal pinged on a particular tower.

Brian wasted a moment feeling too weak to open the door, then opened it, stepped out, and rejoined the others. They didn't appear to look at him any differently than they had before. He tested that impression and decided it must be true. If they'd thought he was making a phone call, wouldn't they have stopped him? Yes, they would. He heard Jane—or not-Jane—coming down the stairs.

If this woman was not Jane Whitefield, he had no idea what these people were doing in her house. All he could think of was that he had to get away from it. He spent the rest of the day watching the ones he could see. The men again took turns talking to him or watching soccer games on television while the others spent their time near the windows, looking out at the street. After a few hours two of them went out, saying it was to do some grocery shopping.

Brian's hopes rose, and he began to feel his lungs taking in more air, his heartbeat speeding up, and his mind waking up. But one man—his name was Daniil—stayed at the front window, and the other stayed near the back door in the kitchen, and the woman came to spend time talking with him, asking him prying questions about what his life had been like and how he would like the new one to be. When the other two men returned, he felt he had missed a chance.

Night was the same. He spent the night watching for a chance to get up and go, but the woman was sleeping thirty feet away in the living room. When he finally got a chance to sneak to the doorway, he tried the door and found that it had an old-fashioned lock that had been locked from the inside and the key removed. Trying it woke her, and she asked him what was wrong. He said he woke up disoriented and had been looking for the bathroom. He would have to wait longer until she was asleep again. Next time he would try to go out a window.

18

Karen Alvarez felt the vibration, looked at her phone's screen, and said, "Elizabeth? Why haven't you called back before now?"

"I was at a funeral in Seattle. I turned my phone off. After that, the main people all got together in a kind of reception with food. It took all afternoon, and I wasn't going to take calls during that either. Then I had to catch a plane home, and my phone wasn't on during the flight. By the time I got home it was after midnight. I knew you wouldn't be in your office, and I wasn't about to call another lawyer at that hour if you were. And so here I am, returning your call. What's so important?"

"I sent someone to see Jane."

"If you want me to help defend you or your client, I'll clear my calendar. Is this call encrypted?"

"Yes. But it wouldn't have to be. The client isn't like that. He's a perfectly law-abiding, innocent person. His former boss is not. He's already tried once to be rid of him. He sent some thugs to kidnap him and drive him out into the desert, presumably to kill him, but he escaped. So I sent him to Jane. The problem is that he's at the house, and she doesn't seem to be the Jane we know."

"You mean she's changed?"

"No. I mean literally. It's a tall, dark-haired woman, but it's not the woman we went to school with. It's a person who seems to be posing as Jane."

"Oh my God."

"I was calling to ask you if you have a phone number that's safe to use to call her—the real Jane—and warn her that this is going on. My client also said that the imposter Jane had four men there with her, all of them Russians. He said that after a day of listening to her, he thought maybe the tiny eccentricities or tonal variations in her speech were similar to their accents."

"What did you tell him?"

"I told him to get out. To run."

"Good. That was the right thing to do, Karen. Have you called Jane?"

"I did, but I never got an answer. Then I thought maybe the number I was calling was ringing, but the imposter was just sitting there listening to the voicemail, so I didn't leave a message."

"I think the last number she gave me is a burner, a throwaway phone," Elizabeth said. "Let's hope she's got it with her. It's 716-555-0119."

◆

The third morning just before noon, Jane heard the sound of Carey's car turning into the driveway. She picked up May and walked to the garage while he was standing by the open trunk and taking his suitcase out. She stood on tiptoes and gave him a kiss and then moved in close so his embrace could take in both her and May.

"You make me glad to be home," he said. "How's everything here?"

"Good. Getting better every minute," she said. "Have you had lunch?"

"No."

"Great. I'll make us something nice."

He took May from her, extended the handle of his wheeled suitcase, and walked with Jane to the house. When they were inside the kitchen, Carey held on to May and he and Jane talked.

After the smell of food had begun to alter the air of the McKinnon house, Katie drifted into the kitchen. She stood there for a moment and then said, "Hi, Carey. If you want to take your suitcase upstairs, I can hold May."

Carey said, "Good idea. Thanks. I'll be back in a few minutes." He handed May to Katie. She watched him as he took the suitcase and walked quickly to the stairs.

Katie turned to Jane. "There's a phone in the bookcase in the den that's been making the signal that you have a text. I don't know if it's—"

Jane said, "Thanks, Katie. I'll see who it was." She turned off the stove and hurried toward the den. She had a few different phones for different purposes. The one on the shelf in the den was a burner phone set aside for calls from a few relatives or special friends. She hoped this call was some kind of friendly check-in, and not another emergency. She unplugged the phone and read the text. "Call me. Urgent. Karen."

Jane felt as though she'd had the wind knocked out of her. She touched the number on the phone screen, heard the ring signal, and then, "Jane?"

"Yep. It's me. Hi."

Karen said, "I sent a guy to see you. He got to your house, then called me and said there was a tall dark-haired woman there. Was it you? There were also four men there who were Russian."

"Do you believe him?"

"Yes. I told him to run. I called the number of your old house, but nobody answered. It occurred to me that they must be afraid anybody who calls will realize she's not you."

"Thanks, Karen."

"What can I do? Should I call the local police, or maybe the FBI?"

"Do nothing. I'll have to handle it my own way. And thank you. I don't know when we'll talk again, but we will." She hung up.

She put the phone down on the desk in the den, went back to the kitchen, turned the stove back on and took a stack of plates out of the cupboard, set them on the counter, put food on three plates, and set them on the table as Carey returned. She said, "You two get started, and I'll be back in a few minutes."

Carey sat down, and so did Katie. Jane set May in her bouncy chair by Carey and hurried to the back stairway, which led up to the attic. The house had originally been the main building of the first McKinnon's trading operation, and the third level was where he had stored valuables received in transactions with her ancestors. She reached the second floor, opened the door of what looked like a closet near the end of the hallway, stepped inside, and went the rest of the way up the ladder that was attached to the wall. She stepped to a spot where the thick, rough boards of the peaked roof met the vertical side wall capped by a wide shelf. She reached the shelf and pulled down two bags, each the size of an airline carry-on.

She looked into the first and verified it was all there—twenty-five thousand dollars in hundred-dollar bills, three passports with her picture in them but different names, a packet of credit cards and driver's licenses from different states, a Glock 17 pistol, and three loaded magazines. The other one had the same variety of items, with Carey's picture on the identification. She took the bags and stepped back to the ladder.

Jane went down the short ladder to the second floor, and closed the door. She walked back along the second-floor hallway to the bedroom she and Carey had shared since their marriage, set the two bags on their bed, and then went back downstairs to the kitchen. Carey and Katie were just finishing their lunch of chicken, mashed potatoes, broccoli, and squash and were amusing May, who was still in her bouncy chair. Jane spent a few seconds looking at the three. They were only eight or ten feet away from her, but they were still in the old, normal life. It was as though they were separated from her on the other side of a glass wall. She had already passed into another phase, maybe even another life. She saw them all become aware of her at once.

"Finished?" she said, and stepped into the kitchen.

Carey said, "I've got to say, this is a wonderful lunch. I don't know how you're always ready for these things."

"Well, I did know your flight number. No secret. Uh, Carey, I've got to talk to you for a minute. Katie, can you please keep May happy?"

"Sure," she said.

Jane took Carey's hand and they went upstairs to their room. Carey sat on the bed and looked at the two bags on the bed beside him. "What are those?"

"Go bags. One for you, one for me. I started them when we got married, and I've kept them up to date since then."

He stared at her for a few seconds, then stood up.

She walked herself into his arms and they hugged each other, rocking from side to side for a long time. "I'm sorry, Carey. I'm so, so sorry."

The hug ended. It changed nothing, accomplished nothing, and became unbearable to them. Jane said, "We've got to get started."

"Tell me what's going on."

"We're all going," she said. "We have to. It's all my fault, of course. If this is the end of everything, please understand that you have nothing to regret. I would have happily stayed with you every day and night for the next fifty years, and wished we had more."

"This can't be," he said. "I can't believe what I'm hearing."

"We don't have unlimited time. I got a call from Karen Alvarez. A man who was in trouble went to her in LA, and she realized his problem wasn't legal help, so she sent him to me. He made it to my old house. There was a woman there who pretended to be me. He called Karen and said things seemed wrong. There were four men with this woman, all of them Russians."

"This can't be the same people as before," he said. "They're all dead. Maybe it isn't the end of the world. It could be squatters. We could call the police. You don't have anything incriminating there anymore, right?"

"They didn't all die," she said. "This woman didn't. I thought she did, maybe even that the rest of her gang in California had killed her for running away and letting the others die. But obviously I was wrong."

"How can you know?" he said.

"This woman, she isn't just some woman. I know her, who she is. When the Russian gangsters caught me in that house, she was with them. She was tall and thin and had black hair, and one of the men with her even made some stupid remark about how I looked like her. When you and Jake came in the morning, all the men who'd slept upstairs were dead, but she and one of the men were just gone. After a couple of years went by, and nobody broke into that house again, I told myself the two of them were gone forever. Maybe they just thought I must be dead like the others. It doesn't matter. She's alive and she must know I'm alive. If she's brought a crew of gangsters to my house, it must be to capture me again. I don't know how long it will take her to find out something that leads them here."

"May."

"Yes," she said. "They can't be allowed to get near her."

"And now Katie too. We can start by getting her out of this right away."

"Right." said Jane. "We do, but not the way you think. She isn't Katie. Or she is, but only because I've been making her into Katie."

"She's one of your runners? You couldn't tell me?"

"I could, but I didn't think I had the right to do that just because it would have been easier for me. She's being hunted by police. She's only sixteen years old, so there's no way she could hide out on her own."

"You were protecting her from me?"

"I was protecting you from knowing something that was against the law, that could kill your career and put you in prison if the authorities found out you knew. If you don't know something, you can't accidentally slip and reveal it, and nobody can hurt you and make you tell."

"What the hell did she do?"

"She stuck a knife into a twenty-six-year-old rapist while he tore her clothes off."

"Wow. So here we are."

"Here we are. We might have hours, but I don't think we have days. The man Karen sent to my house isn't going to survive once this woman realizes he can't take her to me."

"Do you have a plan?"

"I wouldn't dignify it with the term 'plan,'" she said. "If you have one, I'll listen to it."

"I'm starting from way behind. I didn't know the things you knew, let alone anything you didn't know. I thought this stuff was over and didn't know we still might need to run for our lives."

"I think you start by getting the hospital to give you family leave or a sabbatical or something. Then we put everything that might help anyone trace us into a storage pod and have the storage company come and pick it up. That doesn't solve the problem, but it buys us some time. Then we leave by car."

"For where?"

"For what I hope will look like a much-delayed family vacation. Mountains. A fancy hotel on a beach. Whatever you want."

"How long should I say I'll be gone?"

"As long as they'll give you without looking for your replacement. I've got to get started—I suppose I'll have to start by telling Katie what's up—and then begin packing."

"I'll go call Bronson at the hospital and see how much time he can get me."

Jane wrapped her arms around him again and said, "I wish I hadn't been such a disaster as a wife. If we get through this, I'll keep trying."

Jane hurried downstairs, took May from Katie, and said, "We've got troubles. They've got nothing to do with you, but we're all going to have to get out of here within the next few hours. What you need to do now is pack a suitcase and a trash bag. Put the clothes you arrived in into the trash bag. All of them. Then pack your suitcase with clothes we bought. Make sure you include the new clothes we bought when we were shopping for school. We also need to include all of the paper we used to construct your identity."

"What's the—"

"We'll talk about it later on the road."

Katie scurried to the stairs and climbed them two at a time. Jane set May in her bouncy chair again, moved it near the dishwasher so she could see everything, and loaded the pots, pans, and dishes into the machine and started it. Then she searched the internet for the storage company she'd seen leaving storage pods around town, and called them. She asked whether they had a storage container they would be able to deliver to her house immediately.

The man on the phone said, "That's not how we do things. We need some time to get the pod loaded onto the truck and some time to find a place for it in storage. We need to get all of your information and check you out before we even start."

"This is a family emergency. I'm willing to pay an extra thousand dollars for your priority service." She had no idea whether there was such a thing as priority service.

"For fifteen hundred we might be able to put a rush on it."

"Wonderful. Thank you." She told him the address, arranged for a container pick-up at 8:00 P.M., gave him the information he needed, then hung up.

She called Jake Reinert, the elderly family friend who lived next door to her old house. When he answered, she said, "Hi, Jake."

"Janie?"

"Yes. The reason I called is that I just found out that the woman who was part of the crew who chained me in my basement that time is inside my old house right now, and she has four men with her. I'm sure they've come for another chance to kidnap me. When she realizes I'm not coming to get captured, she might try going to your house to ask questions. Get out now."

"Thanks for calling. I'll call Valerie to come pick me up a couple of blocks away, and sneak out the side door that she can't see from your house."

"Be careful, Jake. Don't take chances."

"I'll be fine."

"I'm sorry about this."

"It's okay. I knew what this was from the day you admitted to me years ago who those people coming and going from your house were, and who you had grown up to be. You can't be much of a do-gooder without also attracting some people who are the opposite. If you need anything, I'll be at Valerie's."

"Bye, Jake."

Jane had been prepared, but not for this. For the past ten years she'd always imagined that if a day like today ever came, she and Carey would walk out the door with the go bags she had made containing money and a few carefully built identities, and drive off. What she had not anticipated was that when this day came, there would no longer be just two of them, and the trouble they had would not be one problem, but several at once.

She collected things that she knew would be needed by one member of the family or another, and put them in suitcases. She had always kept her financial records compact and in one place so she could burn them if she needed to, and over the years she had kept the family's records small, and stored them in large safe-deposit boxes in banks. Right now, she was mostly concerned about leaving anything that belonged to Katie, because it might hold prints, and would certainly carry her DNA.

When the whole process was finished, she and Carey loaded his BMW and her Volvo. She told Carey that it was necessary to take both cars because Katie had been in her car nearly every day, and because she'd been arrested, they couldn't leave it in the garage to be tested.

At eight o'clock, the man from the storage company came and set the storage pod in front of the house. He said he would bring the truck back at ten to pick it up. Jane and Carey loaded the pod during those two hours, and when the driver returned and took it away, the house was as empty of documents, evidence of Katie's presence, and other vulnerabilities as they could make it.

At eleven, Jane gathered them in the kitchen. "Carey, I think the easiest way is if you get the kids out of western New York while I stop at Ellen Dickerson's house on the reservation to drop my car off with her. I can't leave it where it can be dusted for fingerprints. When you reach your first destination, call me, and I'll fly there and meet you. Katie, you ride with Carey and help with May."

"I don't know," Carey said. "I think I'd rather just follow you to Ellen's together, and we can all go on from there."

"And then we'd have to explain to her and whoever else is there who Katie is, and why we're taking a baby and a teenager and leaving the house at eleven at night, and where we're going, and on and on. I can handle her questions if I can keep everyone else out of it."

"Okay," he said. "See you later." He handed May to Katie, took the bouncy chair and the two suitcases, and went to his car.

A few minutes later, Jane watched Carey drive down the driveway to the road. Then she went back inside the house and turned on the surveillance system. She'd had keyhole security cameras wired into the house in various places while she was pregnant with May. The rooms on the ground floor had them in unobtrusive spots. There was one in an upper shelf of each of the two bookcases that covered walls in the living room. There was one hidden inside the kitchen clock in the center where the hands joined, and another inside a vent for the heating and cooling system. The staircase to the second floor had two keyhole cameras focused on it.

Jane had never had an alarm system in either her old family house or the McKinnon house. The last thing she'd wanted was security people or police answering any alarms. The surveillance camera recordings could be watched on her phone or computer from anywhere. She locked the door, went out to her car, drove it out of the garage, closed the door with her remote control, and left. She looked at the house in her rearview mirror once more, aware that this might be the last time that she saw it, or her husband or her child.

Getting caught lying to Carey was terrible for Jane. For most of their ten years of marriage she had managed to avoid lying. On the occasions when she'd had to make exceptions to her resolve to never make a runner disappear again, she had not lied to him. She had simply told him she was going on the road again, and that she couldn't tell him anything more. But when Clare had come, she had lied about who Clare was. It seemed to her that once she'd done that, almost everything she'd said to him had been a lie. Her last lie was the biggest.

She wasn't going to drive to Ellen Dickerson's house to hide her car when she knew there was a runner in her house with the woman who had been one of her torturers. The idea was unthinkable.

19

Jane parked her car three blocks away from her old house on Erie Street, a short side street that connected a pair of long straight streets like the center bar of an H. When she was a child, she used to walk one of the two streets to the junior high, and the other one home. Tonight, she was looking at cars. The Russian woman and her crew would have their cars fairly close to Jane's old house, because they might need to get out of the neighborhood in a hurry. If the woman had four men with her and she expected to capture Jane, they might have something like a windowless van. They hadn't done that the last time. They had come to Jane's house in an oversize SUV with three rows of seats. If they were smart they would probably have two of medium size, which would be less noticeable and avoid having every seat filled.

These were professional criminals, and that meant they were probably less predictable. They would know that it wasn't practical anymore to use a stolen car with the original plates on it. A patrol car with a license plate reader could tell in seconds whether a car had been reported stolen. If they hadn't been caught by now, the vehicle or vehicles they'd brought would probably be new or nearly new, with valid New York State plates.

As Jane came closer to the Whitefield house, she recognized a few cars that belonged to locals parked along the curbs, but people in single-family residential neighborhoods in that part of the country were mostly in the habit of parking their cars in their garages at night. In the winter it was almost essential, because cars parked on the street could be buried by snowplows under tons of snow, and in the summer the rains sometimes created streams of water that made it difficult to reach the car doors with dry feet.

She skirted the block where her family house was. She went halfway around the block and then up the driveway of the Volmann house, behind hers, past the garage into the backyard. The fence was only five feet, designed to keep the Volmanns' dog, Ike, secure and available. Ike had lived during Jane's childhood, when most dogs were allowed to roam wherever they pleased as long as they had their collars on. She looked at the darkened windows in her house. There were likely to be eyes watching for her to return. She was sure some of them would be in the bedroom windows upstairs, which would give them an unobstructed view of the street or the backyard. If there were four men, there would be two of them to a bedroom, working in shifts. She directed her attention to the less obvious spots—the kitchen, the den she'd used as an office, the garage.

Jane waited for ten minutes before she was satisfied that there had been no movement, no silhouette behind the glass, no sign that anyone was looking out. She climbed over the fence behind the garage, slipped into the side door, and looked at the car parked there. The license plates were from Illinois. It was too small a car to be the only transportation for five criminals. Was it the runner's? Were the license plates genuine?

She went outside and closed the door, climbed the fence again, and bent low as she walked along the far side of the fence in the neighbor's yard.

She stopped in the dark corner, went over the fence into her own yard, and reached the side wall of her house below the level of the windows.

Three years ago, when she had been chained to the pipes in the basement, she had not been able to move more than a few feet in either direction. What she had used to send carbon monoxide up into the bedrooms was the old coal furnace, which was still connected to its old set of ducts. What Jane hoped to use tonight was another obsolete remnant of coal heating. On delivery day the coal truck would pull up beside the house. The driver would open the coal door, fit the truck's shiny steel chute into it, and raise the bed of the truck so the coal would slide down the chute into the Whitefields' coal bin. The wooden walls of the coal bin had been removed and the floor cleaned to make more space when she was a child, but the coal door was still in the basement wall, as it probably was in most of the old houses in this part of town, because there had been no reason to spend money getting rid of it.

Jane crept along the side of the house on the driveway, reached the coal door, turned the latch, and swung it open. She pushed her feet into the dark space, turned onto her stomach, and lowered herself into the basement. She could just reach the wooden coal door at the hinge side, and she swung it inward, pulled it shut with her fingertips, then went to the cellar steps and began to climb.

She needed to find this Brian Finlay. The fact that they hadn't ditched his car yet gave her hope that he could still be alive. She reached the top of the steps, slowly pushed the door open a half inch, verified that what she could see of the hallway was empty, and sat on the top step listening. There was no sound for several minutes, so she moved her head and shoulders into the hall and looked. The hall was clear, and so was the kitchen.

She stood and moved along the edge of the wall to go up the hallway toward the front of the house. When she reached the living room, she verified that her expectation was correct. The curtains on the front window had been opened a little and then closed imperfectly.

Light from the streetlamp in front of the Ronkowskis' house shone through curtains on the gap, so she could see the living room dimly. The big couch along the inner wall had a blanket folded on it and a pillow on top of that. Someone had either slept here or been planning to. Had that person gotten up to take a shift as lookout?

She glanced through the doorway of the den, and she could see someone was sleeping on that couch. It could be anyone, but if they were still pretending the woman was Jane, they would not have Brian Finlay in an upstairs bedroom staring out windows to watch for Jane to arrive. This must be Brian Finlay.

Jane stepped into the den, saw it was a man, put one hand over his mouth, and used the other to squeeze his arm. His eyes opened, and she whispered, "I'm Jane. Come with me."

He nodded. She let go of him and started down the hallway toward the kitchen. He picked up his shoes and followed instead of putting them on. Jane focused her hearing on the sounds of the house. She listened for the sounds coming from the floor above their heads, for voices, for metallic clicks or sliding sounds that would warn her that someone she hadn't seen was preparing to raise a weapon and pull a trigger.

She opened the door to the cellar and sent him down the steps ahead of her, and then closed the door and followed. She passed him at the foot of the steps. She went to the wall, reached up and opened the coal door, and then went across the cellar and carried a bucket to the spot, inverted it, and set it down under the opening. She stepped up on it, grasped the edge of the opening, pulled herself up, and crawled out onto the driveway.

The man stepped on the bucket, lifted his hands to the opening, and pulled himself up, and as he did, a car came around the corner of Franklin Street. The headlights swept across the driveway and illuminated the man for a second. He was wearing a white T-shirt, and Jane saw the tattoos on his neck and arms, as in a photograph—eight-pointed stars on the shoulders, a pair of scorpions, a Christ on a cross. He wasn't her runner, he was one of the Russian gangsters. She stomp-kicked the door against the man's face and the blow sent him sliding backward into the cellar. The man pushed the coal door open again as he tried to get to her. She kicked the door again, and it caught his face again and then one of his wrists. He bellowed and the weight of his body falling off the bucket pulled his arm free. Jane slammed the coal door fully shut, turned the catch to lock it, and dashed toward the Volmanns' fence, went over it, and crouched there.

There were other voices shouting in Russian, a couple of lights going on, and the sounds of people running on the upper floors of her house. She saw something she had not expected.

The window in Jane's parents' old upstairs room slid open, and a man's legs emerged. Within seconds his whole body was out, and he was descending by clinging to a pair of sheets knotted corner to corner, and sliding down. The sheets only stretched about fifteen feet, and when his hands were all that held him, he dropped the final six or seven feet and ran. He dashed for Jane's garage.

Jane kept low but ran along the back of the Volmanns' fence and reached the garage just as he did. He saw her roll over the top of the fence and froze.

"I'm Jane," she said. "Keep moving."

He flung the door open and ran for the driver's seat. Jane went to the garage door, preparing to open it. The man tried to start the car, but couldn't. He fiddled with the controls some more, and then opened the door and searched for something.

"I'm Jane," she said. "They probably sabotaged your car. Come on."

He got out of the car, ran with her to the Volmanns' fence, and climbed over beside her. They lay still for a moment, silently listening to the sounds of low voices and running feet. Jane tried to get a sense of where the footsteps were going, but they seemed to be heading in several directions, so she couldn't be sure. After another few seconds she heard a car engine start, and then the car accelerating. There would not have been five people getting into a car and driving off, so she remained still and waited. She saw flashlight beams moving around in her yard, saw a beam pass over her head along the top of the fence, and come back rapidly, then disappear. Jane waited, but the lights and sounds had moved away.

She didn't dare to speak, so she tugged the man's hand in the direction of the front of the Volmann house, and began to move. She ducked and ran to the first stretch of thick shrubbery along the side of the house and looked back.

There were still two flashlights, but then they moved off toward the street at a run, and before they reached it, went out. Jane leaned close and whispered, "What's your name?"

"Brian," he whispered.

"Right answer. Now we run."

Jane emerged from the bushes and moved along the side of the Volmann house to the street, and then began to trot. She made it to the cross street, turned, and ran along the side of it. She listened to Brian's footsteps and the sound of his breathing behind her as she increased her speed and the length of her strides. She knew nothing about this man except that he looked about five years younger than she was, so she had hopes he could keep up the pace. The left side of the street had most of the big trees and the taller houses, and the right side had most of the streetlamps.

As she ran, she tried to keep them on a course that kept them in the darkest spaces. She knew the gangsters had gone after them in cars. She was thinking ahead about the moment when the pursuers realized that they had gone farther than anyone could have run in that time, and not caught up with them, so they would pick the next street and drive back toward Jane's house. She hoped they didn't pick this street.

As they neared the end of the residential stretch of the street and approached the old industrial area, she couldn't help thinking about the sleeping arrangements in her house. The man she had guessed would be Brian because he'd been sleeping in the least desirable spot had been a gang member. Brian must have been sleeping upstairs, since he had escaped out an upstairs bedroom window. Brian certainly wouldn't have been up there taking a shift as watchman to help catch Jane. Only a day ago, he had called Karen Alvarez with his suspicions about the people in the house, but he obviously had not had a chance to escape. He was still alive, so the Russian woman could not have discovered he knew she was an imposter. Far ahead there was a curve in the street, and Jane saw the double cone of light from a car coming toward them.

She ran to the right across the street toward a pair of empty redbrick buildings that had been a factory when she was a child but had long ago closed down. There was tall grass growing in the cracks of the big parking lot, and the grids of translucent windowpanes had all been broken out years ago, so the place had a clean, skeletal quality. She got Brian into the narrow space between the main production shop and the warehouse, and stopped.

She listened to the sound of the engine as a car made the turn and kept coming up the street. She was trying to detect the sound of the car coasting as the driver eased his foot on the gas pedal but the driver didn't. He kept his foot on the accelerator, ignoring the dark buildings and raising his speed as he saw that he was at the start of a long, straight stretch of road.

20

"Take the next turn and circle back to those old brick buildings," Magda said. "And turn your headlights off."

Daniil looked at her as though he were giving her a quick sanity check.

"Staring at me won't help find her. Just do as I say," she said. She was not only eager to succeed in the hunt for this Jane woman. She wanted the other one too, Brian Finlay. Maybe she wanted him more at this moment. She had helped to pass the time over the past two days by researching his former employer Bart Stillivant on the internet, and getting a sense of his wealth and power. He could easily pay millions for his former assistant. Right at the start, before she even found the woman who made people disappear, her expedition had been headed for success.

She had been feeling amused and excited about the game she was playing with Brian Finlay. She had immediately fooled him into assuming she was Jane, the one person he thought could save his life, but she was just holding on to him to help her catch Jane. Magda had been constructing a great irony—he would help destroy his own last hope, and then she would sell him to Bart Stillivant. She had begun to imagine the sight of his face when he realized what he had done to himself. He had those earnest blue eyes, and she imagined them opening wide to show his dismay when he would find out, and the strong mouth going slack-jawed in shock. She had begun to relish the power and control she had over him.

A night ago, she had ordered a change in the sleeping arrangements. She moved Maxim down into the den to watch the front door, had Brian Finlay go upstairs to one of the bedrooms, and put Dmitri in the bigger bedroom with Daniil and Mikhail. Two would sleep in the twin beds while the third stayed awake and watched through the back window. When it was night and all were situated, she went to lie on the couch in the living room. As soon as Maxim was asleep, she got up and climbed the stairs to the bedroom where Brian Finlay was. She opened the door, stepped inside, and locked it. Then she began to take off her clothes, draping them over the only chair in the room.

She walked to the bed. She explained nothing, said nothing, simply lifted the sheet, slid in beside him, took his hand, and put it on her waist. The next morning, she was out of the bed and dressed before the darkness was dispelled. She had accomplished exactly what she had wanted. She had sensed some hesitancy, maybe timidity, in him at first, but before long she was sure she owned him, and sure he knew it. She thought he would do anything for her. And she had even managed to hide her tattoos from him in the darkness.

The next night—tonight—she had repeated her visit, and she had been even more certain. Their night had begun at full darkness, and had lasted until they were both asleep. Or maybe it was only Magda who had been asleep. Had he known that Magda was not Jane? Had he been the one to fool her—make a fool of her? As soon as Maxim's yelling and the running noises had begun, she had thrown on her clothes, run out, and locked the bedroom door, this time from the outer side. She ran downstairs, grabbed the gun and flashlight out of her bag, saw Mikhail ahead of her, and followed him to the cellar door.

Maxim was just dragging himself up the stairs, and when he emerged into the kitchen, she could see that his face was covered with blood. His nose was broken, and his eyes were swelling into slits. He said, "She thought I was Brian. I was climbing out with her and she saw I wasn't, and she slammed the door on my face. And I think my wrist is broken."

"Where did she climb out?"

"There, by the driveway."

Magda whirled and ran for the front door, followed by Daniil and Mikhail. They dashed outside and around the house to the driveway, shining their flashlights in every direction. She found the little door because there was a blotch of Maxim's blood on the pavement beside it. There was no sign of her. They ran onward to the backyard, shining their lights at the wall that separated the yard of this house from the neighbors' yard, then spreading out so they could illuminate it from different angles. There was no sign of the woman.

"The cars," she said, and ran toward the one that was parked around the corner, just out of sight. When she and Daniil got there, she said, "You drive."

Daniil started the car, then reached for his pistol and cycled a round into the chamber.

She said, "If you kill her, you'd better be able to make the dead speak."

He set the gun muzzle down into the door cup holder beside him and pulled ahead. He accelerated along the quiet street with the high-beam headlights on. Magda was looking on the right side of the street, and Daniil looked at the sidewalk on the left. They saw only houses with darkened windows and cars left along the curbs of the empty street.

They came to a traffic signal and she could see the sign said Main Street. "Turn right here and go back up the next street. If she's running, she can't have gotten farther than this." She didn't say what she meant, which was "they." A few minutes ago, just as Magda had reached the street, she had looked back toward the Whitefield house, and what she'd seen had shocked her. She had seen the white sheets from the bed she and Brian Finlay had shared, knotted together and hanging from the bedroom window that he'd slid down to escape. When she had left him locked in that bedroom, he had been naked and asleep, but he'd had time to do all that? No. He must have planned every movement, waiting for his chance.

She was trying to keep her mind focused on Jane, the woman who made people disappear, because that was her mission, but it was hard for her to do it. She kept thinking about Brian. He had not been enthralled by Magda at all. He had only been pretending. That was the worst. She had been exulting in the pleasure of fooling and manipulating and controlling this man. Now she knew he was the one who had been manipulating her.

He had gotten the selfish pleasure of having this beautiful woman come to him naked and invite him to do as he pleased with her. And one night had not been enough for Magda. She had gone back for a second time tonight, thinking she was making herself the most important person in the world to him. She had pretended to love every second with him, thinking she would make him like a dog that would follow her anywhere without a leash or a collar. She hated herself for being so stupid.

She watched the dim landscape as Daniil went around the next corner and headed back toward the abandoned factory. She said, "Make sure you stop before you actually get there. Your headlights are off, but there are still brake lights." He saw it and stopped. She couldn't help thinking about killing Brian. He wasn't the main target of their mission, and she had not yet told the Pachan about him, so he wouldn't be counting on the big price he could charge for him. She reached for the door handle and her phone rang.

"Yes?"

The voice was Mikhail's. "Dmitri and I have been going along the road above the river, but we haven't seen them. Have you?"

"Where is Maxim?"

"Still at the house, trying to get the bleeding to stop. Where are you?"

"We're two streets to the east from the one where the car was parked. We're at the back of a couple of brick buildings from an old factory."

◆

Jane and Brian had retreated inside the warehouse, waiting to be sure the car they'd seen a few minutes ago had gone. Jane heard a sound, and looked out the empty frame of one of the back windows near the old loading dock, across the railroad tracks that used to bring raw materials and haul away finished products. She saw a car with no lights parked on the far side of the tracks.

Since it was dark, at first Jane thought the car might be parked for the night. But now she could see the small, bright light from a phone screen that revealed two silhouettes in the front seats. "Come on," she said. "Time to get out of here." She moved out of the side of the building facing the factory shop, trotted to the parking lot, and increased her speed. They ran across the street in front of the factory, kept going onto a lawn, then another, then began a curving path skirting a stand of tall trees, and came out onto a short residential street.

"Not far now," she said to Brian. B

◆

"If you searched hard and didn't find her, come to where we are," Magda said. "Drive up the street where we were parked, turn right at Main Street, turn right again, turn your lights off, and come back toward the house. You can't miss this place. It has redbrick buildings and a big empty parking lot."

"Okay," Mikhail said.

She could hear he was still on the line and driving. "Call me when you're here. We'll go in from both sides at once and trap them inside."

◆

Jane ran hard until they reached the Volvo sedan parked along the curb of Erie Street. She pulled the key fob out of her jeans, opened the doors, and when they were both inside, pulled away.

Brian caught his breath enough to say, "Where are we going?"

"Away from them," she said. She drove to the river road, then made her way out of town toward the Grand Island Bridge, and took the three miles in about three minutes, looking in the rearview mirrors every few seconds. She kept going south to the expressway and on into Buffalo, and then east on the New York State Thruway. She had seen one car at the factory, but if there was another, she hadn't seen it, so she watched for any vehicle going the same direction she was.

She said, "If you want to sleep, go ahead."

"Do you mind if we talk? I'm kind of geared up."

"Feel free. I'm listening."

He told her the story of his years working for Bart Stillivant, his sudden understanding of what his boss's businesses and his partners were like, his resignation from the job and his move to Phoenix, and then their attempt to murder him. Finally, Brian said, "Can you help me?"

"I am helping you," she said. "Right now, I'm driving you to a place where I'm going to try to get you the best new identification that's available. I don't know for sure whether my supplier can help you right now, because he's been busy helping someone else. But I know if he can he will. In the meantime, you've got some work to do for yourself."

"What is it?"

"First, think back over what you've told me. Make sure I know everything that you know. Is there any chance that anyone who's hunting for you can track you here, or trace you backward?"

"Not that I know of. Bart's killers lost me in the desert. They never had a chance to follow."

"Then think about the future. First you have to decide what you want. If what you want is revenge, you're welcome to go get it, but I won't help you. I don't do revenge. If you want justice, I can't help you with that either. I've never been sure I even know what it is, and I can't go near the people who are in the business of handing it out. Their idea of justice would be to lock me up. But if what you want is to run away and disappear, you didn't come to the wrong place, you just came at a very bad time. But I'll give you a chance to do it."

"Thank you," he said. "That's exactly what I want—a chance to keep on living, to be left alone."

"Have you told me everything that I need to know?"

He had to assume that she had seen the sheets hanging from the window and realized what must have been going on in that bedroom. Either way, she didn't need to know that. "I think so."

"There's one more thing you can get started on," she said. "Thinking your situation through. I can help you get very difficult to find, but I can't make you immune to the problems all people have in their lives. You have to live somewhere, do something for a living, take care of your health, and so on. But you have choices about what all that should be. It's an opportunity to make improvements."

"I hadn't thought of it that way."

"Most people don't. Especially people like you, who didn't have a reason to think they were doing anything bad or wrong or even risky. That doesn't change the fact that you have to be different from now on. More advice. Don't pick a place to live that has a meaning for you, or that you've visited before. Not only does that make you easy to find with a simple background check, but you can't go to a place you've visited and have people not notice that this time you have a different name. And here is the big, terrible one. You will have to find a way to live with the fact that you'll have to cut off your relationships with any relatives, friends, even acquaintances. Anybody who knows you. Do you think you can do that?"

"I guess so. Yes."

"You have to try for a clean break—not one thing in common between the person you've been and the person you want to be. And the person has to be somebody you like being, so you'll be able to be him for a long time."

Jane had driven east on the Thruway, never slowing for an hour until she pulled off onto the service area at Clifton Springs to refill the gas tank, buy snacks and water, and use the restrooms. From there she went south on smaller highways. It took nearly three hours to reach the quiet street in Cantrell Falls that went around the park outside Stewart's house. Jane parked her car on the far side of the park, but with an unimpeded view of the front door.

Brian said, "Will anybody be awake in there?"

"These are their business hours," Jane said. "They have blinds and blackout curtains in their studios." The front door of the house opened and then swung shut again without showing a light. "They must have recognized my car. Come on."

They walked to the front steps and up onto the porch. The door swung open and they entered, and it swung shut. While Molly was locking the door she said, "Your timing is perfect, Jane. Your order is ready to go." Her eyes settled on Brian Finlay for a second, but she said nothing.

"My timing is an accident," Jane said. "This is another runner who turned up unexpectedly. He needs the kind of help that you and Stewart can give him. He was sent by people I trust. If this is something you can't take on, I'll understand, and I can take the other order and go."

Molly said, "For you, we'll give it our best shot. Come on up and we'll talk it over with Stewart."

They followed Molly up the stairs to Stewart's studio, where he was in the process of packing a set of papers, cards, and a passport into a stiff envelope liner to go into a padded envelope. He looked up. "Janie," he said. "You're saving me some postage. This is for you."

She accepted it. "Thank you, Stewart. You're the best."

"And this is?"

"This is a man who was sent to me by a friend of mine. I know you don't want to hear names. His situation is bad. There are two sets of people looking. One group works for a billionaire who has already sent people to kill him. Obviously, they failed, but that will probably make the next crew bigger and more motivated. The second group is accidental. I'm being hunted by people who want to know what I know. Some were waiting in my house when he got there. I pulled him out tonight."

Stewart nodded, looked at Brian, and then at Jane. "You should take a vacation."

Molly said, "After this, of course."

"Right," Stewart said. "Right after this. Molly, can you get started on the photography, please?"

"Sure. Come with me, friend."

She and Brian Finlay left the room.

Jane said, "I'm sorry about this. I had to try the first-choice option. You're the first-choice option."

"Don't apologize. At this point I guess Molly and I should do as much business as we can. The way technology is changing, it could be a matter of hours before what we do either becomes impossible or becomes so easy everybody can do it."

"Thanks, Stewart."

"This process is going to have to be the full workup, like the last one?"

"If you can do it, I'd be grateful."

"It's going to take some time. I don't mean hours. Getting this stuff through the government is very tricky for an adult because you can't submit photographs that the face readers will recognize under his old name. If you've got something else to do, you might as well go do it."

"Since this runner isn't dangerous or dishonest, I'll leave him with you. Let me give you the cash to get you started," she said. She set her oversize bag on the floor and began taking stacks of hundred dollar bills out and setting them on his desk.

"You don't have to do that," Stewart said. "You just paid me a lot of money and I trust you for this."

"I know, but a person would have to be crazy to leave this much cash in a parked car." She continued to take out the stacks until the bag was much thinner and lighter.

Stewart knew that what she meant was that she might never be back. He said, "Let's go talk to your runner." They both walked down the hall to Molly's photography studio.

Molly and Brian turned when they appeared. Brian was wearing a tweed coat and a tie in a subdued blue pattern. Stewart said to him, "We're going to give you the best identification we can manage."

Jane said, "It will take some time, at least weeks. I can't stay and wait. I'll send you some more cash by mail to give you a safe start when your ID is ready, but here's some in case I don't get back soon enough." She set another banded stack of money on Molly's worktable. She hugged Molly, then hugged Stewart, turned, patted Brian's shoulder, and took a step.

Brian said, "Thank you so much. I'll never forget what you've done."

"It'll be better for both of us if you do," she said. "Listen to Molly and Stewart. They're the experts at this part. I'll try to get back for the next phase. In the meantime, good luck."

Jane and Stewart went down the stairway to the front door. He stood in the closet beside the door and looked out the disguised peephole lens for a few seconds. "It's clear," he said. "You be safe too." He opened the door.

As Jane moved out past him, she whispered, "Let's all do that." Then she was down the steps and moving across the city park around the antique bandstand and toward her car.

21

Carey had been driving south and east, not being able to plan more specifically than he was taking May and Katie away from trouble and toward the ocean. They were both asleep, but that was probably not going to last much longer. May had taken a bottle and submitted to a diaper change at a rest stop about an hour ago. That had reminded him that the insulated thermal bag was not likely to keep the other bottles of breast milk in it cold enough very long into the day that was about to start. At some point he was going to have to stop and buy some formula and ice as a precaution.

He picked up his phone from the console where he had left it to charge. She still hadn't called or sent a text. He felt tempted to start the thought *What's preventing her from calling me?* but he could think of a dozen possibilities, and none of them made him feel calmer. He didn't want to call her, on the chance that the noise might endanger her.

The phone vibrated in his hand. He said, "Jane?"

"That's me. Sorry to be scarce, but I needed to make a couple of stops on the way, and as usual, they took longer than I expected. Are you still driving?"

"Yes." He fought off the irritation at her for not telling him what her real plans were by noticing how glad he was to hear her voice. "They both fell asleep, so I kept driving."

"Maybe we should both pull over somewhere. We have to talk, and it might wake the girls up."

"You're right," he said. "I'll call you back when we're stopped."

He pulled off the highway and turned into the parking lot of a large shopping center. There were few cars parked this late at night. There were five in front of the supermarket, probably belonging to the workers who were cleaning floors and restocking shelves. He called Jane.

"Hi," she said. "Where are you?"

"Eastern Pennsylvania. I saw a sign that said Interstate 95 a mile or so back."

"Okay," she said. "Stop at the best hotel you can find in or near Philadelphia, and get a suite. Two adults, two kids, two days. Tell them your wife will be joining you later today. I'm coming up to the Syracuse airport in a few miles. I'll fly to Philadelphia on the first flight I can get. I'll call when I have the reservation."

"All right," he said. "Oops. May is waking up." There was a loud cry.

"I can hear her. I'll leave you now. See you in a few hours."

◆

Jane drove, thinking about what she could leave locked in the trunk of her car. She felt glad that she had paid Stewart in advance for Brian's new identities, which meant she wouldn't need to leave cash in her car. She could leave most of her clothes and toiletries and similar things. She had guns and ammunition, which she would have to break down and throw away—preferably in a body of water—before daylight. She couldn't carry them on a plane. But she and her family would be driving south, territory where she could buy a whole arsenal if she wanted. In a pinch she could also take the gun parts and loaded magazines she had wrapped and hidden in the door panels of Carey's car for an occasion like this and assemble them.

She reached Skaneateles on Route 20, where she dropped the lower receiver of the gun into a sewer, the upper receiver and the barrel into another one a few miles on, and the ammunition into a third. She drove on until she came to a vacant lot and eased her car up off the road. She repacked her suitcase with things that were essential to have—the rest of her cash and Clare's new identification and supporting documents and her most necessary clothes—put the things she was leaving into a couple of reusable shopping bags, and put them into the trunk. She used her phone to make her reservation for the flight to Philadelphia leaving at 10:35, texted the flight number and arrival time to Carey, coasted her Volvo back onto the road, and picked up speed toward the Syracuse airport.

Jane was reaching the level of fatigue in which she had to struggle to remember the beginning of the day, and when she did, it seemed faded and vague as though it were a memory from weeks ago. The sun would come up in an hour or so. She would have been awake for twenty-four hours, most of them doing physical and mental labor. She had trained herself over her lifetime to extreme self-discipline. Sometimes when it was really hard, she would think about her father's ancestors, people who fought in endless wars when the continent from the Atlantic to the Mississippi, and James Bay to the Caribbean, was one forest interrupted only by lakes and rivers. Thinking about the grandfathers helped her stay strong many times.

Tonight, she was feeling dread. This time she was a runner too. And because she was, she had put her baby, May, her husband, Carey, and a teenage girl in terrible danger with her.

In another half hour she began to see signs directing her to the Syracuse airport. It was about five miles northeast of the city center, and as she got closer there were signs that reminded her of its official name, Syracuse Hancock International Airport. As she drove in, the big parking structure appeared on her left. She could see there were plenty of spaces. She knew there were no long-term parking lots at this airport, and the prices for parking were ridiculous, but that didn't matter. She entered, said she planned to park for a month, and paid in advance. Her car was registered in the name Susan Mason, so she had her Susan Mason credit card ready.

She took her suitcase with her, walked across the street to the terminal, and waited until it was seven-thirty and she could check in for her flight without being early enough to attract attention. The time went slowly, but it went, and then she was at the ticket counter, checked her suitcase, and walked through security to the concourses. She wore an N95 mask while she was in the airport and she watched the crowds around her for any face she'd seen before.

She only removed the mask while she ate breakfast in the deepest corner of a restaurant and charged her telephone. She thought about texting Carey, but she was afraid even that would wake the baby up.

She sat in the waiting area across the concourse from her gate so she could study the people about to board her flight, and soon she was on the plane. As usual, the pilot's announcement sounded like a dog growling into a metal garbage can, and the only recognizable human word was "Philadelphia," which was sufficient. The flight attendants' speakers were, as always, better than the pilot's.

When the plane began to move, she felt elation. It picked up speed and lifted above the tarmac and she felt a surge of relief. She had not felt this way in an airplane in a long time. Her trip to Oklahoma had been the first in two years, and that had not ended happily. She stared out the window while the plane rose and passed through the clouds, and then her eyes got tired. She closed them, became aware of the steady buzz of the jet engines, and then not aware.

When she was deep asleep she heard a rushing of air and then the sound of a hatch closing. She dreamed she was opening her eyes, and saw at the front of the plane an old man, thin and slightly bent over, wearing a gray sport coat he had obviously bought during the years when his body had been big enough to fill it, stepping away from the main hatch. A female flight attendant sidestepped him to engage the latch that sealed the exit.

"Thanks, honey," he said, and turned to walk down the aisle of the plane. As he reached Jane's row, the woman in the aisle seat stood and went to the restroom, and the old man sat in the middle seat next to Jane. When he turned his head toward her, she could see the stitches that the undertaker had used to close his cut throat. They always reminded her of the seams on a baseball.

She said, "Hi, Harry. Once again, I'm sorry."

"Jesus," he said. "Will you stop that? The last time you dragged me into your life I recall that you had said sorry a thousand times. So now it's a thousand and one."

"It was my fault. That can never change. I led John Felker straight to you."

"Not straight to me. You took me to Lewis Feng in Vancouver, the best forger available, which I still thank you for. And years later you took Felker to the same guy—the logical thing to do. Nobody knew that he kept a record of every false ID he made. My death was his mistake, not yours. And Felker killed him too, and he almost killed you, so he and I are even, and you and I are pretty close. You haven't lost anybody since me."

"How do you know?"

"Because I'm just a weird electrochemical short circuit your brain triggers on you sometimes. An altered protein causes a synapse to fire and brings an image of me to become your go-to nightmare pal. You pay attention to it because dreams are part of the religion you were raised in. Maybe another part of the religion, about the twins, is true—that there really is a right-handed twin, Hawenneyu, the Creator, and a left-handed twin, Hanegoategeh, the Destroyer, and they need you to help keep your tiny part of the universe in balance, so they send me to be your spirit guide."

"Which is it?"

"You don't know, so I don't know. I'm just a memory of a dead man you used to know. So I'll pick the simplest. I'm your spirit guide."

"Then for once, you've come to tell me something?"

"No. I came because you're ignoring what you already know. This time you've taken on too much. The left-handed twin took your parents, but the right-handed twin gave you a husband who loves you. You finally had a baby. A beautiful, perfect baby, your biggest preoccupation. Now you have these Russians after you again, and the woman who has seen you and will recognize you from a hundred yards off. You also have Clare, so you're raising a teenager who is wanted for murder. And last night you've picked up Brian Finlay, or whatever name Stewart, your current best forger, comes up with for him."

"So what have I done wrong?"

"You said yes too many times," Harry said. "You're spread too thin."

"How can I fix this now?" Jane said.

"Think."

"What does that mean? Do I have an answer already in my mind?"

"Of course you do. The world is beautiful to all creatures, but that doesn't mean it isn't cruel. We eat, but that means animals that are as good as we are—just not as smart—get eaten. Somebody has to die or nobody lives."

"Who? Tell me."

"I can only know what you know. You're going to be the one who has to choose."

"I don't pretend I have the right to do that," Jane said.

"You've done it."

"I fought back."

"Take it from me, dying happens billions of times a day," Harry said. "It isn't as bad as you think."

"Oh? What am I missing? What does anyone get from dying?"

"A break," he said. He got up and walked up the aisle to the flight attendants' galley and turned left toward the exit hatch. The pressure in Jane's ears increased.

There was a *ding-dong* tone, and Jane opened her eyes. The overhead lights came on, and the flight attendants' public address said, "We're making our final approach to the Philadelphia airport. Please check that your seat belts are fastened, your tray tables are closed, and your seats are in the upright position. All personal belongings should be stowed under the seat in front of you."

Jane caught herself looking ahead at the front of the aisle, which was empty. The woman in the aisle seat of her row was in her place, where she had always been.

22

In the morning Magda, Dmitri, Daniil, and Mikhail arrived back at the house owned by the woman who called herself Jane. They had been searching the town, driving or trying to flush their prey from likely hiding places since around 2:00 A.M., and now people were beginning to fill the roads on their way to work. That made it difficult to capture someone who was aware that getting caught would probably be fatal. Magda was convinced that they had not stayed in this little town but had gotten into a car and kept going. She was the boss, but she was also the most light-footed, so she was the one most likely to check on Maxim without waking him. She found him asleep in the den. His nose, lip, and left eyebrow had bled for a while before he had managed to stanch the flow with rolled-up toilet paper in his nose and plasters made of it stuck to his head and lip. The pillow had scarlet stains ruining its bright white pillowcase. His nose was broken and swollen, and both his eyes were blackened. She closed the door quietly and joined the others in the kitchen.

"It's not serious. He's going to be miserable for a few days or a week, and it will show for a month."

"What do we do now?"

"You sleep. I want all of us to be rested and alert as soon as possible."

The three all went upstairs to the bedrooms. As soon as they were gone, she went back to the den where Maxim was sleeping. She shook his shoulder and he blinked his eyes. "Hello, Maxim," she said in Russian.

He stared at the ceiling, raised his hands intending to rub his eyes, and then winced in the first instant when his fingers touched his skin. She could see he was remembering what had happened. He turned his head toward her and looked at the bloody pillow, felt the toilet paper stuck to his skin, and sat up.

Magda said, "What I'd like you to do is go into the bathroom down here and start cleaning yourself up. Try to make yourself look as good as you can, ready to travel."

"Where are we going?"

"I don't really care where you go, but I would think it should be back to Boston. You're no use to me looking like this. You remember I picked all of you because you seemed most like Americans and spoke most like Americans? Now you stand out. People will look at you and remember you. It will take a week or two before you heal. If I were you, I would see a doctor right away to make sure your face heals right."

"They'll look at me in the airport here, and on the plane, and at Logan Airport."

"Then drive. You can take Brian Finlay's car. He parked it in the garage, and I took his keys and his gun, so the car is still there. You can ditch the gun for me on the way to Boston, and have the car chopped for parts after you get there." She went into the kitchen, opened the pantry door, reached into a box of crackers, and took out the key fob. She opened a kitchen cupboard, took the top off a fry pan, and produced the pistol. She brought them back to the den and set them on the desk where Maxim could see them.

He nodded, stood up, took his suitcase, and walked to the bathroom connected to the small bedroom near the kitchen. In a moment she could hear water running.

Magda thought about whether she should call the Pachan in Boston to tell him what had happened and ask for another man. After a moment she decided that asking for anything extra was showing weakness. Without Maxim they would be four—two men in one car, and Magda and one man in the other. As long as she kept alternating which vor she rode with so they didn't start thinking of themselves as partners, she would be able to control them. Right now, she was tired.

Eight hours ago, or maybe more recently than that, Magda had been sure she had everything moving along smoothly. She had Brian Finlay as tame as a pet. He was worth at least a million dollars to his former employer, and she had been practically counting the money. Now he was gone. This Jane she had been sent to capture had walked straight into the ambush Magda had prepared, sneaked into the house without being noticed, gotten back out again, found Brian Finlay, and vanished with him. She had also left Maxim's face looking like he'd been hit with a bat. Magda had been up the rest of the night chasing hunches based on which directions looked as though they would appeal to a person trying to escape from someone like her.

The whole experience had left her confidence diminished, and that made her feel as though she'd been hit in the face too. She gathered the bloodied sheets and pillow and stuffed them into a big black plastic trash bag from the kitchen, tied it off, and left it by the back door. She sat down at the desk in the den and began to search the drawers. She had given everything a cursory search when she and her men had arrived, but what she had been searching for had been mail or papers that had the name of the woman on them.

When she hadn't found any of the usual papers, photographs, or anything else of use the first night, she had reluctantly granted the woman respect for maintaining a general void around herself. That had never made her question the fact that the woman lived here, or used it as a home base. Magda had been part of the crew who had caught her here before. That time when the woman had arrived, she had not knocked on the door. She had opened it with a key, stepped inside, and been dragged to the floor and overpowered by four men and Magda.

This Jane had not received any mail or a newspaper or anything else since Magda and her men had arrived. It was time to start looking for other ways of learning things. Was there a key to a post office box hidden somewhere? Was there a plugged-in cell phone hidden that never rang, but recorded her calls? Had she been watching her house with pinhole cameras set into walls or shelved books or furniture?

Maxim came out of the bathroom wet-haired and clean-looking, in neat and well-pressed casual clothes. "I'm ready to leave," he said. "I'm sorry I failed, Magda."

"We only got set back. Delayed," she said. "Go get yourself healed. When we have her, I'll ask the Pachan to give you a chance to hurt her more than she hurt you. How much cash do you have?"

"About a hundred."

She went to her purse and pulled out two thin sheaves of money. "That's five hundred in fifties and a thousand in hundreds. It will hold you until Boston. Use some to stop overnight somewhere so you don't fall asleep on the highway."

"I will," Maxim said. "Thank you." He picked up Brian Finlay's car keys and his gun, hid the gun in the outer pocket of his suitcase, and went out the kitchen door.

Magda stood a few feet back from the kitchen window and watched him open the garage, pull Brian Finlay's car out, close the garage door, and then back into the street and drive south toward the road they had taken from Buffalo to get here. She turned around, walked back to the den, and lay down on the big couch to think.

She took her phone out of her purse and pressed the number of the man who had selected her and freed her for this job, Pavel Obolonsky.

Her phone gave the ring signal and she heard Obolonsky's voice. "It's me," she said. "Do you recognize me?"

"What's wrong?"

"I just sent Maxim home. He's driving, so it should take about two days to get there."

"What for?"

"I brought the crew here, to the place where we caught her last time. A man was already here looking for her, wanting her to help him disappear. Two nights later she arrived at the house in the middle of the night. She ran into Maxim, and at first, she seemed to think he was her fugitive. She didn't talk, so Maxim didn't either. She led him to the basement. She climbed out a little door that opened outward in the stone wall. He started to follow. When his head and hands were out, she kicked the door shut in his face, locked it from the outside, and got away. Her fugitive seems to have been aware of what was happening, and he used the time to sneak out a window and join her. They disappeared before the rest of us woke up to the sound of Maxim shouting in pain, and went after them."

"Was Maxim hurt so bad he couldn't help?"

"He has a broken nose and a big wound on at least one eyebrow. He may also have a broken finger or two. When I looked at him this morning, I realized I have no more use for him. He stands out too much with the bruises and swelling. I can't use him."

"Do you want me to send you a replacement?"

"No, thank you," she said. "Things might take a little bit longer than I had planned, but we'll find her again."

"All right," Obolonsky said. "Let me know when that happens."

"I will." She poked the red circle to end the call, and then felt the exhaustion like a weight pushing her back onto the big leather couch. She had made sure her boss had the self-satisfaction of learning that his confidence in her had been justified. She had found the woman that so many experienced people—dozens, maybe even hundreds—had hunted with no success, and she had lured her into an ambush. She'd had to acknowledge to him that her carefully selected crew had failed to spring the trap and capture her, but she had managed to shift the blame for it from her to one of them—the one who was most likely to tell him a story that would be worse for her. She closed her eyes for a moment and sleep caught her.

23

Jane hurried out of the airport baggage area to the next cab in the line and said, "The Rittenhouse Hotel, please." Jane had found over the years that choosing a very good hotel was not a bad idea. They tended to cater mostly to wealthy people, and they protected their guests' privacy and safety better than bigger and cheaper ones. When she'd called Carey and he'd told her where he had checked in, she had approved.

She had stayed at the Rittenhouse twice, the last time over five years ago. Her first worry was that some hotels had employees who stayed for decades, and she didn't want one of them remembering her under another name. When the cab driver pulled up to the entrance and took out her suitcase, she waved off the bellman, took it herself, and walked inside and straight across the lobby to the elevators, pressed the up button, and stepped inside.

She pressed the 6 button and rose to that floor, then found her way to the room and knocked lightly. She saw the peephole lens darken and the door swing open. She gave Carey a hug and a peck on the cheek and kept going into the suite. Katie and May were both asleep in the second bedroom. She just looked at them for a moment. Carey had placed May in a crib that must belong to the hotel, and Clare looked very small in the middle of a queen bed. Jane closed the door. "How long have they been asleep?"

"This is part two," he said. "They both slept a few hours on the drive, and then we checked in here, and they were still groggy. We all had a snack and got them settled, and they lay down again about a half hour ago."

Jane looked around her. "Beautiful suite." She pointed at another door. "Is that one ours?"

He nodded and then followed her as she wheeled her suitcase into the other room.

When they were inside, she put the suitcase into the closet, turned around, and gave Carey a much stronger, longer hug. "Did everything go smoothly?"

"The drive was okay, because I didn't have to do much except drive. I asked the phone for the best hotels, and it gave me a list of five. This was the most familiar name. When they saw me come in carrying May, and with Katie, people appeared. They asked me if I would like this, that, and something else. I said yes. There were bellhops to take the luggage, a guy who brought the crib in, and so on. So here we are. Now comes the part where you tell me about your trip?"

"I know you thought I would be right behind you, but I had to go back to my old house to pick something up. I'm sorry it took so long."

"You went back to that house when you knew the people who had tried to kill you once were there? That guy told you they were there already."

"He didn't tell me. He called Karen Alvarez, and she called me."

"So what did you pick up?"

"Him. The runner."

"You're not kidding, are you?"

"I couldn't leave him there. They would have tortured him to find out more about me, about us, and when they realized he didn't know anything but that address, they would have sold him to the man who's been trying to kill him, or killed him themselves."

"Where is he now?"

"There's a couple who live in a small town near the south end of the Finger Lakes. For a few years now, whenever I've needed to get IDs and papers for anyone, I've brought them to this couple. I did that for Katie. Even some of our newer identification came from them—yours and mine. What they'll have to do for this runner is going to take time, because it's complicated."

Carey stared at Jane, then stood up. "I think this is the point when we've got to ask for help from the police, the FBI, or somebody."

"If we go to any law enforcement agency, they'll have to be told that the reason the gangsters want me is that I've spent half my life making potential murder victims disappear. Everything I've done to accomplish that is a felony. A couple of those agencies were founded just to make what I do not happen. And right now, you and I have become the de facto foster parents of a young girl who is wanted for murder. Do you imagine there's a police force anywhere that wouldn't be curious enough about who she is to find out?"

Carey sighed. "Everything is getting worse and more precarious. I think getting in trouble might be better than being dead. I don't know much about getting into trouble. I know a whole lot about being dead."

Jane said, "This is one of those times when I want to say 'Trust me.' But you have trusted me, and here we are, up to our ears in it. You're angry and you have a right to be. So let me just say, I'm sorry. I love you, and if I could, I would do just what you're saying. But I can't. I'll do everything I can to get us through this, but I can't give up voluntarily or turn Katie in."

"So what do you suggest we do now?"

"You and I need to sleep too. I'll leave this door open so we'll hear May if she cries."

Two hours later Carey heard May start to make little noises. He got up and changed her. He had put the remaining bottles of milk in the small refrigerator in the room. He took one of them out and put it in the plug-in bottle warmer from the baby bag, and held May while it warmed up. In a few minutes he was sitting in the big armchair and feeding her. He could tell that he'd had more sleep than Jane, and he was also sure that whatever she'd had to do to rescue the man who had been sent to her house had been more strenuous than his night of driving two sleeping girls on a trip on the New York State Thruway.

By keeping both bedroom doors closed while he played quietly with May, Carey was able to keep Jane and Katie asleep for another hour and a half. When Jane appeared in the doorway, May was suddenly excited, reaching out with hands, feet, and voice for her. Jane scooped her up from Carey, took her around the living room to look out the windows at the city and the cars driving past the building on the street far below, and then took her into the parents' room.

"Katie is up too," he said. "Would it be a mistake to order room service?"

"It would be a mistake not to," Jane said. "Just be sure to use the same name that's on the credit card you used to check in here."

"Good point," he said. "I had figured that out. We're the Buckleys. Here's the menu. Decide what you want and I'll call down the order."

"Are they still serving breakfast?"

"No." He pointed. "This page from here on is lunch."

"Good enough. Caesar salad, small steak, medium. Fresh fruit for dessert. And coffee. Make sure Katie knows she can order whatever she wants, including snacks for later."

"I'll do that." He went out to the living room, and in another few minutes she heard him talking in his professional telephone voice.

Jane ran water in the bathtub in the grown-up part of the suite, got into the water with May, and gave May a bath. She dried her and wrapped her in a big fluffy white hotel towel and called Carey in. "My turn for a bath. You hold her, and then I'll take her and it'll be your turn." A few minutes later she dressed and took May into the living room with her.

Katie was sitting in a big overstuffed chair along the wall under a big painting with splashes of bold color, reading one of her textbooks, her head down and her black hair hanging straight. She looked up. "Good morning," she said. Her voice sweetened. "Hi, May."

"Good morning," Jane said. "I stopped on the way last night and picked up your new identification. I can bring it out and we'll sort it after lunch. Now that we've got the ID, it's getting to be time to start calling you Katie in every situation. Are you ready for that?"

"I have to be, and I'm already starting to get used to the idea," Katie said. "I picked the name, and we did it to help me, so I can't complain."

Jane stepped closer and touched her arm. "I've been thinking about that too. You never complain. But I want you to remember that complaining is sometimes necessary. I'd love to know what's on your mind when you're happy. But I've absolutely got to know it if you're unhappy, or scared, or worried."

There was a loud knock on the door. Katie set her book on the chair as she stood up. Jane handed May to her and said, "Take her into the bedroom and close the door."

Jane went to the door, looked out the peephole, and opened the door. A smiling waiter said, "Room service," and wheeled a cart into the room.

He started converting a nearby table with a folding top to a dining table, put a white tablecloth over it, and set three places. "Should I leave the plates covered to stay warm?"

Jane said, "Please do." She picked up the folder with the bill and signed it "Marie-Louise Buckley." She added a large tip to the total. The big tip was always a problem of proportion. The Buckleys would want be liked, but if their tips were too big, the risk was that the Buckleys might also be remembered. The waiter seemed pleased, but not overwhelmed. He said, "Thank you," and left, and Jane immediately reset the locks, went into the adult bathroom, and said to Carey, "Our food is here."

He came out and he and Jane set out the plates and removed the silvery plate covers. Jane held May while Carey and Katie ate. Then Carey took May while Jane ate. The conversation was soft and for the moment, concentrated on the hotel and the food and the long drive.

Jane checked the camera recordings in the McKinnon house. She had gotten her family away, and there was no indication that the Russians had known anything about the connection between the house where she was raised and the McKinnon house, where she had lived since her marriage. If they had known about it, they would have gone there. As of this morning, they hadn't.

She still had some hope that they would not find the McKinnon house. The house had been in Carey's family since before the Revolutionary War. Jane had never let Carey add her name to the deed. He had been the sole owner from the time his mother had died while he had been in New York City working as a resident in surgery. For a group of strangers to find out about the McKinnon house, it would probably require them to talk to random people, find the right one, and ask the right questions without appearing to be too nosy or threatening. Jane estimated that she and her family would have three more safe nights in this hotel before it was time to make a decision about their next refuge.

24

Magda woke just before noon. The men were making their breakfast right down the hall from the den. Men banged pans down on the burners and set stacks of plates on tables too loudly, and while their voices began as whispers, about once a minute one of them would forget and raise his voice.

She got up and climbed the stairs to one of the bedrooms, took a shower, washed and dried her hair, dressed, and went back downstairs. She saw they had saved a chair for her, then decided it was probably the one Maxim had left vacant. She cooked herself some eggs and bacon and sat down to eat while the men were clearing their dishes.

She said, "Today I want to go through the house carefully. Now that Brian Finlay is gone, we don't have to worry that he'll wonder why I'm searching my own house. You're looking for anything interesting, but especially anything that points to another address. I think she may have another place to live. It might be two blocks from here or two hundred miles. It doesn't matter if it's her place or someone else's place. She's not here, but she's somewhere."

Dmitri, Daniil, and Mikhail appeared to agree that this was a wise plan, but it might be that they were anxious to be doing something, and didn't much care what it was. Over the next few hours, she was pleased to see them working, searching, up on their feet and moving.

It was late afternoon before Mikhail approached her in the first-floor bedroom. She had pushed the bed aside and was on her knees, moving from one floorboard to the next, using a knife to try prying up each one, hoping to find one that could be lifted to reveal a cache of documents or something else that would provide a lead. She heard him and turned to look up. She kept her eyes on him and waited.

He said, "That house—the next one over—have you seen anybody coming or going?"

She stood and looked out the window where he was pointing. "I don't think so. Have you asked the others?"

"Yes. Nobody else has seen anyone either. At first I didn't wonder about it because the lights would go on downstairs in the early evening, and then they'd go off and then the upstairs ones went on at around eleven and off around eleven twenty. But that never changed, and the curtains in the windows never moved."

Magda said, "Go take a look."

"Yes," Mikhail said. "I will."

He left, and then she watched through the upper window as he made the short walk to the back of the other house. He crouched beside it, bending and leaning to put his eye to the corner of a window to peer at the inside through a spot the curtain didn't quite cover.

When a light beyond a curtain came on, she saw him give a startled jerk and then recover. It made her smile. He turned and looked up at her window and nodded. She walked to the stairs, hurried to the kitchen door, and went to join him.

He said, "There are no signs or stickers for an alarm system. I saw a plug-in timer for the pole lamp in the living room, but I haven't seen an alarm keypad."

"Can you pick the back door lock?" she asked.

"Yes. But I can't be sure the door won't have a deadbolt set from the inside."

"There may be one without a deadbolt set. If not, you can kick the door in."

He climbed the steps to the door, knelt in front of it, stuck his tension wrench into the keyhole, used his pick to rake the pins into line, turned the cylinder, and pushed. The door opened, and Magda walked past him into the house. He followed her and closed the door.

The house was structurally similar to the house where they'd been waiting to catch Jane, but there were differences that mattered to Magda. There was clutter—*AARP* and *Field & Stream* magazines addressed to Jacob Reinert on a table beside an easy chair that tipped back to semi-recline, a buffet counter with a tray, a bottle half full of brown liquor next to a clutch of crystal glasses, a big television screen on the opposite wall with a few fingerprints on its black surface. They went deeper into the house. There was another envelope on a table in the small room across the hall from the dining room. Magda saw that the letter was not addressed to anybody named Reinert. It was addressed to Ms. Jane Whitefield, from the Cornell University Alumni Association.

"He has to be the one who keeps her mail for her when it gets delivered," she said. "This is probably an old address." She looked among the magazines for anything else. Then she said, "Keep looking, the same as we did next door. Don't ignore anything. Everything that tells us something we didn't know will help. But don't leave any fingerprints." She turned and started to go back toward the kitchen.

"Are you leaving?"

"Just for a minute. I'm going to get the others over here."

Mikhail heard her go out and close the kitchen door. That was when he noticed the address book on the bookshelf. He opened it at *W*.

25

Officer Dave Fenton hit the door frame outside Chief Henderson's office with the flat of his hand in a military knock. The Chief looked up and saw who it was, so instead of just calling "Enter" or something, he got up from behind his desk and met him at the door.

"Hey, Dave. Come on in. What can I do for you today?"

"If you've got a couple minutes, I wanted to talk about my brother's killer."

"What about her?"

Fenton said, "It's been six weeks now. We had mug shots, prints, the police report, and all the usual information. As soon as we found out that she had run to avoid prosecution, we sent the package everywhere. Nothing's happening. A sixteen-year-old girl from a family that doesn't show signs of having ever had any money, just vanished from sight in the middle of summer and nobody anywhere in the country has come across her in six weeks. Usually with a fugitive like that, they have to hitchhike to get anywhere, and beg for money and food. When they leave in the summer most of them don't even have a jacket. They turn up as runaways in a big city, or they get picked up on misdemeanor theft or prostitution."

"I've assigned the detective work to McEvoy. Do you think he's not doing his job?"

"I'd hesitate to imply anything like that about Paul. But I don't think he's been able to find a way to bring the case to people's attention, to make this case stand out among the thousands that happen every day. I've even thought that what we're expecting him to do is just too hard. When there's a big search for a female and the whole law enforcement community gets involved, it's because it's a woman who's the victim. We've been sending out this picture of a sixteen-year-old girl who's a killer. Nobody sees her as a threat to anybody, so they're probably throwing our bulletins away or giving them a permanent place at the bottom of the stack."

"You could be right."

"It's the numbers. Not just criminals, but anybody who's disappeared. I just looked up the statistics from the Justice Department's National Missing and Endangered Persons System. Six hundred thirty thousand people get reported missing each year. Ninety thousand are never found. Forty-eight percent are women. It's hard to make anybody you're looking for stand out."

"I don't see what we can—"

"I just came here because I know I should tell you what I'm going to do."

"What exactly is that, Dave?"

"The first thing is, I'm going to offer a reward for information. I've got nearly fifty thousand dollars to contribute to it, and I'm going to set up a GoFundMe page to bring that number up, maybe even double it."

The Chief said, "I don't know what to say about that. I know you're desperate to get this done, but it takes an honest cop a long time to save fifty grand. And if you take some time to look into the cases behind some of those big statistics, you'll see that a lot of them have rewards offered already. Big rewards, and they're years old. You're also forgetting that rewards don't just motivate witnesses. They also attract crackpots or liars looking for a big payday. That can bog down an investigation."

"I've been at a loss. This is something I can do, and still be a cop."

"There's nothing illegal about what you're planning. In your place I might consider the same thing." He paused. "I hope somebody would talk me out of it."

"I don't want to tell you I haven't been doing anything else. I've mostly been trying to think of things that haven't been investigated yet, trying to find ways to pick up a lead. I know it's not going to be a huge reward, but the people who will be most likely to run into her are other teenagers. It's a hell of a lot of money for a teenager. It turns out Clare Markham is an Indian. At first we assumed she was Cherokee, because there are so many more of them around here than any other group. I found out she's a Seneca."

"So what?"

"History. Hardly any of the tribes in Oklahoma started out here. They were forced here by the government in the 1830s. Most of them were from the Southeast. The Senecas' home country was the western part of New York State. The ones sent here were just a small splinter group who had spread into Ohio. There are three reservations in New York that are still inhabited, and one in Canada. We looked for relatives the girl might have gone to live with, and didn't notice any. What I realized is, there are something like ten thousand of them, at least eight thousand registered with the Bureau of Indian Affairs."

"I've got to say that's good thinking, but what we need is something small enough to wrap our arms around. Our little police force can't send enough officers to another state to investigate ten thousand, or eight thousand, or even eighty people. Particularly people we don't even suspect had anything to do with a crime."

"I know that, Chief," Fenton said. "That's the other thing I needed to tell you. I'm planning on taking my vacation time in a month or so. Wednesday, August 20, through Wednesday, September 10."

"Have you cleared the dates with Sergeant Cochran?"

"Yes. Everybody else will be back by then."

"Okay, then," the Chief said. "You're good to go, as far as I'm concerned."

"Thanks, Chief," Fenton said. "And thanks for talking to me. I'd better get back out there. The kids will be getting out of school soon." Fenton left the office and walked off down the hall.

Chief Henderson leaned both elbows on his desk, clasped his hands in front of his chin, and watched him go. He remembered Dave Fenton from the days when he had been Patrolman Henderson and Dave had been a high school kid. He had been one of those kids everybody knew was going to grow up to be a solid citizen. He was a good student and an athlete who played football in the fall, basketball in the winter, and baseball in the spring, but he was kind of quiet and thoughtful too. He never had a big head or lorded it over anybody, never got in trouble. He had enlisted when he graduated, served in Afghanistan, came home, used the GI bill to get a degree, and joined the police force. Henderson had assumed he would go into something that would pay better than this, but everybody had been glad to have him.

Henderson took a deep breath and blew it out. The thing that never seemed to come up was the actual case. Gerry Fenton had not been much like his older brother. He'd stolen his first car for a joyride at fourteen, gotten off because he was underage and drunk, beat some other kid up a few months later but his family paid the other kid to drop the charges, took another car, got caught with enough meth to warrant a charge of selling it, but the first weight was declared inaccurate, and the corrected weight turned out to be low enough so the charge was just possession. By the time he reached eighteen he'd committed a couple of other felonies that should have stuck but didn't.

The other things that Henderson was bothered about were stories that had never become police business. There had been two or three girls over time who were rumored to have had things to say against Gerry. That hadn't slowed down the DA's eagerness to prosecute a murder case that might get him some recognition, and knowing the little that Henderson did wouldn't get the charges dropped.

He watched Dave Fenton go out the double doors that opened onto the parking lot, and couldn't identify his feeling, except anxiety for the whole set of circumstances. He didn't know if the girl was guilty or not. What he did know was that the most fearsome instrument that law enforcement had was a competent cop who was positive that what he was doing was right. Dave was determined to find that girl. He was in the research and planning stage right now, and in a month, he would hunt her down.

26

Magda studied the address book, a task that irritated her. She had grown up with the Cyrillic alphabet but had gotten used to the alphabet used for English. Still, she found reading American handwriting a chore, because everybody seemed to write it differently and carelessly. She took her time until she could decipher the personal style of Jacob Reinert.

Under the *W* section, there was no entry for Whitefield. The man who lived here didn't need the address, because he lived next to her. He apparently kept her mail for her, and he didn't need the house number. He could look at it from his front porch. If he'd needed to write something he could leave it with the envelopes he was holding for her. She supposed he didn't really need her phone number either, but most people would have written it down anyway.

She leafed through the other pages rather than putting the address book back right away. There were many people whose names began with *S*, but the middle of the alphabet was very large in his book. The *O* section had lots of people who were Irish—O'Connor, O'Manion, O'Day, O'Malley—and others who were not—Olson, Odette, Offerman,

Osherovsky. But it was the *M* section that was the thickest. It had Moore, Monroe, Montrose, Mervin, Manke, Michaels, March, Melman, Marx, Marsh, and the flood of Mc and Mac names—McNalley, Mary and Bob; MacIlhenny, Ray and Anne; MacNamara, Sean; McKinney, Karen; McKinley, Dave and Ruth; McKinnon, Carey; McGraw, Ted and Lana; McHale, Don and Nan; and on and on. She looked for the sort of thing that people with secrets sometimes did: addresses or phone numbers with no name, or symbols or signs on any page, but there were none. She handed the book to Dmitri and said, "I don't see anything useful. You give it a try, and then put it back on this shelf."

She was getting tense. What she had learned by coming into this house was that the woman who was calling herself Jane Whitefield was still actively using her house, the place where Magda and Oleg Porchen and the others had caught her a few years ago, and that her neighbor, maybe all her neighbors, were helping her. She was clearly operating as she had been before, which was a surprising mistake. Could she have thought that nobody had recovered from her attempt to poison them all? It didn't matter. Magda would find out everything Jane Whitefield had been thinking eventually.

But now Magda had a problem. Jane Whitefield was aware they had been waiting for her in her house. She wasn't going to come walking in to be captured again. She looked around her at her three remaining men.

"Time to go back to her house," she called out. "Put everything back where you found it."

She said to Mikhail, "When we're all out, make sure you leave the back door locked."

She went back to Jane Whitefield's house and sat at the kitchen table. The men came in and joined her. She said, "She's not going to come back while we're here."

"What are we going to do?" Dmitri asked.

She said, "We should clean this house, so after we have her, the police don't find our fingerprints and DNA all over her house. It could take a day or two, so we might as well start while it's still daylight. We'll do shifts, with one man watching the street while the rest of us work."

"Where are we going after this?"

"When Brian Finlay came here, he didn't know her, or know very much about her. Now he's been with her for days. He knows what she does for her customers. He's gone, but he told me the name of the lawyer who sent him to her. She had told him that Jane Whitefield was an old friend."

They went to work. They had all been soldiers or prisoners in Russia, so they weren't at a loss when somebody told them to clean. They got rags and buckets and made sure every surface got rubbed hard, every floor vacuumed and mopped, every window washed, every towel, sheet, or blanket washed, dried, folded, and put away. A small house was not much of a chore for their combined physical energy. Magda made sure she was the last one to take the more restful job of lookout, patrolling the house from window to window.

Now and then during her shift as lookout, she passed by one of the others scrubbing some surface. She was aware that they were probably under the impression that because she was a woman, she was acting out a feminine urge for domestic order. Magda only cared about not getting arrested. While she had been keeping watch, she had been thinking about something else.

She'd been thinking about torture and the vulnerability of the human body, and the way the prisoner's mind worked on the side of the torturer to make the treatment more effective. Whatever the torturer did first was a promise that other, increasingly terrible things were coming, a proof that the torturer was not reluctant to do worse. The prisoner's mind would be conducting a survey of his own body, listing the places where the next damage might be done. Eyes? Teeth? Genitals? Fingers? Always, the deepest instincts of the human animal to preserve itself intact would be at work. The deepest part of the mind feared that something would be taken from it permanently—power, capability, mobility, hope.

Karen Alvarez was the lawyer's name. Magda had some time to think of how she would proceed. It would be like a little play—show her rather than tell her the consequences of resisting. Every no would have a cost, and the price would keep going up.

27

In the night, Jane and Carey lay on their sides facing each other with their heads on the same pillow and whispered. "We can't keep the kids here for too long," Jane said.

"We've only been here for two days," Carey said. "People go on vacations that last three or four weeks."

"Right," she said. "But when you're running, whether you get found or not depends mostly on who is looking."

"Are a bunch of gangsters going to look for us in a nice hotel hundreds of miles from home?"

"The gangsters who are after me aren't the only threat we have. The Oklahoma police think that Katie is a murderer, and that means they're hunting for her the way they hunt murderers. They send information and pictures all over the country. One way that local police search for fugitives is to ask hotels if the person has been there. And now we have Brian Finlay to worry about. His former boss is a billionaire with connections to the sort of men who kill people for money."

"I get all of it," he said. "What are you thinking we can do about it?"

"Our first responsibility is the kids," she said.

"Agreed."

"There are a few people around the country who think they owe me their lives. More than a few."

"I'm sure they're right."

"They're alive, but it's mostly because they did it themselves—lived wisely, year after year. They're new people now. They sometimes send me things to let me know they're safe and happy—cards, presents, always unsigned, always mailed from cities where they don't live."

"I know."

"A few of them have kept themselves invisible for so long that the ones who wanted to kill them have died. This may be the time when I need to accept help from one of them."

"Do you have somebody in mind?"

"Several, actually. They've thrived since I left them. Some were people who had just started out with a lot of bad luck—born in the wrong place, met the wrong guy, whatever—and ended it by starting fresh. Others had realized that if they could change something about themselves, they would do better, and they did. A few met and married somebody who was good for them."

"What do you want them to do?"

"Hide the girls. Hide you."

"Not you?"

"You asked me what I want them to do. I told you what I want most. We have to keep the girls safe, and what we've done so far has been good. It's like chess. We jumped from one city where we were in danger to another where we weren't. We didn't get caught at it, and it's bought us at least two days of going dark."

"What's next?"

"We're a frog on a lily pad in the middle of a shallow lake. Under the water are a lot of big frog-eating northern pike swimming around. What we've got to do is stay absolutely still and watch for signs of where they are, then when it seems safe, jump to the next lily pad."

"I don't exactly understand what that means."

Jane gave him a kiss. "I'll think of another way to say it in the morning. Sleep tight." She turned away from him and the silence and accumulated exhaustion let them sleep.

In the morning Jane was the first one awake. She bathed, changed, fed May, and packed a small bag with a few essentials. When Katie and Carey were awake, she took their orders for breakfast and called room service. As soon as they'd finished eating breakfast, she said, "I've got to go out alone for a while."

Carey looked at her with curiosity.

She said, "Checking lily pads."

"Good luck."

"Thanks."

As she went down the hall to the elevators, she thought about the people she was considering asking for shelter. There were the two women in the Midwest who had thanked her by creating birth certificates in false names, different sexes and ages, inserting the originals into the records of the counties where they worked in the county clerks' offices around Chicago, and sending copies to Jane. That was a long distance to drive. Chicago was also where Bart Stillivant's headquarters were, and Brian Finlay was going to need to be out of sight for a while. Bringing him back to Chicago might be asking for a chance encounter with some employee of Stillivant's.

There were quite a few runners who had made successful transitions to new lives. One of the most recent runners who came into Jane's mind was Sara Doughton, now Anne Bailey. She was bright and flexible, but she lived in Quincy, Massachusetts, and that put her near Boston. The faction of Russian gangsters who had supplied the men who'd followed Jane into the Hundred Mile Wilderness a few years ago had come from Boston.

There was Jimmy Sanders, a Seneca man she had known since they were both toddlers. When her parents had taken Jane out to the Tonawanda reservation for visits, they used to play together. She had helped him get through an attempt to frame him for murder. He had come back to live on the reservation afterward. Anybody looking for Clare Markham would eventually get around to checking each of the reservations for her, so he was out.

The person Jane asked for help would have to be one of the people she had helped at least ten years ago. One part of Jane felt that it was unfair to ask someone who had survived and succeeded in making a new life to bring themselves back into jeopardy after this much time. These people, however, were older and better established than newer runners, and far less vulnerable. The hunters searched hard for a week, a few months, even a year or two. They seldom kept looking hard after that, and once the trail was cold and the traces faded, no place was more promising than another.

Carolyn Anne Striker. The name came into Jane's mind and it seemed promising. Jane had just begun helping people disappear from the places where people wanted to kill them, teaching them to become new people, and establishing the new people in new places. The woman had originally been Lois Polk, and she had been about Jane's age at the time—twenty-two or twenty-three.

At nineteen, Lois had been partway through college in New York City. The job that her university had given her as financial aid—working in the library—had not brought her enough to feed herself, so she had used an older friend's driver's license to get a second job waiting tables at a bar until late at night. In those years about half of all college girls had the same long, straight brown hair, and so the license easily satisfied the bar manager. The result was a semester that put her on probation, and a second semester that flunked her out.

Her parents gave up on her, so she stayed in New York, moved into another friend's dorm room, and took on more hours at work. She met a boy at the bar, got to know him, and when her friend graduated a few months later, moved into his apartment with him. She didn't know that what paid for his apartment was selling cocaine. One night some competitors followed him home, killed him, and took his supply and his money. Lois came home from work and saw them leaving. She remembered having seen them at the bar talking to people she knew, so she went to the police and told them.

As soon as the police questioned the first killer, the others knew who the witness was. Probably what saved her was the false driver's license she had used to get the waitress job, because people at the bar knew no other name for her. She hid with another university friend, who began asking others if they knew of a way to keep Lois from getting killed. There was someone who knew someone who knew about Jane, and how to find their way to her.

Jane had taken Lois out of her life as Lois and changed her into Carolyn Anne Striker. She found her a hybrid half-rural and half-suburban town in western Pennsylvania where most people at the time were not interested in cocaine and wouldn't have known where to find a dealer if they had been. Jane had manufactured a college degree for her, a BA from Carstonia College in Missouri, a liberal arts school that had closed its doors about five years earlier. Jane had ordered a stack of diplomas from an engraver. She had already established that one of her post office boxes was the current address of Carstonia College, so she was able to answer potential employers' inquiries. She had manufactured a work history for her, and helped her invent a biography that would be difficult to challenge. For years afterward, the frauds Jane invented for Carolyn Anne Striker, she also used for later runners.

Carolyn Anne Striker had, during the succeeding years, been careful to use what Jane had taught her. She had also become famous, something that had been so unlikely that Jane had never thought of cautioning her against it. Carolyn had started writing stories because it was something that helped relieve the boredom of living a quiet life in her Pennsylvania suburb. She had been very reluctant to date after her first serious lover turned out to be a dealer. Most of the men in town were either married or too young for her, but that never prevented them from trying, so she had an exciting but quiet social life. While her solitude lasted, the stories she wrote became longer and more structurally complex, and then more subtle and nuanced. She specialized in novels that had a distinctly romantic tone.

At the age of thirty she wrote one that seemed to her to be good enough to share. She invented the nom de plume R. J. Rakuse, and began writing letters of inquiry to literary agents. In two years, R. J. Rakuse's books were earning hundreds of thousands of dollars, and then more, and then much more. There were no photographs of R. J. Rakuse, she never agreed to public appearances or even business meetings, never agreed to interviews. Her agents helped protect her privacy and wrote the appropriate rules into her publishing contracts.

Jane used her burner phone and called the number that Carolyn Striker had sent her a few years earlier. The phone rang only three times, and then a voice came on. "Thank you for calling Temp-Fine Cookware." It was Carolyn Striker's voice. "The associate you are calling is not available right now, so please leave a message after the tone."

Jane said, "Remember me?" then ended the call. She kept walking because that was the way to avoid being really seen and remembered. She looked in store windows as she went, not because she was interested in the displays, but because large store windows gave her a chance to scan the reflections in the glass to detect people who might be watching or following her.

The phone in her pocket vibrated. She looked at the number and tapped the screen. "Hi," she said.

Carolyn's voice said, "What happened? Have they found me?"

"Not you," Jane said. "Me."

"Oh my God. Come right away. I'm still in the place where you planted me. Can you remember your way?"

Jane said, "There's a complication. In fact, three of them. I have a husband, a baby, and a teenager."

"Good for you. Bring them with you."

"I'll call when we get close." She ended the call and kept walking.

The call had taken about fifteen seconds, and neither of them had mentioned a name or an address. Jane's past had become so complicated that she couldn't ever be sure who else might be hunting her in addition to the ones she knew about. There were the assorted criminals she had robbed of their victims, but there could also be law enforcement people who might have stumbled on one of the deceptions she had used to help her runners assume new identities.

She continued walking, watching for the signs as she always did—people who were sitting in parked cars or trucks that never moved, sets of workmen who didn't seem to have an obvious project or purpose, vehicles that went by the same spot more than once, people who stared. When she was satisfied, she went back to her hotel. Before she went upstairs, she watched through the entrance windows to see if anyone reacted.

When she returned to the suite, she saw that a waiter was moving off down the hallway pushing the breakfast cart in front of him.

She used her key card to get inside and then looked through the peephole in the door to see if the waiter produced a phone. He didn't.

"What's wrong?" Carey said.

"Nothing," she said. "Not a thing."

"Good," Carey said.

She said, "This is our last morning at this hotel."

Carey said, "That's right. Of course, if we wanted to stay longer, I'm sure they'd let us."

"Not necessary," Jane said. "I've arranged for us to stay with a friend."

"Where does the friend live?"

"A suburb of Pittsburgh. It won't be as fancy as this, but it's not a hotel, it's not in the middle of everything, and there's no reason anybody would expect us to turn up there. It's a nice area, and it's quiet."

"You seem to know a lot about it," Carey said.

"I picked it out for her about twelve or thirteen years ago," Jane said. "She's still there."

Carey said, "That's long enough to sound like a good bet."

There was little packing to do because Jane, Carey, and Katie had not taken more out of their suitcases than they needed each day. Jane soon turned her attention to making sure nobody was forgetting anything. She sat down on the bed beside Katie. She said, "Have you been paying attention?"

"Sure," Katie said.

"Is there anything else you want to know?"

"The woman we're visiting. Are you able to tell me anything?"

"About my age, smart. Was once in trouble through no fault of her own. She loved to write stories and things, which was something she never mentioned to me at the time. She only told me about it after she had sold a novel to a publisher and wanted advice about how to keep from putting herself in danger. I gave her some—to use a pen name and not get her picture taken. People liked her books, and over time, they began to sell well enough so she could live on the proceeds. I haven't talked to her in maybe four years, until this morning. The name I gave her was Carolyn Anne Striker. The name she made up for writing is R. J. Rakuse."

"Oh my God," Katie said. "I've read about three of her books."

"You're worried about something else. What is it?"

"We worked pretty hard to find me a school and get me in and everything. What are we going to do about that?"

Jane hugged her and said, "I don't know yet. If we have reason to stay away past the day when school starts in the fall, we'll let them know we've changed our plans. We'll try to get you into a good school wherever we are. If that fails, Carey and I can homeschool you for this year. If we don't know something, we'll learn it with you. But first choice is a good school."

Carey appeared in the doorway. "How's the packing going?"

"It's done," Katie said.

"Give me a minute to change May," Jane said.

"I just changed her," Carey said. "I also left the tip for the housekeeper, and called to ask the parking people to bring the car."

"Then we're set," she said. "Let's go."

They all left the suite and walked to the elevators. When they reached the lobby, Carey went to the desk and turned in their key cards while Jane and Katie and May waited across the room for him. The car was waiting for them, and in a few minutes, they were all buckled in, and the car was moving toward Route 76 and the long drive west from Philadelphia toward Pittsburgh.

After a few minutes Katie fiddled with her phone, and then announced, "Philadelphia to Pittsburgh by car is three hundred and five miles, and takes about five and a half hours."

"Okay," Carey said. "Let's do it."

It took them seven hours, with Carey and Jane taking turns driving, and stopping at intervals for baby care, restrooms, food, drinks, and gas. Jane drove the last stretch because she knew the way to the house. The town of Lowery had changed in the past twelve years. The house Jane had found for Carolyn Anne Striker had been on the outer edge of the town, with a rail fence beside the yard that kept a few of the neighbor's dairy cows in their pasture during the day. Now, the hundred acres where the neighbor's farm had been was a residential development four blocks wide and even longer the other way.

There was a new Audi parked in the street in front of the house. Jane pulled up behind it, and the driver's door opened, and Carolyn got out. She walked up to Jane's window, leaned in, and said, "Don't turn off the engine. I still own this house, but I don't live in it anymore. I rent it out. Follow me to my new place. If I lose you, it's 440 Old Pike Road."

She got into the Audi and drove. Jane said, "I don't love changes of plan, but I'm sure she has a reason, and she's a smart person."

They followed her for about a mile, until they saw the Audi drive along a stone fence and turn at a gate on the left and go up the pavement about fifty feet. She stopped her car until they were inside the gate too, and then pressed a remote control and the gate moved along its track to close. She drove up the farm road made of fine gravel and Jane followed her to a large white farmhouse. There was a traditional-looking red barn with a circular Pennsylvania Dutch hex sign above the loft that showed tulips in the center and the phases of the moon around the rim.

Carolyn got out of the car, opened the barn doors, drove her Audi in, and beckoned Jane to pull in beside it. Jane drove in, got out of the car, and as Carolyn stepped up to hug her, Jane took a good look at her. She hadn't seen her for several years, but she still looked about thirty. She was a small, thin person, with very good posture that made her seem to be about five feet eight. She had long, light brown hair and wore a good pair of jeans and a work shirt.

"You look great," Jane said. "Obviously you're taking care of yourself. Are things good?"

"Yes," Carolyn said. "Thanks to you. It occurred to me after you called that you probably have so many people praying for you to so many versions of God that they're all getting sick of hearing about you."

"I've got to hope not," Jane said. "Thank you for inviting us."

"So let's see who 'us' is."

"This is my husband, Carey," Jane said.

Carolyn shook his hand and smiled. "I always thought there must be a husband somewhere. I'm pleased to meet such a lucky man." She turned to Jane. "I guess the luck started with being handsome."

Jane lifted May out of her car seat and held her. "This is May."

"You're a wonderful baby, May," said Carolyn. "Lots of potential."

Jane nodded to Katie, who overcame a bout of shyness or possibly fear, got out of the car, and shook Carolyn's hand while Jane said, "And this is Katie."

"Your older daughter?"

"No, but we're relatives, and she's living with us now."

"Wonderful to meet all of you," Carolyn said. "I wish it were under other circumstances, of course. But I'll do whatever we can to make this work. Let's get you into the house and show you around. It's roomy and has a lot of bedrooms because farm families in the old days had lots of children. Whenever they needed another room, they would just add one to the house."

Jane handed May to Katie, and the three adults each took a suitcase and a smaller bag, and walked to the white farmhouse together. Jane was taking in everything as they walked—the traffic passing on the road, which was about two hundred yards away, the house, the big expanse of grassy land within the stone fence, the woods to the north and west that included big old trees, probably left standing by the farm family as a windbreak.

Carolyn said, "After I had lived in Lowery for a few years I saw that the farms were being bought up. It was inevitable that the farms around here would eventually be divided into a lot of regular blocks with houses on them. Fortunately, by then I had a little money, so when this farm came up for sale, I could put in a bid. I only kept the fifty acres with the house and barn in the middle and sold off the rest after the prices went up. It gives me a little permanent space, so people aren't ever very close to the house unless I invite them."

The house had seven bedrooms, five of them upstairs. Jane and Carey chose one of the two bedrooms downstairs so they would not disturb the others if May cried in the middle of the night. Next, they all went for a walk on Carolyn's property. The sun was still high in the west, and the warm fresh air moving across the skin felt good after the hours sitting in the air-conditioned car. Fifty acres let them stay a comfortable distance from the road, but they spent most of the time in the back parts, near the woods. Carey wore May in a front-facing rig that allowed her to see where they were going. They talked to May, pointing out the things they saw as though she understood. She did seem to be aware that they were bringing things to her attention and she showed some interest in each of them.

As Jane explored, she was assessing risks. They were far enough away from the road and from neighboring properties to be nearly invisible, and it was possible to walk in the wooded areas and be actually impossible to see, except from the air.

Jane could see that both Carey and Katie were less tense than they had been for days, and that helped her to feel slightly better too.

That night after Katie went upstairs to the bedroom she'd chosen, Jane and Carey took May to their room and put her in the travel crib they had brought. It had high sides like a playpen, with a mattress at the bottom. They talked about the things they had done and seen during the day, about Carolyn's farm, house, and loyalty. It was a way of not talking about all the things that were uncertain and threatening.

Hours later, while Jane was deep asleep, she heard footsteps on the front porch, and the front door opening and closing. She looked beside her for Carey, then for May, but they were both gone. She stared at the bedroom door, but that part of the room was so dark that she had trouble seeing it clearly. When the door opened, she saw Harry clearly enough, because in dreams people see what the mind tells them is there. He came into the room and closed the door.

He stepped forward, and she could see the familiar shape, and the gray sport coat hanging from his bony shoulders. From where she lay, she was looking up and could see the big stitches the undertaker had used to close the slash across his throat that had killed him.

"Hello, Harry. What brings you into my dream this time?"

"Sky Woman's twins are keeping an eye on the way this is going. They seem to think you're causing a balance problem. Hawenneyu the Creator and Hanegoategeh the Destroyer, they're like two kids of exactly equal weight on a teeter-totter. Theoretically they could just sit there perfectly still and the board would stay horizontal and balanced, but they don't, because the universe doesn't work that way. Things are moving and changing every second. A mountain over here is getting pushed up higher by two tectonic plates colliding, and over there another mountain is getting rained on and eroding. A war is killing people off, but it ends tomorrow, the boys come home, and the baby boom starts in ten months. We little humans can predict things, but mostly it's massive things. One is that new people will be born, and every one of them will die. Everybody dies, no exceptions."

"I noticed that at age five and learned I had to accept it as part of the bargain."

"Yeah. You accepted the good stuff—delicious food, mind-bending sex—so—"

"—Harry?"

"—And the beauty of nature, great arts, and great thoughts, etcetera, that the Creator gave you, so you have to remember that it's a take-it-and-leave-it deal. You're slowly delivering yourself into the hands of the Destroyer, who has to clear the field for the next person. 'Nature, red in tooth and claw,' you know?"

"The brothers read Tennyson?"

"I don't know where that came from. Maybe you're so worried that your memory is leaking into your dreams. You're trying to ignore the fact that you can't save everybody you think might get killed. You're one puny human who has been allowed to play a tiny part in the immensity of reality. But be careful. This time your boat is already too full. You're going to have to be ready to decide who goes overboard."

He went into the dark space toward the door and she lost sight of him. Jane heard the bedroom door open and close, and then she was awake. There was light coming from the window. Carey was beside her, and she could hear little sounds of movement in May's crib. She got up and picked up May, and her day had begun.

28

Jane's phone rang, and she looked at the name. It was Molly. Jane knew instantly that it was an emergency, because Stewart and Molly had never done this before. She looked at the message.

It wasn't exactly from Molly. "Jane?" The voice was Brian Finlay.

"Yes."

"I had to get in touch. I realized I had made a terrible mistake."

"What was it?"

"The night I got to your house I knocked on the door and a woman's voice answered from inside. I asked to be let inside, and I said, 'Karen Alvarez sent me to you.'"

Jane froze. "What did she say?"

"I don't remember exactly, but she let me in right away. She didn't ask who that was, just asked a lot of questions about me. As soon as I remembered this afternoon and realized what danger I'd put her in, I tried to call her, but so far, I haven't reached her. Calling you was all I could think of to do next."

Jane froze. He had told that terrible woman that Karen Alvarez was her friend.

She said, "You did the right thing, but only call me again if you reach her. I've got to go now." She ended the call and touched the name in her phone's directory for Karen's cell phone. It was 7:00 in New York, but 4:00 A.M. in California. Karen certainly wasn't in court or something. Jane hoped her phone wasn't turned off to protect her sleep. Karen didn't answer, so Jane left a message. "This is urgent. Call me." She left the same message on Karen's private office phone.

Jane's mind raced. During the night drive away from her house, she'd had Brian tell her his whole story. When she was sure he'd told her everything important, she had started giving him lessons about how to stay alive. She should have grilled him longer and harder, and maybe she could have jogged his memory and found out this one essential thing he had told that woman. During the time since then, he must have been going over and over what had happened, and the one small sentence he'd said in a moment of desperation had come back to him. This time he had realized how important it was.

Jane walked back into the bedroom carrying May as Carey was getting up. She said, "Good morning. I love you."

"Something's wrong. What is it?"

"I just found out that Brian, my runner, has remembered that he told the Russian woman that the one who sent him to my house was Karen Alvarez."

"Oh my God," he said. "But wait a minute. That must have been four, maybe five days ago. Maybe she didn't hear it or realize what it meant, or something. Have you already tried calling her?"

"I called Karen to warn her, but it's night there and she probably has her phone off. I left messages on her phone and her office."

Carey said, "I'll take May while you get the first shower."

"She's hungry. I've got to feed her first." Jane fed her, burped her, and then handed May to Carey, gathered fresh clothes from her suitcase, and took her phone into the bathroom with her. When she came out, she took May back while Carey took his shower and dressed.

Part of Jane's mind kept returning to the dream she'd had just before she'd awakened. She had let the lifeboat get too full. Now Karen was in danger and might not even know it. Whatever Harry was—a manifestation of guilt that she'd had a runner she'd failed, a spirit guide sent to give her a message, a personification of her mind's disquiet—what he had warned her about was happening right now.

When Carey came out, she took May to the kitchen and began making breakfast for Carey and herself. When they had eaten and loaded the dishwasher, Jane sat back down at the big kitchen table with May, set the phone on the table, and looked at the screen. "Carey," she said, "I'm going to need you to drive me to the Pittsburgh airport. Give me a little time first to see what flights are available today."

Carolyn Striker came in and saw their faces, and said, "Is there anything I can do to help?"

"Yes. Please keep giving my family a safe place, at least until I get back."

"I owe you everything," Carolyn said. "You're all welcome to stay forever if you want."

"Thank you." She saw Katie was awake and coming down the stairs.

Jane said, "Katie, sit down with me while I do this." When Katie was seated, she handed May to her. "I want you to get familiar with how to think about this. I need to get from Pittsburgh to Los Angeles. When I went on a plane to Oklahoma, I was Nora Jean Gibbs. When I built her identity, I had her live in Los Angeles, so it's tempting to use the same name now, but complications made Nora memorable, so this time I'll be someone else with another name. She has a good American Express card, and she's from Chicago. This is one reason why I set you up with a couple of extra names. We'll have to keep them up and keep their credit good. There will need to be a different residential-sounding address for each one, and when I set mine up years ago, I needed the addresses to be mailing services that would forward them to me. Now you can do almost everything online: no bills in the mail."

She looked at the schedules of two of the biggest airlines, made her selection, and had the QR code for her boarding pass appear on her screen. "Now I've got to do a few things to get ready. Will you help me by keeping May happy?"

"Sure," said Katie.

"Thanks." She got up and beckoned to Carey. They went into their first-floor bedroom and closed the door.

"Karen hasn't called."

"I figured."

"I can't just keep waiting. I've got to start moving in that direction as soon as I can. If Karen already knows she's in danger and has herself in the protection of the police or the FBI or something, I'll get on the next flight back here."

Carey said, "I'm pretty sure I know what happens if this trip goes wrong. I never see you alive again. What happens if it goes right? If it goes perfectly? Are you going to take Karen on as another runner?"

"It will take me about seven hours to get to the airport, board the plane, and fly to LA. There's a lot that can happen in seven hours. If she needs help of some kind, I'll try to help her. Then I'll come back. I don't know enough to give you a decent answer. You're the man I've chosen for life. If the only way to get back to you is to walk back, I'll start walking as soon as I can, and I'll be eager to start. I know you'll take care of our kids, and I know you'll be strong, so I'll try not to worry about you. Try not to worry about me."

"When do you want to leave for the airport?"

"I'll be ready in fifteen minutes."

Carey held her close, and she knew that she was doing something that she would probably regret when her eyes were closing for the last time. "Come on," she said. "We've got to get started or I'll miss my plane."

29

The pilot lowered the plane onto the runway at LAX and Jane felt the touchdown bump and then the plane hurtling forward, its brakes straining to slow it down, her seat belt keeping her from lurching forward as it rattled toward the end of the pavement. She watched impatiently as it taxied up to the side of the terminal and the deplaning ritual commenced. She reached under the seat ahead of her to retrieve her bag and hold it on her lap. She slipped its strap over her shoulder and then turned on her phone. There was still no message from Karen Alvarez.

When it was her turn Jane walked down the aisle to the hatch and along the Jetway. She hurried to the escalator and rode it down to the ground floor. She picked up her rental car and drove toward Karen Alvarez's house in West Los Angeles. She drove past the house, taking advantage of the slow traffic to study the windows, then turned and looked at the rest of the neighborhood, giving special attention to the houses on both sides.

She parked on Robertson in front of a high-end outdoor sport and camping store, and bought a watch cap, an all-steel rip hammer with a wide head for tent stakes, and a pair of long, straight, sharp claws, presumably for pulling them out. She added a five-inch spring-assist pocketknife that was nearly flat. She drove back to the street behind Karen's house and parked. She hid her hair under the cap and walked two doors up the street to a house with a carport instead of a garage, saw there was no car and no other place to put one, went up the driveway to the back of the property, and looked over the fence.

There was no visible or audible activity in the house behind this one, and none she could see at the back of Karen's house, so she went to the corner of the fence and climbed over it into Karen's patio and moved close to her house. She looked in the kitchen window, moved to the door and looked, then saw an alarm keypad on the wall close to the door. The keypad's red light was not on, but neither was the green one. The keypad had no power. She walked to the circuit box on the back wall of the house and found that inside the door each circuit was neatly labeled. Someone had found the wire going from the alarm circuit, and cut the connection. On nearly all the systems Jane had seen, a battery backup should have sent the company a wireless call that the power had been cut. Karen's alarm system was basic and outdated, probably as old as the house. She had been a prosecutor and a defense attorney, but had little fear for her own safety.

Jane went to the back door, opened the pocketknife, inserted the blade into the crack between the door and the jamb, gave the knife handle a gentle tap with the hammer, and tugged the door open. She took a step into the kitchen and waited. The room was cool compared to the outside, which was at least ninety degrees. The air-conditioning system had obviously not been cut. Jane heard no sound. She walked deeper into the house, toward the living room. Every space she passed was modern and trendy, remodeled and professionally decorated.

The living room was the culmination, a showpiece made for entertaining guests. Everything was stone or polished hardwoods, and wherever the eye was drawn there was art—except one place. On the white couch nearest to the front door was a black Hermès purse, beside it a set of car keys, and a wallet lying open, so Jane could see Karen's driver's license. It looked as though the contents of the purse had been dumped on the couch and the purse tossed beside it. Karen would not have done that.

Jane stepped quietly back to the kitchen. She took the boning knife from the butcher block, slid it up her left sleeve, and hid the pocketknife in the ankle of her right boot. She held the hammer in her hand and went to the staircase. She climbed with each footstep directly in front of the last one on the edge of the stair that was closest to the wall. Boards gave a bit near their centers, and that movement caused creaks. The edges were where they were nailed in place.

She got to the first landing, where the stairs turned ninety degrees, and started up again. There was a sound, and she stopped. A voice? She felt hope coming back. Maybe Karen had been spending time with a man. She was an attractive single adult.

Jane heard the voice again. Female. Maybe Karen was on the phone. Jane went up a few steps, listening for the voice. She heard it again. Was someone crying?

The next sound was a loud, horrible shriek, and this time Jane knew the voice—Karen.

Jane took the last two steps in one stride, saw that there was only one door that was closed, and knew that they had closed it to muffle Karen's cries so the neighbors didn't hear her.

Jane dashed across the hall, used her left hand to turn the knob, and her left shoulder to make the door fly open. It hit a man standing to the left and knocked him off balance. He was reaching for something in his pocket as he steadied himself, but Jane's right arm swung the hammer downward onto his head and he dropped to the floor. A second man was standing to her right and lunged toward her, intending to wrap his arms around her to pin her arms down to her sides, but she swung the hammer toward him and struck his arm. He instantly used the other arm to grip the injured one and shrunk back, but then launched himself toward her again, and managed to grasp the head of the hammer.

Jane tugged hard, then let go, slid the boning knife out of her left sleeve, stuck it under his rib cage, and drove it upward toward his heart.

The third man was in motion and took advantage of the time to get around behind her and threw his arms around her neck. He jerked Jane backward in a choke hold, and her face was aimed at the other side of the room.

She saw that Karen Alvarez was bound by zip ties at her wrists to the brass spokes of her bed's metal headboard. The Russian woman was standing over her with a knife at her throat.

She said, "Hold tight to her, Dmitri, but don't kill her. We need to have her last as long as possible."

The arm around Jane's neck tightened as though to argue against what the woman had said. The man who was choking her walked her forward to the bed and forced her to look down at Karen. She had two blackened eyes, big bruises, and long, straight burns on both of her arms. She had blood that had run from her nose and from a split lip, dried, and then bled again. Jane saw there was a tray on the night table by the bed, that held a curling iron plugged into the wall.

Karen looked up into Jane's eyes and her face muscles contracted into a mask of pain and sorrow, and tears welled in her eyes and streaked to the sides of her face. "Not you too. You were supposed to stay far away from here, Jane. I'm so sorry."

Jane tried to speak, but keeping her neck muscles tensed to prevent the man's arm across her throat from breaking her neck made her voice strained. "My. Fault."

The Russian woman looked at the two men on the floor, and said to Jane, "You're right. And you'll remember while you pay." She walked to the two men and knelt beside the first one, whose head wound had bled into a pool on the floor. "Daniil is dying. His heart is still pumping blood out, but he's got a broken skull." She looked closely at the one with the boning knife in his torso. She listened at his mouth for breath, then felt his carotid artery. "Mikhail is done already." She stood and came close to Jane and looked at her closely, as though she wanted to bite her.

The woman made a fist and punched Jane in the jaw, and when she was knocked back against the man, punched her again in the stomach. Jane doubled over in pain and the man released her, letting her collapse to the floor in the pooled blood. The woman gave Jane a hard kick in the ribs. She stood over her, looking at her as though to judge whether she was in enough pain.

After a few seconds she said to the man, "Everything's different now. We've got to get her back to Boston and deliver her to Mr. Obolonsky alive. We can't leave Daniil and Mikhail here like this. We obviously can't take a plane. We've got to drive and we've got to get a new rental. A big van or a truck. We'll also need to clean this room up enough so they don't use the blood to know who we are and where we're going." The woman picked up the knife from the tray beside Karen's bed and held it in her hand as she stood over Jane while the man walked across the room.

Jane had heard Boston, and she had heard a name. She repeated the name to herself silently, then again. *Obolonsky. Obolonsky.*

Jane lay where she was, drained by the exertion of her attack, stunned by the retaliation, and trying to gasp her wind back. She assessed her situation. The surviving man was much stronger than she was, but the woman had not hit Jane with as much force as Jane could have produced. Jane had taken the two men down by surprise and ferocity, and they were dead. Jane had been lucky that they had obviously come to California by plane, and so they could not bring guns, or she'd have been dead in the first seconds.

Jane had been disarmed, but she still had one thing that was precious, a hope, the pocketknife she'd hidden in her boot. The boots were nearly calf high, and she had stuck it into the top, where the leather had held it.

The man came back and wrenched her arms around behind her and secured her wrists with a zip tie, like the ones on Karen's, then wrapped them in duct tape so she couldn't rub the release tab against something to loosen them. Jane's optimism waned, but she told herself that nobody bothered to bind a person if he intended to kill them. She still had the pocketknife. It would be harder to reach, but she'd find a way. Then he grasped her ankles, probably to tie them too. He stopped. Jane lay there, holding her breath, not fighting him. He held down her leg, jerked up the pant leg, and took the knife out of her boot. He held it up and said something in Russian. The woman took the knife, opened and closed it, and then pocketed it and held the butcher knife close to Jane's face, snatched a fistful of her hair, and tugged it so her head was lifted, and said, "What else do you have?"

"Nothing."

The woman released her hair, patted her down all over, nodded to the man, and got up, the big knife still in her hands. She said, "When we get you to Boston, I'm going to advise the Pachan to blind you so you can't hurt anybody and get away again."

While she stood over Jane, the man went out and came back with blankets and bedspreads taken from other rooms. He went out again and returned with an armload of towels. He made a body bag for each dead man by covering the man's top half with one plastic trash bag and his legs with another and taping them together. He rolled the two bodies over onto the blankets and wrapped them up, dragged them onto the bedspreads and wrapped them again, and dragged them out into the hallway. He returned and went to work cleaning up the two pools of blood on the hardwood floor with the towels, wiping it up and putting each soaked towel into a big plastic trash bag, and taking another, and tying each bag when it was full.

He was a hard worker and he had stamina, so the work went quickly. When he had finished with the towels, he went downstairs carrying them in the plastic bags and returned with a mop and bucket. He cleaned the bedroom for some time before he was satisfied. He had a whispered conversation with the woman, and then went out the door again. Jane expected to see him return immediately, but this time he didn't.

Jane watched the woman, using every moment that the woman wasn't looking at her to strain and twist her body to put more pressure on the duct tape and the zip ties that held her to the bed's steel frame. She had to be watchful, because she knew that if she managed to break a tie she would be committed. If the woman noticed, she would get nervous and think she had to do something sadistic and debilitating to make Jane too weak and intimidated to fight. Jane couldn't see the ties because her wrists were behind her, but she suspected the ties were the kind that the police used, not the ones people used to bundle wires and things, because she'd worked at it for an hour but wasn't making much headway. She felt anxious because she had noticed that the woman seemed to have completely forgotten about Karen.

The woman had brought her men out to California to find Karen, presumably to get her to tell her how to find Jane, or maybe to hold her hostage. It occurred to Jane that maybe the plan had been to lure Jane into a futile attack and capture her, which was exactly what had happened. The way the woman was behaving now worried Jane. If she wasn't interested in Karen, it might mean that she had no further use for her. If that was true, then she would probably kill her. Jane heard heavy footsteps on the stairs. Too late.

It was dark outside when the man came back into the room. He talked to the woman in Russian again, and then turned his attention to the two wrapped-up bodies in the hallway. He took the roll of duct tape and ran it around the bottom ends of each corpse, then the middle, then the top, so each was like a cocoon.

Jane wondered what they were going to do with those two bodies. Would it give her more time to work her way out of the ties and tape? He dragged the first body along the hall to the staircase. Then she heard a bump-bump noise as the body slid down the stairs to the first landing. She heard the man go down the stairs and drag the body to the second flight and launch it the rest of the way to the foyer. He came back up the stairs and repeated the same process with the second body, sending it bumping down the first flight of stairs, and then the second.

The woman never left the room except when the man was there to watch the captives. When he was, she busied herself with searching the upper rooms of Karen's house for cash and valuables. The world outside had been in full darkness for hours when she and the man had their next conference in Russian. Their faces were serious, maybe even anxious. Then the conference was over and they became active again.

The man and woman wiped down the smooth surfaces in the room, and the tools for torture that she had used, and then she raided Karen's closet for extra clothes. Rather than search for suitcases, she put the clothes in the same kind of trash bags the man had used to wrap the bodies.

The last thing they did was to cut Jane and Karen loose from the bed and make them stand. Then they herded them down the stairs to the foyer. The two wrapped corpses were lying together beside the front door. The man went out the door while the woman kept the knife blade pressed against Jane's side so she could feel the prick of the tip against her skin. They heard an engine noise and some scraping. The woman turned off the light.

When the door opened again Jane could see that he had backed a rental truck up over the curb nearly to the house so its tall, broad cargo section was blocking the view of the house from the street. He'd opened the cargo bay doors and extended a metal ramp down to the ground. The man said to Jane and Karen, "You two, drag the bodies over to the ramp. Now! Get going!"

The two women were tired and hurt, but they had no choice. Jane did most of the dragging. The man stayed within a few feet of them while they worked to move the body. "Get it up the ramp. You pull it up, and you push."

When they had strained and dragged it up onto the floor of the truck, he said, "Pull it all the way into the back." That part was not as difficult, so Jane did it herself, and then came down. The second body was easier for them, but it felt a bit heavier.

After that, they had to lift the trash bags full of bloody towels and rags and things into the bay. Their captors were determined to leave as little as possible in Karen's house to be found by the police.

During this labor, the woman hovered near them so that she and her knife were never far from Jane and Karen. Either she or the man would be able to kill at least one of them in any struggle.

The man ordered Karen and Jane to get inside the truck, and he zip-tied their hands behind them again. He went down the ramp, pushed it back into its place under the truck bed, and closed the rear doors. Jane listened while he turned the lever to seat the lock bar into its socket. A moment later the engine started, he eased it down the front lawn, and bumped it down off the curb to the street. He swung it around and made a series of stops and turns that she could not keep track of, while she sat in the locked cargo bay in the dark.

30

"Is Jane going to come back?"

"Sure she'll be back," Carey said. "We miss her and we worry about her, but try to remember she's only been gone a day, and for most of it she was on an airplane. She's about the least eccentric or unreliable person I've ever met, and what she cares most about is here." He was holding May, and he gave her a kiss on her soft baby cheek. "Jane's done a lot of very difficult things to help people, and she's very smart and very brave. I admire who she is, but mostly I worry. I didn't know she was doing these things until I was already in love with her and trying to get her to marry me. And it's not something you get used to."

"I'm sorry," Katie said. "I didn't mean to make you feel worse. It's just that things aren't the way she thought. She told me what these people had done to her before. And she told me they were all dead, but there could be others looking for her, so it would be dangerous for me to be around her. She said she would never leave May."

"I'm not saying that there's anything irrational about the way you're feeling tonight," Carey said. "I've always resented it when somebody would try to cheer me up by telling me I had basically imagined some situation that was seriously bad. Jane really did think she could keep that part of her life in the past, and she was wrong. But bad things have happened before, and so far, she's always made it home."

"I was just letting myself be weak, I guess," Katie said.

"That's perfectly understandable too," he said. "Let's say the very worst happens, and Jane can't make it home. You'll still be a sixteen-year-old who is in trouble, and you didn't ask for that or deserve it. Jane and I have put a lot of thought into how we can help you build a good life for yourself. If she can't keep helping, I'll help you alone. You'll still have a home where somebody's always glad to see you, spend the next three years in a good high school, and then go to college. You'll still have to be Katie and not your old name, but I'm sure you can handle that."

"Thank you," Katie said. "Can I take May for a while?"

"You must be tired," Carey said. "You should probably try to get some sleep. I'll bathe her and feed her a bottle and put her to sleep."

"Okay," she said. She got up and walked upstairs toward the other side of the house. Carey couldn't help feeling a mixture of sorrow for her predicament and envy that she was probably young enough to be able to sleep tonight.

◆

Officer Dave Fenton was thinking about the girl who had killed his brother Gerry. Michelle didn't intuit this because she had loved him for so long and so deeply that she could feel his thoughts—although she could. She knew because he didn't hide things. Every night after dinner he came into the living room and woke up the computer so he could get back to work on the case. Half the time, he barely said anything to the kids during the evening hours when he used to help them with their homework, or listen to somebody's presentation about refrigeration or aerodynamics.

She knew he had been sending himself reports and evidence evaluations and things from work. She was pretty sure doing that was against policy and maybe even illegal. She was also pretty sure that the IT people could detect things like that, and if they did, they would report him. They weren't cops; they were civilian technicians. They were more like the machines they operated than like the men and women who went out in a patrol car and saw blood and realized that the next blood might be theirs and that they'd already said the last things they were ever going to say to their families.

He had been receiving things that he had asked for on his own, too—information from other police departments, county clerks, departments of motor vehicles. He said he had asked for out-of-step vacation time too. Usually, he took his three weeks when the kids were out of school in the summer. He had told her that wasn't happening this summer because he was saving his time to follow up on some leads. He said he had to do it after school had started up again because she was a sixteen-year-old girl. If she wasn't in school somewhere she would stand out. If she tried to enroll in a school somewhere she would get caught because she would need a parent to show up with her and furnish paperwork from her last school.

He was a really good cop. The worst thing she kept picturing was that she would be in some other state and he would find her there. He would try to arrest her and she would try to stick a knife in him and he would shoot her.

If only she could tell him.

31

It was pitch dark in the cargo bay of the truck. There was a straight, smooth road under them and Jane felt the truck moving faster, felt the automatic transmission shift to a higher gear, and finally rose to her knees and moved close to Karen. She whispered to her, "I'm sorry you got involved in this. But now we've got to find a way out of it. How badly are you injured?"

"They hit me, and she burned me with my curling iron. You saw I could walk and move my arms. What are we even going to do? We're tied up and we don't have anything to fight back with."

"I watched that man wrapping up the two bodies."

"Yeah. I couldn't believe what you did to—"

"—I noticed something when he was getting them wrapped. He didn't go through their pockets or get their wallets or anything, just got them ready to put them in the truck and haul them away."

"I guess these two got what they came for and wanted to get away as soon as they could."

"When I came in, the first thing I saw was the man to my left reaching into his pocket for something. They must have flown here, so they couldn't bring guns with them. To me that means he was going for a knife."

"Oh my God," Karen said. "Which one is it?"

"This one. He's in the flowered bedspread. You can't see that, but I made sure I knew where we were putting him." Jane moved herself with her feet so that her back was close to the man, and she tried to reach his tape with her hands behind her back. After a few minutes, she said. "This is not working. I've got to try something else first."

Jane leaned forward, moved her wrists, and strained her legs to slip her backside into the circular space her bound wrists made of her arms. She worked to slide her arms down her thighs, then under her knees. When her hands got down to her ankles, she said, "This is where it gets really hard." She bent her legs to bring her knees up to her chin, worked her bound wrists under the heels of her feet, and stopped. She said, "See if you can pull off my boots."

Karen slid herself close to Jane so her back was to her, and her fingers felt around until she could feel Jane's boots. She tugged and then pulled the first one off, then worked on the other and pulled that one off too.

"Thanks," Jane said. She felt the change. Her heels were much lower than the heels of her boots, and she could point her toes to bring her heels up and slide her wrists under them. "Okay," she said. "My hands are in front of me."

"I can't do that. I'm not limber enough."

"You won't need to." Jane turned to the nearby corpse, and felt with her hands until she could feel the tape around it. She worked at finding the slightly raised beginning of the strip and then pulling the strip off until she couldn't go any further, then moved to find the next strip of tape and got that tape about as far, and then moved to find the third, and the fourth. She rolled the body to reach the next few inches of tape, then the next.

It was a slow, frustrating process, but at last she rolled the body, and the blanket and bedspread stayed flat. She had removed the tape. She could reach under the covering and feel the man's clothes. The body was getting stiff, and the smell of the blood was strong. She felt the right leg of the trousers and realized she had been right. She had difficulty reaching into the pocket because her hands were still bound together, but she managed to work the object up out of the pocket. "It's a knife," Jane said. "It's odd, though. The blade isn't exposed. I can't see anything, and I don't want to cut myself."

Jane found a slot at one end of the handle. She ran her fingers along each side until she felt a place where it was raised, and pressed it. There was a click, the handle gave a little jump when the spring was released, and the blade jutted outward. Jane ran one finger along the blade from the slot in the handle to the tip. "The blade is about six inches long, shaped like a stiletto, sharpened on both sides, with a blood gutter down the middle."

"Sounds awful."

"It's wonderful," Jane said. "I'm going to use it to cut your tie now. Make fists with both hands so there are no fingers out, and pull your wrists apart so the tie is tight. Don't move." She felt Karen's wrists, then sawed at the tie, and felt the knife cut through. Karen's wrists jerked apart.

"It worked," Karen said. "It feels so good."

"Now cut mine. Open your hands and feel where mine are. The knife blade is pointed down touching the floor."

Jane put the handle in her hand and then made fists and pulled her wrists apart so the tie was taut. Karen sawed through the tie and freed her. "It does feel good," Jane said.

"What's next?"

"As long as we have the chance, we should find out what else these two have on them."

They found the man's wallet, and Jane took the money and cards out of it, and put the wallet back in the same pocket. Next, they rolled him back up in the blanket and bedspread and used the tape that Jane had pulled off him to restore the four bindings so his bundle was tight again.

Next, they both worked to unbind and unwrap the second corpse. This one also had a wallet with money and cards in it, and two knives. One was like the knife they had used to free their hands. "It's like they bought them together. Or this guy liked his friend's knife and asked him where he bought it," Karen said. The man's other knife was short-bladed but razor-sharp, carried in an ankle rig. Jane took that too. Then she realized that among the other odors was a tobacco smell. She ran her hands over him until she found a pack of cigarettes.

"Is there something we missed?"

"He was a smoker," Jane said.

"I don't get it."

"That means he had something to light them with." She stuck her hand deeper into his pocket. "There it is." She pulled out a plastic disposable lighter and her thumb clicked it. The light illuminated the cargo bay, and it felt almost too bright after their hours in the dark.

They looked at the bodies and at each other's bloody faces and hands, and made swift adjustments to the tape strips, rewrapped the second man, and used the tape they'd taken off to make the bundled corpses look the same as before. Jane released the thumb switch and the truck went dark. "It's hot. I've got to let it cool off," she said.

"When it's cool again I want to get all of this blood off of us."

"Don't do it," Jane said. "When he opens the door, he's got to see us the way we look now, or he'll know we got our hands free."

"Oh, of course. I can't believe I was too stupid to remember that."

"What I think we need to do most in the light is be sure there's nothing in this truck that looks different from the way it looked before he locked us in. No pieces of the zip ties or duct tape lying on the floor. We stick leftover tape across our ankles so it looks like they're still bound together. We practice sitting down with our hands behind us so our wrists seem to be zip-tied. We study the way the switchblade knives work, and get used to holding them, so we can use them when the time comes."

"Use them?" Karen said. "I don't know—"

"I'll teach you and we'll practice. Usually, the first time people use a knife to fight for their lives, they don't get a firm enough grip on it, and their hand slides off the handle to the blade and gets cut. That's especially likely after the first stab and there's a lot of blood flowing. The handle gets slippery. Let's start with that." She lit the lighter again.

Karen stared at the knife in her hand, turned it over and over, pressed the switch to free the catch so she could push the blade against the hard floor and force it back into the handle. She pressed the switch and the blade shot out of the handle again and clicked into place.

Jane held up her identical knife and showed Karen the two horizontal protrusions at the top end of the handle. "This is the hilt. It can prevent your hand from sliding forward onto the blade. Get the feel of it and learn to grip the handle as hard as you can with your fingers tight against the hilt so your hand won't move."

"I don't think I can get into a knife fight."

"You're brave. These people tortured you to get you to help them catch me. They wouldn't have hurt you so badly if you had given in. But next time they'll keep torturing you until you'll do anything for them, or they'll kill you outright because you've served your purpose. When they get me to Boston, they'll start in on me to make me give them all my runners. Then they'll finish killing me too. To avoid that, we've got to kill this man first. It's a homicide in self-defense. You're a lawyer. You know all about this." She moved her thumb and let the flame go out.

"Yes," she said. "It's a defense I've used a few times in court. But—"

"So you understand. There are other things that you need to learn right now. In any kind of combat, but particularly with knives, the one who draws first blood probably wins. Speed is everything. There's no brandishing or letting him see the knife so he'll leave you alone or something. He should never see it until you strike. The instant he's vulnerable, spring at him and stab him as hard as you can and keep pulling the knife out as fast as you can and stabbing him anywhere you can reach—face, neck, back, chest, belly, thighs—until you can't anymore. Don't stop when you think he might be too far gone to hurt you. That won't be true until he's dead."

"It's all so horrible."

"Yes, it is. But if you understand that this is the only chance for either of us to stay alive, you can do it. The lighter is cool enough again. This time we place ourselves the way we want to look when he sees us. You go first."

She lit the flame and Karen sat next to one of the bodies with her arms behind her in the same position as when her wrists were bound together. Jane was at the spot where the truck's two doors met. She came forward, adjusted Karen's pose a little, took the knife handle, and moved it so she had a good grip but the man wouldn't see it behind her. "There. That's good." Then she let the flame die again. "Next it's my turn. When we have light again, sit at the center of the doors and see if I look right or if there's anything that I should change."

After a few minutes Jane handed the lighter to Karen, who took her turn lighting it and adjusting Jane's pose so her body hid the knife and Jane looked helpless. Then she gave Jane the lighter again.

An hour later, they felt the truck begin to slow down, then felt the transmission downshift. Jane lit the lighter again. "This is it," she said. "Take your place." She kept the flame lit while Karen returned to the position she had learned. Then she let the flame die and moved herself to the pose Karen had approved, and relit it. She said, "Do I look right?"

Karen nodded. "Yes."

Jane said, "Remember to breathe. Inhale through your nose, exhale through your mouth. Not so fast, but deeper. Good. We can do this."

32

The truck coasted off the highway, and then went along a slower, rougher road that sometimes made the truck bounce, and twice required a complete stop for what felt like thirty seconds while Jane and Karen waited, their muscles tensed to fight. Then the truck would back up or go around something and then go on.

Karen said, "Where do you think we are?"

"I know that after driving a few hours from LA we're not in Boston. They might be switching to another interstate that heads more northeast. If they were on the 10, they might be heading north to 70 or 80." Jane suspected that they might be doing something else. She judged that they could have reached the desert some time ago. They could have decided this was a good time to kill Karen, and be looking for a remote place to do it and leave her body and maybe the bodies of the two men.

The truck slowed some more, and then stopped. After a few seconds it turned to the right and lurched downward, then tilted to the left, as the right front wheel went over something, then tilted to the right as the left went over it. The two bodies slid as the truck bumped along.

Jane could hear gravel being kicked up by the tires and peppering the underside of the truck.

"Be ready," Jane said. "They won't go too far off the road."

The truck kept going for another few minutes. This time after the truck stopped, the engine stopped too. "This is it," Jane said.

After a pause they heard the clank of the lock bar being turned and sliding up, and then the latch being turned to keep the bar up. The door on the right swung outward and Jane could see the man's arm and hand, and then the other door. The world outside was dark, but the man held a flashlight in his hands. He aimed it into the bay of the truck and into their eyes. Then he said, "Okay, time for a pee stop."

Jane was hopeful for a second because for now he was fooled. If he had realized they were free, he would have slammed the doors and locked them in. But she knew that what had made him stop out here was that the woman had ordered him to kill Karen. What he had told them to do was certain to show him their hands weren't bound behind them. She rose to her knees, stood, and walked to the edge, sat, and slid off the edge of the cargo bay floor to the ground, then instantly lunged for him. He jumped back away from her, crouching to prepare to fight, but when he did that, it brought his upper chest and head closer to her. Jane slashed his neck, and she instantly knew that his left carotid artery had been cut, because blood was spurting out with each heartbeat. He dropped the flashlight and clamped his hand over the wound, staggering backward away from Jane.

Karen jumped from the truck behind him. When her feet hit the ground, she ran two steps and stabbed him in the back, withdrew the knife, and stabbed him again and again. He fell to the bare, sandy ground among clumps of weeds, quickly bleeding out.

Jane ran forward along the right side of the truck. When she reached the cab, she saw that the woman was gone. She spun around and ran for the back of the truck and found Karen still holding the knife, standing a few feet from the man's body. Jane slammed and locked the back doors, then patted the man down. She found the keys in his pocket and took them. She snatched up the flashlight that was still lit and lying near him, and said, "Come on."

They both ran to the cab, and Jane got into the driver's side, locked the doors, and shone the flashlight on the area around the steering wheel and found the ignition. She started the truck, turned on the headlights, and drove forward, but could see only about sixty or seventy feet ahead. The dashboard was lit now, and she found the switch and turned on the bright high-beam headlights. They lit up the area ahead of them for at least a hundred yards. She handed the flashlight to Karen. "Use this where the headlights don't reach. We've got to find her."

First Jane drove in a slow circle so the headlights would shine in every direction, but they didn't see her. Jane said, "I've got to guess that she's headed back toward the road. If she tried to go across the desert she'd die." There was only light in one direction, a faint glow like a haze along the black horizon. Jane drove the truck toward it at a steady ten miles an hour, weaving to make the headlight beams sweep while they both looked for the woman.

"There," Karen said. "What's that? It looks like tracks."

Jane turned right toward the spot where Karen was aiming the flashlight, and in the brighter lights the tracks in the sandy earth stood out. The woman seemed to have been at a dead run, with about a yard between steps. Jane straddled the tracks and sped up. As long as she could see the tracks, she raised the speed to twenty-five miles an hour. There were places where the woman had intentionally diverted her steps into patches of weedy plants, but each time, Jane's high-beam headlights would reach the space beyond, where they illuminated the tracks farther ahead.

After a few minutes, they made out the tall, thin woman in her dark jeans and black pullover running far ahead. As soon as the headlights reached her, she looked back over her shoulder, and her pale face flashed white in the light. Jane said, "Now she'll try to get out of the light."

The woman veered to the left, toward the distant light of the road. When Jane followed, gaining speed and moving the light beams to center her again, she tried the right. Jane kept the lights on her and accelerated. The woman stumbled, fell, pulled herself up, and kept running.

"What are we going to do with her?" Karen asked.

Jane said, "She beat you and burned you. Twice in three years she tried very hard to drag me off so her friends could torture me until I betrayed all of the people I ever helped. They would have been auctioned off to the people who want them dead."

"That's not really an answer."

"She knows where my family lives. My husband and our baby."

"That doesn't tell me what you're going to do."

"Yes it does."

Jane sped up until the woman was caught in the headlights with the truck only ten feet behind. Jane stood on the accelerator and saw her go down between the headlights. The truck ran over the top of her. Jane stopped the truck, took the flashlight from Karen, and said, "Stay here." She jumped from the cab and trotted back to the place where the woman lay.

Jane found the woman in the flashlight and stopped about eight feet from her prone figure. She said to the woman, "When you hit somebody with a truck, you might not see everything happen, but you hear it, and feel it. And then there's blood and broken bones."

The woman suddenly rolled and charged toward Jane. As she dashed toward Jane, she reached behind her and her hand came back with the ten-inch butcher knife she had taken from Karen's house. Jane waited as she came, then feinted and stepped aside at the last moment. As the woman passed, Jane jabbed the switchblade knife in beneath the woman's ribs and withdrew it. The woman seemed to falter in indecision for a second, and then decided to keep running.

Jane sprinted after her, grabbed her hair, and jerked her head backward, then brought the knife across her throat. She released the hair and said, "All you ever had to do was leave us alone." She walked back, picked up the flashlight again, and shone it on the woman until she was dead. Then she walked back to the truck where Karen waited. "Help me load her into the back of the truck with the others. We can drag her up the ramp. Then we'll go back to get the man too."

An hour later they were back in the truck's cab bumping the wheels up onto the main road. Jane said, "We'll have to find a place where we can wash while it's still dark, and then open the bag that woman filled with clothes from your closet." She looked at Karen, who was sitting beside her crying. She left her alone and kept the truck moving.

About ten minutes later she saw a sign that said they were on Interstate 15, and then another that said that they were passing Halloran Springs. Another sign told her that there was an exit ahead that would take her toward Laughlin, and soon they were crossing the state line into Nevada and heading for Arizona.

After a while Karen seemed to run out of tears. "I'm sorry. It's just nerves and fear. I wouldn't be alive if it weren't for you. And I started thinking about the horrible things you've had to live through to know how to do all this, and then I was stabbing him too, and I just—"

Jane said, "And now you have some horrible things in your memory too. I'm sorry for that, but I'm glad you were there to fight for my life."

After a long drive, she stopped the truck south of Las Vegas and north of Bullhead City, Arizona. She found a boat launch that was deserted at night, backed the truck to the edge of the water, climbed into the cargo bay, and dragged the first body, which was the woman's, along the floor, and pushed it out the back of the truck into the water. Then she got into the water to drag it out away from the boat launch ramp.

Karen joined her and helped her to unload the bodies of the three men. Then she got into the water with Jane to drag them out as far as she and Jane could pull them. They ducked under the water and washed the blood from themselves and most of it from their clothes. They got back into the truck dripping wet, and Jane turned on the truck's heater to dry them. She turned onto Route 68 because there was a sign that said it led to Interstate 40. When they were dry, they stopped and put on some of the clothes that the dead woman had stolen from Karen's closet. Before dawn, they stopped again at a gas station outside Kingman, Arizona, filled the gas tank, and drove on. When it was daylight, they parked a few blocks from a supermarket and walked to the store to buy food, bottled water, and over-the-counter wound medication with some of the money Jane had taken from the dead men's wallets.

When they returned to the rented truck, Jane started the engine and said, "Try to get some sleep. I'm going to need you to take the wheel in a couple of hours."

33

During the next full day, Jane and Karen drove on smaller roads roughly parallel to Interstate 40 East because the cameras that took pictures of vehicles and their drivers were more common on major highways than small roads. They dressed in more of the clothes the dead woman had taken from Karen's closet.

On the second day, they saw a self-service car wash with power hoses, stopped, and thoroughly cleaned the truck, with particular attention to the cargo bay. They put the clothes they'd worn with traces of blood on them into a trash bag and stuffed them into a dumpster behind a store near Lubbock, Texas.

On the third day, they left the truck outside a U-Haul lot in Dallas with the keys in it and walked a mile to a hotel-rich area, where they took a cab to the bus station and bought tickets to Chicago.

The travel became easier after that. During a stop in Indianapolis, Jane and Karen walked to a big drugstore and bought another burner phone, and then abandoned the idea of continuing to Chicago and bought tickets to Cleveland. While they were on that bus, Jane used the phone to call Carey.

"It's me," she said. "Karen and I are on our way to you. Tell me how everybody is."

"May and Katie and Carolyn are fine. Me too. I'm more than fine, as of now. I'm relieved. When do you expect to be here?"

"I'm guessing about three more days. I've got to go, but I love you." Once again, she'd said it, but she hated the inadequacy of it. She really did love him, but throughout her marriage to him, she seemed to say it most often when she was far away and not telling him what she was doing there, so saying she loved him felt like a lie, a way of diverting his attention from things she didn't want him to ask her about.

They kept going, and reached Syracuse a day earlier than she had predicted, and took a taxi to the airport to pick up Jane's Volvo from the airport parking lot. When she started the car, Jane said, "What happened to us in California and what we did afterward is a secret. If one of us ever told anyone anything about it, the consequences would be the kind we could never recover from. It's not easy to be a person who can't ever talk to anyone about big things that have happened, but this is one secret you have to keep forever."

Karen said, "I'm a criminal lawyer. I know what the legal consequences would be. I've thought about the rest of it since the minute it happened. The fact that the two of us know what we did and why we had to do it is enough. I don't need to have anyone else know. As far as I'm concerned, you came to my house for a visit."

That night they took the county road into Cantrell Falls, the small central New York town where Stewart and Molly lived. They parked for five minutes before Jane saw the front door open for a second and then close again. Then they got out of the car and walked across the park to the big old house and up onto the dark porch. Molly opened the door, let them in, and then looked out at the circular street around the park, the quiet streets radiating from it, and then closed the door. Molly hugged Jane and then looked at the woman she had brought with her.

Jane said, "Molly, this is my friend Karen."

Karen said to Molly, "Thank you so much for lending my client your phone to call Jane about me. I'm very grateful."

Molly smiled. "I'm glad you're here. Your client will be very glad to see you."

They climbed the stairs to the shop where Stewart was at work. He looked up. "Hello, Jane."

"Hi, Stewart. This is Karen," Jane said. "You happened to be on our way, so I thought we'd stop and see if Karen's client was ready to go to his next stop."

"I'm pleased to meet you," Stewart said to Karen. He looked at Jane. "I finished his order the day before yesterday. He's ready to go."

Jane said, "I think that if you have time, Karen needs one identity that's good enough to get her on an airplane. It's a precaution, not for a specific emergency in the present. A birth certificate and a Real ID driver's license. It doesn't matter what state, as long as it's not California."

"Have you told her what it will cost?"

"It's a present," Jane said. "I don't have the cash with me right now, but I'll get it to you when the work is ready to pick up. Can you do it?"

"Sure," he said. "I can mail it to your PO box."

Molly said, "Karen, come with me. We need some pictures and we need to talk about a name you'd like to use." She and Karen went down the hall to the photographic studio.

Stewart looked at Jane. "I may have to do some photo magic on the pictures. The bruises and cuts and the split lip may show if I don't." He said, "You too, now that I see you in the light. Your face is healed up better than hers, but the scrapes on your hands and that bruise on your neck are still pretty clear."

"What can I say? Rough trip. It's too hot out for a turtleneck or a scarf, but I'll use more makeup."

"Molly probably has your shade in the studio. It's on the house."

"Thanks, Stewart."

A moment later Brian Finlay leaned in the door. Jane said, "Hi, Brian. Are you ready to move on?"

"Yes," he said. "Stewart and Molly have been great, but I'm sure they'll be ready to start missing me as soon as possible."

"Okay," Jane said. "We'll go as soon as Molly is done with Karen."

Ten minutes later the three were walking across the city park to the space where Jane had left her car. Jane clicked the fob to unlock the doors, and Brian said, "I'm feeling fresh and ready to drive. I've gotten used to being awake when Stewart and Molly are awake."

"Great," Jane said. "We've been navigating with this burner phone I picked up. We want to go south into Pennsylvania and head to a farm outside Pittsburgh. It belongs to a friend of mine. She doesn't know what I've been doing all these years, so don't talk about being on the run or anything. I'll enter the address for you." She typed in the information and put the phone into the cup holder, where he could see and hear it.

As soon as she had watched Brian drive a few minutes and had assured herself he was a good enough driver to trust—he had driven himself across the country to reach her just weeks ago—she allowed herself to lean her seat back and fall asleep. The others talked in low voices for a while, and then Karen fell asleep in the back seat, and the only voice in the car was the female phone app voice telling Brian when a turn was coming up.

When Jane woke up, it was because the morning sun was in the east. They were in Pennsylvania, only a few miles from their destination. Jane brought her seat back up and used the visor mirror and the brush she had bought during a visit she had Karen had made to a big Target store in Syracuse to brush her hair. Then she handed the brush to Karen. She put on a little makeup and perfume, and waited.

"In one mile," said the female phone app, "your destination will be on your right."

Jane put everything except the phone away in the overnight bag she had bought during the trip. She picked up the phone and said to Brian, "Do you need this anymore? I'll warn you when I see the place."

"Then I don't."

She called Carey's cell phone. "Hi," she said.

"Where are you now?" he said.

"If you were to pick up May and walk out the front door onto the porch, you would probably see us in a minute."

She turned to Brian. "See the big white farmhouse up there? That's it. Stop at the gate so I can open it. Carey? See you in a minute."

34

During the next few weeks, Jane and Karen rested and recovered, and Carey took over the care of Karen's wounds and Jane's. Karen's burns were going to need some plastic surgery, but the rest of their injuries would heal without it. Jane called the mailbox rental store in Chicago that she used as a mailing address and had the owner forward her mail to her at a new box she rented in Pittsburgh. She put May in a sling and, usually with Carey, or sometimes Karen or Katie or Carolyn, walked the big farm. On the eighteenth day, Karen's new birth certificate and Real ID driver's license arrived. Jane and Karen drove into the city to pick them up and mail the payment in cash to Stewart.

Karen and Katie became friends. Jane had told Katie that Karen was not a fugitive, but a friend Jane and Carey had made in college who had become a successful criminal lawyer in California. Jane also mentioned that she was brave and could be trusted.

Within a few days, Katie had told Karen about her case, and Karen told her that most of the time the legal system came up with the right answers, but that sometimes it didn't. In rare instances, a victim was justified in refusing to allow it to determine her fate, at least temporarily.

Katie was one of those people. She had taken a big risk, but if she did exactly as Jane was teaching her, from now on, she was very likely to live a free and happy life.

As soon as Karen was ready to travel, Jane took her to the Pittsburgh airport, where she caught a flight back to Los Angeles under the name Stewart had put on her documents, Laura Shepherd.

Almost as soon as Jane returned to the farm, she was in the barn opening the door panel of Carey's car's left front door and retrieving the Glock 17 pistol and loaded magazines she had hidden there when the car was new. She took out the clothes she had left in the trunk of her Volvo, packed them in the new suitcase, put the pistol and ammunition inside, took the two switchblade knives out of the space under the spare tire, and slid them into the outer pocket, and carried the suitcase inside to the bedroom she and Carey shared.

While she was taking out pieces of clothing, holding each one up to look at it, and then laying it on the bed, she heard Carey come into the room behind her. He said, "Are you unpacking or are you packing?"

"First one, then the other," she said. She waited for a few seconds, but he didn't say what she was dreading. He said nothing, which she thought might be worse.

She stepped close to him and put her arms around his neck and hugged him. "I'm sorry," she said. "I know I've probably said that a hundred times since this started, but I am, so I say it. Karen is safe, and she's on a flight home. Katie is safe with us here. Brian has his new identity documents, and I've been giving him lessons about how to be a new person since we left my old house. The people I took him to for identification papers spent the last couple of weeks teaching him more. As soon as I can get him transportation, he'll be ready to go too. There's just one more person I have to go see."

Carey said, "I know you wouldn't go if you didn't think you have to."

"Thank you. I wouldn't."

"But do you?"

"Yes."

"When do you leave?"

"As soon as I've gotten Brian out of here in a car that will take him where he's going, and can get some laundry done and my suitcase packed again. Probably two days from now."

Carey nodded. "I'd better go take May from Katie now. It's my turn."

Jane closed the suitcase. "Let's take her for a walk together. She hasn't seen enough of me lately, and I can't ever see enough of either of you."

That night after May was asleep and they could hear her on the baby monitor where she slept in the next room, Jane and Carey had a bath together in Carolyn's oversize bathtub and made love. After that, Jane fell asleep with the soft sound of May's baby breaths amplified in the monitor.

Jane dreamed that she heard the sound of footsteps coming from the monitor speaker, and sat up, alarmed. The steps came closer, and she looked up and saw the door swing open. The bent-over, shrunken shape and the loosely fitting jacket over it were a relief. Harry said, "No need to get up. We've seen enough already."

"Don't be disgusting," Jane said. She pulled the sheet up to her neck and glanced at Carey's sleeping face.

"He won't wake up."

"No?"

"No," Harry said.

"What are you here for, Harry?"

"Recent developments. You were always the woman who decided to do something that made sense to her. Working to make more machines that were turning the world into an overheated desert, or working forty years to add a few bucks to some guy's hundred billion dollars didn't make sense. Keeping a person from being killed always made sense. Remember that?"

"That's what I've been doing. You can't be saying that the twin brothers think I've changed my mind or that I want something different now."

"The brothers are about keeping the world in balance, not making moral judgments. An island volcano erupts molten lava and burns the plants and trees, and all the people and animals vacate. When the lava cools, the island is much bigger and there's a fresh bunch of minerals that help grow things. Right away the island starts getting repopulated, but also getting eroded by rain and wind and time. Something is destroyed, something is created and then destroyed too. The brothers are busy with the big picture, which is balance, which is health."

"What do they want, Harry?"

"Did I say they sent me? The only place I'm alive is in your mind. The one who conjures me into her dreams is you. You took in Katie. You rescued Brian Finlay. A few weeks ago, you dragged your family away from your husband's home. Then you found out Karen was probably in danger, so you went there and saved one life too. How many lives did you take there? My count is four people. The term 'bloodbath' comes to mind."

"Do I have to relive that now?"

"You've been reliving it since it happened. Your number of people saved has stayed about the same, on a per annum basis. None during the couple of years since the Russians caught you the first time, of course. Having the baby might count as one life contributed. The number of people you've killed has been growing much faster."

"I never wanted to kill anybody, ever. That hasn't changed," Jane said. "The world has changed."

"Okay," said Harry. "No argument there. In each instance you've been trying to save somebody from being killed. You might have known at the start that it meant going up against killers. And how about right now? You're packing to go on another trip. Is it unavoidable? Are you being forced to do it? Who are you saving?"

"May, Katie, Carey. Everybody I've ever taken out of their old lives and given new ones. And me. I can't just say it's over. That was my mistake three years ago."

"Then there's nothing more I can do. I've done my job. You're welcome. I hope you get what you want." He turned and walked out through the closed door.

Jane heard Harry's voice in the baby monitor. "Hi, baby. Go back to sleep now."

35

One of the attitudes among Jane's ancestors, even up to the present generation, was that when they prayed, they didn't do it to ask for favors. They did it to give thanks. It was a sense of proper behavior and the relationship between people and the universe. Jane walked up behind the farm buildings to the woods alone. She thanked the universe for having allowed her and her family and friends to survive the latest attacks. She gave thanks, as she was taught, in the timeless order, from beneath her feet upward and outward—the earth, the waters, the fish, the plants, the edible plants, the medicinal herbs, the animals, the trees, the birds, the four winds, the thunders that bring rains, the sun, the moon, the stars, all spirit messengers, the Creator.

She walked back down to the farm buildings to be with her family for a few more minutes, and then she said, "I'd better get going." She hugged and kissed them, starting with May and ending with Carey.

Jane started her car in the barn, then drove out past the farmhouse where Carey and Katie and Carolyn stood on the porch and waved. Seeing them like that, standing there and waving in some strange, smiling tableau of family contentment and safety, was—her mind had reached for *surreal* but the world had become so strange that the word was getting faded from overuse, not strong enough, or crude enough. *Crazy* seemed closer. She turned her attention toward the highway as she made her way down to the gate. It was early, but she had a long way to go.

She got out to open the gate, drove past it, then got out again to close it. Then she waited impatiently for cars to pass until she had an opening for a left turn toward the east. She accelerated until she reached the right speed. She caught herself whispering "Obolonsky."

She set her telephone to use the app that gave her directions, and then she turned on the radio to a rock station. That seemed to silence the part of her mind that kept repeating the man's name, but she noticed that the first three songs were ones she had not heard before. Since May was born, she had not played rock stations when May was with her because she had been trying to talk to her and teach her a couple of languages, and May was with her all the time.

Jane made the best progress she could without violating any traffic laws or speed limits. She wanted to get there before the bodies of the woman and her crew were either traced to the Boston gang or made it to national news. She was sure they had been found by now and identified, but she had seen no mention of them in the national media, so there was a chance she'd get there in time. The first thing was to cover the distance, which her phone said was still 482 miles.

Jane reached the car rental lot in West Springfield, Massachusetts, over seven hours later. She used the name and credit of Denise Hutchens again to rent the car because if things went wrong, she wanted to give the authorities a chance to go wrong and make up a story about Denise Hutchens avenging herself on a Russian gang. For the moment she wanted a nondescript car with legitimate Massachusetts license plates. She parked her Volvo on a residential street lined with single-family homes that was within walking distance. When she had picked up the gray Nissan Maxima from the lot, she came back and took the suitcase from her car and put it in the Nissan, and then she was gone. Boston was still a long distance away, but the drive was easy, and most of the traffic in the evening was commuters heading away from the city.

When she arrived in Boston, she checked into the Lexington Hotel and immediately began charging her phone and going down the list she had made of addresses connected with anyone named Obolonsky, re-examining the order that she had arranged to visit them. She made a few revisions, and then took the knives and the pistol out of her suitcase, reloaded the pistol, selected, and laid out her outfit for tomorrow, choosing her clothes for their ability to hide weapons.

She had already completed a day-long drive, but only after those preparations did she feel that she was ready to run a bath and soak in the hot water. When she had done that, she dried off, put on a warm, soft robe, and sat in the room's easy chair to think and prepare herself.

She fell asleep in the chair and woke sometime in the middle of the night, turned the light off, and slept again. In the morning, Jane went over the list of people named Obolonsky who lived in Massachusetts that she had compiled from the internet during the past couple of weeks. Her problem was that there was no way to eliminate any of them. Just because somebody put *MD* or *LLD* after his name on LinkedIn didn't mean he wasn't the head of a Russian crime organization. The fact that a person named Obolonsky was a woman might mean she had nothing to do with crime, or it might mean she was the gang leader's wife or sister or mother.

Jane had read that there were neighborhoods in Boston where large numbers of Russian speakers lived. Gangs made up of immigrants often lived in areas among lots of other people from the same country. It was easier to be unnoticed there, easier to recruit new members, easier to know a person's background well enough to detect undercover cops and infiltrators. The neighborhoods mentioned most often were Allston, Newton, and Brighton, so whenever she could find an Obolonsky whose address was in one of those neighborhoods, she had moved that Obolonsky to the higher-priority list.

She had made a list of Russian grocery stores, but then she had read that the people who missed Russian food the most and frequented these stores tended to be the older immigrants. The men she had seen and fought were young. The man she was searching for would not be elderly. He would be young—someone who had arrived after the collapse of the Soviet Union. She learned that there was only one Russian Orthodox church in Boston, the Church of the Epiphany, and she knew that being the boss of a criminal gang didn't necessarily mean he had never been in a church, but on any given day, she was pretty sure that was not a likely place to find him.

Jane took her high-priority list of Obolonskys and began to search for the addresses where they lived. She used her rental car to give herself tours of the neighborhoods, driving past the addresses she was interested in, and when she could do it without standing out, she would park and walk to get a better sense of what a house or apartment building contained. She only used the car once for each address, because she was sure that this gang was sophisticated enough to have security cameras and watch the footage to see if one car kept going by.

After three days she bought a seven-day pass on the MBTA and began using the subway to reach the neighborhoods where there were Obolonskys, and walked to the local restaurants and bars to watch for the sort of men who might be part of the Russian gang. She watched for men who had the sort of tattoos she had seen on the men she had fought, but the tattoos she saw were the sort that anyone might have.

She listened for the Russian language and accents, and she heard a few snatches of conversation—people making phone calls or ordering something—but the talk meant nothing to her, reminding her that expecting it to mean more than that the person was Russian-born was foolish. After a few days, she started driving around to Russian restaurants that were too far from MBTA stations to visit on foot.

And then, while she was sitting at a table in the back of a restaurant, she saw a man walk in whose face meant something to her. The last time she had seen his face, he had been trying to climb out of her basement into her driveway. She stared at him for no more than a second, and ducked her head to look down and turn the other way. She gave him time to take a few steps. Then she shouldered her purse, took her check to the cashier by the door and left it on the counter beside her with a fifty-dollar bill, and was out the door in five more seconds.

Jane hurried down the street toward her car. She was feeling the seconds going by, and when she felt enough had elapsed for the man to make it back to the front door, either to see if he had recognized her or see which way she was going, she reached into her purse to put her hand around the pistol grips of her Glock and looked over her shoulder. He was not on the sidewalk or standing at the front window. As she walked the remaining steps, she kept her hand in her purse as though she were feeling for her car keys, and when she was at the car, her hand came out with them, and she got in the driver's seat and stared down the street at the restaurant.

Jane thought about the man. He was the one she had mistaken for Brian in the darkness on the night when she had gone back to her house to try to rescue him. She had led him as far as the coal door in the basement in the darkness and climbed out, but as soon as his upper body was in the opening and he was pulling himself up to crawl out, a car's headlights had passed across him and she'd seen his tattoos, kicked the coal door shut on his face, run to the other side of her house, seen the knotted sheets hanging from the upper window, and realized Brian had gotten out.

During the long drive away from her hometown across the state to take Brian to get his new identity, they had talked about what had happened to bring him to that moment, and he had mentioned the name of the man whose shouts had raised the house. Maxim.

Jane sat in the car for about half an hour waiting for Maxim to come out of the restaurant. She tried to understand what she had heard and seen. Over the years she had found herself facing members of American organized crime groups. In the northeastern part of the country the most common form they had taken was the Mafia, which in the Buffalo area was sometimes referred to as "The Arm." The bosses tended to be, or pose as, businessmen, wearing good suits and expensive shoes, driving big fancy cars long after the era when that sort of behavior wasn't dangerous. The lower-level men, the ones who went around collecting payoffs from restaurants, bars, and small businesses, or collecting the money from football pools and so on, tended to dress less expensively so they didn't attract attention. Jane still hadn't been able to identify a common look for people from this Russian gang, except for the tattoos. All she had right now was the face of Maxim—not an unusual-looking man. She only remembered his face so clearly because in that single moment in her house's driveway, he had been caught in the bright headlights of the car turning at the corner of her street. And there he was, coming out of the restaurant now.

He was carrying a large, square cardboard box. It looked cumbersome, and he was being very careful to keep it level. He was bringing somebody—a group—lunch from the Russian restaurant. Jane's heart began to beat faster. She used her phone to film his progress across the street where there was no crosswalk, moving fast but being careful not to tilt the box. She needed to be sure she didn't lose sight of him and she needed to get an accurate record of the car he would be driving, so she rested her phone on the door to keep it steady.

He stopped at the trunk of a dark blue Lexus sedan. He opened the trunk and leaned in to put the box inside, and that gave Jane a chance to take several still shots of the front license plate. She put her phone away and started her engine while she watched him walk to the front door of the car and get inside. Jane pulled away from the curb and drove away from him in the opposite direction before he had started his car, so he wouldn't focus on her. She turned left at the first small street and extended the maneuver into a U-turn, then stopped at the corner and waited while he accelerated out into the street, waited for two cars to pass by her, and then followed him at a distance.

She assumed that Maxim was on the way to some place—maybe an office or a shell business—in the immediate area, or at least the first mile, but he kept going past that range. He was driving out of the city westward on Route 9 into the suburbs. Jane stayed far back, keeping the blue Lexus in sight, but making sure there was always a changing string of other cars between the Lexus and her rental car. He turned onto Interstate 95 South and Jane stayed after him. There was no telling how good Maxim was at detecting someone following him, or at drawing a follower to reveal himself. Jane decided it was good that Maxim was so careful about his box of take-out lunches. He wasn't about to speed up or stop abruptly, or to weave in and out of traffic, or to veer across several lanes to take an exit.

When Maxim reached a sign that read "Needham," he signaled, coasted onto the exit ramp, and turned right at the foot of it. Jane didn't signal, so if he saw her at all he would think she was continuing on the highway, but she drifted over one lane to glide off after him just as the Lexus accelerated onto a surface street. She turned after him, her eyes scanning for the sight of him. She saw he was approaching a street with a traffic signal, and a pedestrian crossing signal that displayed a red hand. The green was about to switch to yellow. Instead of speeding up to make the light, he slowed gradually, and when the yellow appeared, he stopped.

The soup didn't spill, Jane thought. She slowed to let two cars get into the lane between her and the Lexus, and then followed. Three blocks later he made a left turn. She gave him time to complete his turn, then turned left, prepared to pull over and stop if necessary. Maxim kept going. After a few more blocks, he reached a yellow house on Grove Street, turned to pass through an iron gate onto the long, wide imitation cobblestone driveway and up to the broad parking area in front of the house. Jane slowed down and kept taking pictures as she approached.

As Maxim got out of the Lexus and walked to the trunk, a man opened the front door of the house and held the door while Maxim brought the box inside. The door closed. Jane kept going five hundred feet, pulled to the curb, and watched the gate in her rearview mirrors, but Maxim's blue Lexus didn't leave. She reviewed her pictures on her phone. This house was big and beautiful. The paving stones were perfect—not one of them different from the thousands of others or eroded out of place. The house looked like something out of the late nineteenth century, about ten thousand square feet of it, but it was new. There was nothing that wasn't freshly built or planted on this plot of land. She estimated that, since it was also in a neighborhood where this level of excellence was common, it had cost somebody between five and ten million dollars. That was not Maxim. That was the man who had sent a crew out to hunt for her.

She was too far away to take more pictures of the house, but she took a few more of the walls and the gate, then started the car. She spent some time exploring the area, looking for places where she could leave the rental car, and then kept going to the east, back toward Boston. She stopped in a hardware store and bought a small, powerful flashlight, and went to her hotel to prepare for the night. She left her rental car parked on a side street a few blocks from the hotel.

36

Jane spent time online. She had finally found a way of separating the one Obolonsky who mattered to her from all the other Obolonskys in the Boston area. He was the one who lived at the address on Grove Street. She learned his first name was Pavel. She ran several searches for him, and finally found a photograph. His picture taken at some charity event showed he was about fifty years old with a slightly receding hairline and a face that struck her as so untroubled and relaxed that he seemed almost featureless. She found another picture of him as a member of a business group, identified as an investor and entrepreneur. She studied his pictures until she was sure she would recognize him if she saw him. Then she studied the pictures she had taken of the big house and its grounds, expanding the images and looking for its defenses and vulnerabilities.

It was dark outside when Jane decided it was time to examine the things she had brought in her suitcase. She laid out a pair of black pants, black running shoes, a black long-sleeved pullover shirt, and a lightweight black men's-style jacket. She took out the black balaclava she had brought, the two identical switchblade knives, and the Glock 17 pistol and loaded magazines. When she had reassembled and loaded the pistol in the barn at Carolyn's farm, she had worn rubber gloves so there would be no prints or DNA on any of its parts, or on the ammunition. If she lived through this, she could wipe the gun and toss it away without fear that it would be traced to her. It had been a present given to her by a man named Randall she had helped once. He had inherited it from an uncle who had until recently been a cop in Minnesota. When he'd died, he'd left a collection of high-quality handguns he had come by in various unethical ways. Randall had suspected he'd kept them in case he needed to plant one on an unarmed dead person he'd shot. He had sent Jane five Glocks, a couple of Sig Sauers, and a Beretta. The serial numbers couldn't be traced to the uncle, who was dead, to Randall, who was somebody else now, and certainly not to Jane.

Jane stood in front of the bathroom mirror and tied her hair in a tight bun. She put on the black clothes, and then slid one knife into her left-side pants pocket and the other into her right. She put the Glock into the inner left-side jacket pocket and stood in front of the full-length mirror on the closet door to be sure the jacket hung naturally and hid the pistol.

When she walked across the lobby, she placed herself among a group of people who were going out the front entrance to ask the parking attendant to bring their cars. As they lined up along the street to wait, Jane separated herself from them and walked down the street toward the side street where she'd left her rental car.

Jane drove west to Route 9, then to Interstate 95 and the Needham exit, and then to Grove Street. When she passed the house, she saw that Maxim's Lexus had not left, but had been moved away from the front of the building. Now it was parked on a paved strip along the side of the house with two others.

She looked at her car's dashboard clock. It was after ten. She drove to the space where she had stopped early in the day and parked at the side of the road. She sat in her dark car, watched the gate and the lighted windows in her mirrors, and waited.

As she sat in the dark, she thought about the old people, the ancestors. There was always war or the possibility of it. Warriors would appear out of the forest, some of them from far away—Hurons and Ojibways from the western Great Lakes, Cherokees and Catawbas from as far south as what would later become Georgia—kill a few people and disappear again. Or they did what she was doing now. They would go out in parties as large as a thousand, as small as three, or even one man, and make their way to the villages of enemies, either to strike to prevent an attack or to exact a price for past battles. Sometimes they would be out for as long as two years at a time. Jane waited two hours.

In her rearview mirror she saw first one car, and then a second car, drive out of the gate. She leaned to the right so she would not be visible, pulled out her pistol, listened for the approaching cars, and watched the car ceiling for moving light, but neither came. The cars were both moving away from her. She put the pistol back in her jacket.

She got out of her car and walked along the perimeter of the property, going slowly with her left shoulder almost touching the wall so she would not be visible to the security cameras she had noticed on the eaves of the house and would not trigger any motion detectors she hadn't seen. When she reached the corner of the wall she put on the balaclava and thin leather gloves, hoisted herself up and over, then took two steps to crouch behind some thick rose bushes and became motionless. She listened and watched the house for any sign that her presence had been detected.

The lights were still on, and she could see a man who looked like the pictures of Pavel Obolonsky sitting at a dining room table across from

Maxim smoking a cigarette and talking. If he had been aware that an enemy was in his side yard, he would have been worried about a rifle shot. If he had been aware that the woman he had been planning to kidnap and torment was in his side yard, he would have been making arrangements to have men come and surround the property, then move in and capture her. That thought made Jane look in every direction to be sure that was not happening.

She leaned her back against the wall, and returned her attention to watching the two men in the dining room. She could see that they were drinking. There was a bottle on the table that contained a clear liquid, and as they talked, they kept refilling glasses that were wider and deeper than shot glasses. She was delighted. Alcohol would dull their senses, make them slow to make decisions, and if they kept it up, make them likely to sleep deeply for the first hours of the night.

Jane waited. It took only about ten minutes for a drink to start to affect a person, and about an hour to reach its full effect. She would see when that happened if they stayed in front of the window. After a few minutes it crossed her mind that if she had come to murder them, she could probably have simply walked along the house to the window and shot them both with her pistol. Her plan was different.

She waited and watched. Finally, a few minutes after 1:00 A.M., Obolonsky stood up, screwed the cap onto the bottle, set it on a sideboard with others, and walked out of the room. Maxim stood up and carried the glasses into an area near the back of the house that had to be the kitchen.

She saw the lights turn on in a series of windows that traced Obolonsky's progress up the stairs to the second floor. Then there was a light on in an upstairs bedroom, and a light in a window that was translucent rather than clear and so was a bathroom. After a time, that one went out, and then the bedroom light. She checked the time on her watch: 1:37 A.M.

After that she saw the light on the staircase go out, and then a light go on in a window on the first floor, and go out a few minutes later. Apparently Obolonsky had Maxim sleeping on the first floor to be his watchdog.

She gave them time to get settled and fall asleep. One hour later, at 2:37, she walked toward the house. She went around it to the kitchen door and looked in the windows for alarm keypads, but saw none. She used one of the switchblade knives to cut away the dried and hardened putty around the glass pane closest to the doorknob and then to pry it out of place. She set it down beside the steps, reached inside, felt for the deadbolt and disengaged it, turned the knob lock and then the knob, and entered. She could hear the faint whisper of a central air-conditioning unit, and then she separated that sound from the quieter sound of the refrigerator.

Jane made her way deeper into the house, keeping her steps small and tentative. This was a practically new house, but sometimes a new house would settle in the first years, so she walked slowly and with care to make her progress silent.

She identified the room where Maxim was sleeping by the sound of his snoring. It was the first door in a hallway near the front of the house, probably so he could control the entrance and stairs. She was worried about getting up the stairs without waking him, but she had no other way, so she kept moving to the staircase.

In a moment she was climbing the stairs with her eyes on the hallway where Maxim would appear if she woke him. She would take a few stairs and then stop and wait for long enough so a sleeper's mind would not connect two faint sounds into a pattern and wake.

She reached the top of the staircase and stood still. The second floor was silent except for the slightly closer hum of the air-conditioning system. She remained motionless while she looked back at the bottom of the stairs and the mouth of the first-floor hallway. There was still no sign that Maxim was awake.

Jane concentrated on the second floor. There was a big window at the far end of the hall, and it admitted the dim light of the moon. The hallway consisted of a row of doors on either side of the long hardwood floor. It was very good news to Jane that down the center of the hall floor was a long, narrow rug that would absorb sound. There seemed to be eight bedrooms along the hall to the left side of the staircase, and a single set of double doors to the right. Those doors would be the master bedroom.

She moved toward the doors, taking small steps. When she reached the double doors, she found they were locked. She had a few cards in her pocket in the name of Denise Hutchens so she could return her rental car and pay for it. She selected one by feel. It had to be thin enough to slide between a pair of well-fitted doors, bendable enough to get into the depression behind the strike plate, but thick enough to push the latch bolt aside.

She picked one, slid it in, bent it with her thumb and forefinger while she pushed, and opened the door on the right, crouched low, and stepped in. She closed the door with extreme care, knelt and listened, letting her eyes adjust to the deep darkness. After a few seconds she heard the slow, heavy breathing of the sleeping man. She counted to two hundred, then began to crawl toward the sound.

As she crawled, she got a sense of the size and shape of the space she was in. This was the bedroom proper, just a large bed, a table and chairs, and a chaise longue that felt like part of the same set. To her left was an open walk-in closet the size of a second bedroom. Beyond that was the open door to the bathroom. To her right was another big open space, but she could not see well enough to determine anything else about it.

When Jane reached the bed, she could hear that the man was breathing with a slight snore. She pulled the pistol out of her jacket, pointed it toward the bed, and reached up to the lamp beside the bed and switched on the light.

The man in the bed was Pavel Obolonsky. His eyes opened in alarm and he raised his head, squinting and blinking. "Maxim? Is something—"

"Put your hands on the bedspread where I can see them," Jane said. "Do not reach for anything, or raise your voice, or you are going to die."

"Who are you?"

"I'm the one you sent the woman and her crew to kidnap," Jane said. "I came to tell you that she and the others are dead."

"I guessed that," Obolonsky said. "You wasted your trip. Or maybe not. If you're ready to make an agreement with me, I can pay you a percentage of the money I get for each of the people that you've hidden. We'll take them one at a time, so it's easy, quiet, and efficient. If anything goes wrong when we take one of them, we can wait for a while before we go out to get the next one."

"I came for a different kind of deal."

"Tell me."

"I came here to show you that I can find you and get to you any time I want to. I want you to think about that. I want you to understand that you are not to bother me again. Don't send any more people, don't do anything else. If you do, make sure that you have your funeral planned and paid for in advance. The last man I said that to was a big boss too, but he was wise enough to do what I asked. He lived for years and died of old age." She saw his eyes shift slightly away from her eyes and back. Had he focused on something behind her for a second?

His face changed and looked cold and angry. "Don't you have any idea who you're talking to?" He used one hand to brush back his hair in a gesture of frustration, but Jane saw the movement was a distraction from the other hand sliding under the covers.

"Don't!" she said, but he was committed and moving quickly.

She saw a section of the bedcovers rising, and fired her pistol at his chest. The gun he held under the covers went off and puffed the covers toward her as a hole appeared in the bedspread where he'd fired through it. She placed her second shot through his forehead, ducked, and spun around.

She saw Maxim in mid-charge and she fired three rapid shots into his torso as he dived toward her. He flopped on the floor five feet short and lay still. She fired once more into the back of his head and stepped past him through the double doors into the hallway. She closed the double doors and went down the stairs and out the kitchen door.

She drove back to her hotel, showered, put on fresh clothes, stuffed everything she had worn or used into a plastic bag inside her suitcase, left a large cash tip for the hotel maid, and used the automatic service on the television set to check out of the hotel. She went out, walked down the street to the side street where she'd left her rental car, and began the long night drive toward Springfield. She was sure that the rental car lot would be open by the time she got there, and she would clean the prints and DNA from this one and turn it in, and then pick up her own car and head for Lowery, Pennsylvania.

◆

Jane got out of the Volvo, opened the gate, pulled in, and closed it again, and then drove up the long farm road to the barn and parked inside. As she came out and headed for the house, the back door opened and her family poured out and met her. Carey hugged her. "Why didn't you call us?"

Jane said, "This time I thought I'd surprise you."

They walked to the back porch of the house, where Katie was standing holding May. Jane stepped up and put her arms around both of them and kissed them both. Katie handed May to Jane. Jane spoke a couple of sentences to her in Nundawaono.

Carey said, "Have you got luggage to bring in?"

"One suitcase, and it's practically empty. Might as well bring it in, though, because we'll need to start packing again tomorrow."

Carey looked at her. "Where are we going?"

"Home."

37

Officer Fenton had two suitcases lying open on the bed. Each one had two or three thick file folders on the bottom and a couple of flash drives in the inner pockets, and the smaller suitcase held his laptop computer. Now he was rolling his clothes up and packing them the way they'd taught him in boot camp.

He had compiled an itinerary of stops for himself to begin as soon as he arrived in Albany, New York. He had already made contact with the law enforcement departments in charge of runaways and delinquents because she was still sixteen, so he'd start there. He'd also made contact with the departments that dealt with the Iroquois nations, because she was a Seneca Indian. He would go there second. After that, there was the education department. State governments at least had the names of all students in their states, and they could find the names of the ones who had just entered the state and were registered for the school year about to begin. All these people would be very interested in helping him find a teenager wanted for stabbing a man to death.

As he packed, his wife, Michelle, watched. He was completely absorbed in what he was doing. He was never really unaware of her, but his mind was somewhere else right now. He was making sure that he had all the information he had collected on Clare Markham, and all the results of the inquiries he had been doing through these weeks, mostly in the evenings and on his days off. There were probably people in the law enforcement community of Oklahoma who would have heard what he was doing and thought he was overconfident. How could one lone cop do a successful hunt for a murder suspect across the whole country all by himself? Michelle knew better. Fenton had decided it was now his job to take it on himself to find the girl who had killed his brother. She was as good as caught.

It had finally come to this. His plane would leave tomorrow morning. "Dave," she said.

"What?" he said, but he didn't look up from what he was doing.

"I really need to talk to you."

There was something in her voice that he sensed wasn't routine. He put a rolled shirt into a suitcase and turned to face her. "Is something wrong?"

"Yes," she said.

"Is this about my using vacation time to go after the girl?"

"Sort of. No." She stood there looking in his eyes. "This is hard for me. I want you to look at me."

He nodded.

"I've been trying to bring myself to this since Gerry died, but I thought something would happen if I waited. Somebody else would do it, or something. But that was stupid. You and I have been together for a long time, and I love you very much, and I always will until I die."

"I feel the same about you," he said. "You know that."

"You and I also know that Gerry did some wild things, some of them things that made us worry about how he was ever going to keep from having his record spoil his chances to have a decent life or a career."

"I could hardly forget."

"I've been thinking that there might be more to what the girl said happened than the DA believes. Than you believe."

Dave said, "Well, I understand that. You're a woman, and you see this kind of thing a little differently than the DA or a cop sees it. But we've seen some things in the years in our jobs that nice women haven't seen. We've also seen the evidence in this case."

"Dave, I know that what I'm going to say is going to put a terrible strain on you. It may even be the end of everything. But I know something that you have to know too, and right now. I know that Gerry was capable of raping that girl. I know it because he did it to me."

"What? When?"

"It was right after we got married. You were in Quantico taking a class from the FBI. I was home alone for about a month. He called and said he wanted to come over, said he had something for me to welcome me to the family. He came in, and we made some small talk, and I could tell there was something up, but I had no idea what it was. I went to the kitchen and got him a beer, and when I brought it into the living room, he was waiting for me. He dragged me into the bedroom and . . . did it. I was trying to fight him off, and when I screamed, he hit me so hard I saw a flash."

"Why didn't you tell me?"

"I was pretty sure you would kill him. Your life would be over. You would go to prison forever. He wouldn't have hurt just me, he would have ended the bright new life we had just started. I thought about it a long time, and decided I was not going to let him do that."

"Oh my God," he said. "I don't know what to say."

"I'm not done yet. I need you to know this part too. I cried for days. After a week went by, he called me up again and said he was coming over because we needed to talk about what had happened. I said I was willing to talk. When he walked in the door, he saw that I was aiming your .44 Magnum at him with both hands. I told him that if he ever came within three feet of me again, I would kill him, and that the only reason I didn't do it right then was that I would have to tell you and it would break your heart. For the rest of our marriage, I've had to see his smirk when he looked at me, like we had a secret. It wasn't like he had some crush on me, he was just mean. You and the other cops know a lot of things I don't know. But I know for certain that Gerry got stabbed because he was raping that girl and she had a chance to stop him. I didn't.

"I'm going downstairs now, to get started making dinner. When you've had time alone to think about it, you can either come down and tell me that you and I are done, and I'll come up and pack myself and the kids, or we'll all sit down together like we always have. Either way, the kids have to eat." She walked out of the bedroom, and he heard her going down the stairs.

He found himself sitting on the bed and realized his knees had buckled. He wondered if he had suspected his brother was capable of molesting anybody. Maybe he had years ago, but he had told himself that Gerry had matured into a fairly solid guy. His mind had never traveled into this territory, that his own brother would do this to his wife, or that he himself had put her in the position where she'd thought she had to cover up this ordeal for all these years. He realized that he was being a fool again, that he was just sitting up here when there was something he had to do right now. He stood and hurried to the staircase. In a moment he was down the stairs, and he could see her in the kitchen standing over the stove, just starting to cook. It took a dozen quick strides to reach her.

"I'm sorry, Michelle. I'm so sorry." He put his arms around her and held her gently. It was a long hug, and after a minute or two she could tell he was crying, something she'd never seen before, even when his parents died. Finally, he let her go, facing away, not letting her see he had tears on his face. "If I could dig him up and kill him again I would."

"I'm glad that isn't possible," she said. "I want it to be over. I don't want you to leave, and I don't want you to be the one to hunt down that girl."

"I'll cancel my flight tonight. Tomorrow I'll see if I can change my vacation days back to August."

38

The storage pod was delivered to the McKinnon house the day after the family returned from their two and a half months away. It took Carey, Jane, and Katie a week to put everything they owned back in its place, restock the house with food and supplies, and recreate the routines that they were used to. The special telephone that Jane reserved for conversations with a very small number of people rang as August was about to turn to September.

The voice on the phone was Karen Alvarez. Jane said, "I didn't expect to hear from you this soon. Is everything all right?"

Karen said, "With me? Sure. You know, over the past few weeks I've discovered that it takes a lot to get to me. Maybe I'm starting to grow up, finally."

"It's a theory."

"The reason I called is that I promised our friend Katie that I would keep track of a legal case she's interested in. There are developments."

Jane carried May and the phone into the room where Katie was reading. "Here you go," Jane said. "It's Karen Alvarez. There are developments." She handed Katie the phone and started to leave.

Katie said, "Wait. Karen, is it okay if Jane stays to hear this?"

"Only if you want her to."

"I do."

"Okay, then. Put me on speaker."

"You're on."

"Katie, a few days ago the district attorney in Oklahoma announced that they were dropping the murder charges against Clare Markham due to insufficient evidence. He didn't disclose any plans he or the State of Oklahoma had for the future."

Jane used her free arm to hug Katie. "Great!"

"Thank you, Karen. I can't believe it."

Karen said, "Let me explain the legal situation as clearly as I can. It's good news, for sure, but it's not everything. The death of Gerard Fenton has been ruled by the coroner to be a homicide. That isn't going to change. Somebody stabbed him and he died. So while the DA doesn't think they have enough evidence to convict Clare Markham, there is no statute of limitations on a homicide. If, ten or fifteen years from now, some cop finds something that changes the DA's mind, he can refile the charges. Or if he loses the next election in a year and there's a new DA, the new DA might decide that the evidence they have is sufficient and refile the murder charge, or file a charge of manslaughter, which is usually easier for a jury to convict on. He or she might instead charge Clare Markham with fleeing to evade prosecution for a felony, which could carry jail time, allowing them to imprison Clare and keep her available for a while—years—until they can make a case."

"Wow," Jane said. "That's a lot of information to think about. Thank you, Karen."

"I also consulted Elizabeth Howarth, who is another lawyer friend we both know," Karen said. "One of the points she made was that this Clare Markham person is a sixteen-year-old girl. It would take a couple of years, maybe much more, before a trial could happen. By then the defendant is likely to appear much more mature, and some of the jury could be swayed by that."

Jane said, "That is something to keep in mind."

Katie spoke in a voice so soft that it was hard to hear what she'd said.

"What?" Karen said.

"I said I'm not going back."

"No?"

"I'm grateful to you for all of this, Karen," Katie said, "Right now, it seems like I would be stupid to put my life in the hands of a DA who doesn't believe my story and already charged me once, or maybe some random person who wins his job next time. I would miss May and Jane and Carey. And Jane went to a lot of trouble and risk and got me into a good school. I want to stay here."

"Jane? What do you think?"

"I think she's a smart kid," Jane said. She watched Katie carry her book out of the room. "She's gone."

"So tell me what else you think," Karen said.

"When I went to her hometown, I didn't see much reason to believe that they could guarantee her a fair trial. I think the only way I would advise her to go back there is if a court dismissed the case because it was self-defense and ruled it could not be refiled in the future. I mean, this was a child defending herself against a grown man, using the knife he had on him. There was no way for her, or for anyone, to be sure he wasn't planning to kill her afterward."

"It happens," Karen said.

"She'll probably do very well in school here. She spent some time this summer reviewing last year's work and getting a taste of next year's, and since then she's been doing a lot of reading. She's a relative of mine and May's, and we all love having her here."

"I understand. I'll let you know if anything changes," Karen said.

"Thanks. How is your medical treatment going?"

"Three operations so far, and two 'procedures.' They seemed suspiciously like surgery too, but those are the terms. There will end up being some marks, but clothes will cover them, and when there are no clothes involved, I'll be very sexy and very responsive so the guy doesn't notice them."

"Is there a particular guy?"

"Well, there's a promising candidate, but this one is too smart and too attentive to fool, so I'm not sure. I told him I'd been in a car accident. I can tell he knows I was lying, but he still keeps coming around."

"Give him a chance."

"As soon as the bandages come off. I'll talk to you soon."

"Bye."

Jane ended the call and carried May upstairs to the bedroom she and Carey shared. She set May in the room's playpen and talked to her while she picked out the clothes she would wear that night, carried them down the hall to one of the spare bedrooms, and hung them in the closet.

◆

It was after 2:00 A.M. when Jane opened her eyes and slipped out of the bed. She looked down at her sleeping husband for a full minute to be sure he was not about to wake, then walked to the spare room. She dressed, went down the stairs and out the door without making a sound. She'd had a decade to learn the places to step and how to navigate the big old house in the dark without disturbing her husband, or more recently, her baby.

She went outside and started her car while it was still in the closed garage, and only opened the garage door after the engine was idling. She shifted, let it drift out of the garage, and then turned it and let it coast down the long driveway to the street and make the turn without stepping on the brakes or switching on the headlights. In a moment she was driving along the road at forty miles an hour, heading for the small town along the Niagara River. It was where her mother, the blond, blue-eyed woman who never said much about her past, and her Seneca father had raised her. Her mother had told her that the only part of her life that she was willing to spend a minute remembering had started on the day she'd met Jane's father in New York City, where he and some friends had gone to work on the steel skeleton of a tall building.

They had both been dead for a long time now, her father from a fall from a bridge under construction in the state of Washington, and her mother from cancer's slow, painful descent. They had been the best kind of parents, an unlikely matching of opposites. Jane hated what she was going to have to do tonight, which was why she was going about it so quickly.

The house had been one of her easiest ways of feeling closer to both of them, and to her grandfather and grandmother, the young couple of almost a century ago, the man who built the house and the woman who had inhabited it and loved it and scrubbed every inch of it so each floorboard gleamed at sunrise when the light shone in the front windows and down the hallways.

It had been a special place then, and it had played a big part in everything that Jane had done since then. There were a lot of people who were alive and living under names Jane had given them because that house had been there. It was their first stop after terrifying escapes from monsters.

While she was waiting at the light at Amherst and Delaware, she took out her phone and pressed the name Jake Reinert. The silence was replaced by Jake's voice. "This is Jake."

"I'll be there in a few minutes."

"I'll be awake."

"Thanks, Jake. I'll talk to you in a day or two."

"Right. Good-bye."

The red traffic light went off, and the green light came on.

Jane drove the rest of the way into town, left her car between the buildings of the long-closed factory, put her hair under a cap, and trotted along the empty street, reached the inhabited section, and used the deeper darkness under the old trees to keep herself invisible. She had run this route with Brian Finlay weeks ago, and had never heard anything to indicate that they had appeared on anybody's security cameras. She had noticed a long time ago that a person who looked like she was out jogging wasn't of much interest to the suspicious, even at some weird hour.

She made it to the house, kept going to the kitchen door, opened it, and went inside. She walked through it without stopping, opened the door in the hallway, and went down the stairs in the basement. She didn't turn on the light, simply turned on her phone. She looked up at the five rounded air ducts that extended from the top of the old coal furnace, along the wooden boards above her head and then upward into the first floor and beyond. She had used those old ducts since her mother died to hide things—guns, money, documents—and only removed the last of them a few days after she'd returned from the West. She walked to the far end where her father's old workbench was.

The bench had a number of paint cans, a few cans of thinner and turpentine that dated from the days before he had died. She had selected one of the turpentine cans a few days ago because it had apparently been left outside at some point, and had rusted along the bottom edge. She had used a nail file to scratch at the thin, rusted area to find the weakest spot, made a tiny open space in the rust, set it on the wooden workbench, and refilled it with another can and watched the turpentine drip its fresh contents onto the unfinished wood. The smell was strong right now. She looked at the nearby outboard motor that was clamped to the wooden stand her father had made. There was a five-gallon can of gasoline beside it. The big oil tank along the wall in the middle of the basement near the furnace had been refilled during the spring, as always.

Jane went to the bench, took the lighter out of her pocket, and flicked it. She looked at the flame, then held it to the dark spot where the turpentine had soaked into the wood. The flame flickered, then caught, dancing on the wood, making the basement brighter as Jane walked away from it and climbed the stairs, two at a time. She took a last look from the top, and the whole bench was going up, the flames rising toward the old rounded wooden beams that supported the planks of the ground floor of the house.

Then she went out, leaving the basement door open so the fire wouldn't run out of oxygen. In ten steps she was outside, turning around to lock the kitchen door. Then she stood still. In the old language she said, "Grandfather, Grandmother, you know why I couldn't use your house anymore. You know why I couldn't sell it or have anybody living there when the next bad people come. Father and Mother, you know that I had to do this. We're done here. I'm turning this place into memories. Nobody else is going to die here because of me."

She took a last look, turned, and began to run. She kept her face lifted to the night sky and breathed so deeply that the air felt like freedom.

39

Carey walked around in the kitchen carrying May. "These are my keys. One of them starts the car, one of them—this one here—opens the door to our house, this one opens my office at the hospital. Here are my sunglasses, to protect my eyes while I'm driving to work. In the winter it's usually dark when I drive in, because I start doing surgeries at seven o'clock, but near the end of summer, like today, the sun is already low in the east, but it can be very bright. I'm going to give you back to your mother now. I hate to leave, but there are people waiting who don't feel good, and I can help them."

He kissed her cheek softly, handed her to Jane, and leaned close so he could give Jane a grown-up kiss. He said to her, "See you later. Love you."

"I know," she said. "But I still like it when you remind me like this."

As soon as she heard Carey's car go down the driveway, she began to be aware of the sounds of Katie coming down the stairs. She looked at the open doorway, waiting for her to appear.

She came in, her eyebrows knitted and her eyes studying Jane for a reaction.

"Wow. You look great, honey." It was true. Katie was lucky that she didn't have any of the complexion problems that made a lot of teenagers suffer. She had wonderful black hair that hung straight down her back, and an athletic body. The new clothes that she and Jane had picked out over the past weeks looked good on her.

Jane knew that last evening Katie had laid out the things she was going to need for her first day of school. Jane had pretended that she was utterly confident that Katie had packed all the necessary and appropriate things, but after Katie had gone to sleep she had secretly checked her bag. She saw her printed class schedule, pens and pencils, laptop, phone, notebook, and so on. Jane had also found protein bars and fruit, obviously put there in case Katie wanted to retreat from the cafeteria at lunchtime. It had made Jane feel sad for Katie, but she was pretty sure that when she looked in Katie's bag later, she would find the emergency food was still in there.

"You really think I look okay?" Katie said.

"Better than okay. Definitely. You're all set—clothes, makeup, everything. Just remember to smile at people, respond to anybody who talks to you, and be confident. There's likely to be nobody in your new school who has lived through anything like the things you have. You're as brave and strong as anybody, and very smart. Relax and jump in."

"Thanks, Jane."

"What do you want for breakfast?"

"I'll make it."

"No, I insist. You hold May and I'll make you something. How about an omelet?"

"That sounds good." Katie smiled. "I woke up kind of early, so I'm pretty hungry."

Jane made Katie's breakfast, went upstairs for her shower, dressed, and came down to drive her to the Stanhope School. While she was driving Katie to school, Jane talked to keep her mind off her anxiety. "I'll be driving you to and from school until you get your license. You're the right age for that. We made your birthday be in August, so we can get you started whenever you want."

"I already know how to drive. I got my permit the day after I turned fifteen. That's the age in Oklahoma, and I was about to take the license test when my grandmother got sick. Then she died and I never got around to it."

"I'm sorry about that," Jane said. "I'm glad you can drive, though."

They talked about other things that had little to do with school all the way until Jane drove up through the tall iron gates to the parking lot of the school. Other students were already getting out of cars and walking toward the front entrance of the main building, talking with first-day excitement with friends they saw every day and friends who had been away for the summer. Jane said, "What do you think? I'll bet it looks a lot like your old school on the first day."

"Right," Katie said. "I'm ready."

"You can call me if you want."

"It's against the rules except in emergencies and stuff. I'll call you when it's over." Jane watched her as she got out of the car and headed for the front entrance. Jane inched her car forward in the drop-off line. The parents ahead of her had to wait for openings to turn onto the street, so the process was slow. She scanned the high school kids near the front steps and spotted Katie. There were three girls her age looking at her, and then Jane saw them approach Katie tentatively. Yes, those were smiles. Katie said something too, and her smile matched theirs. They all started up the school steps, still talking. Jane exhaled. One win.

Jane moved her car ahead again, and swung out between the gates of the school, looking much the way two or three hundred other parents looked that morning.

As Jane drove toward the expressway, she glanced at May in her car mirror. "We're going to do something different today. We'll stop and see Jake." She returned her eyes to the road ahead. "He went around to all the neighbors and woke them up and made sure they were safe the night of the fire, and timed the 911 call so the fire department got there just at the right time. He'll want to tell us all about it. Maybe we can watch the crew drive the big bulldozers through what's left of the old house, truck the wreckage away, and level the lot, so the ground can go back to being just green land.

"Another day maybe we'll plant something there. What about flowering bushes? Or a garden? The old people used to plant big gardens. They planted corns, beans, and squash. They called them 'The Three Sisters.' We'll have nearly a school year to think about it, because you have to start those crops in the spring. They used to figure out when it was time by looking at the first leaves that grew back on the trees, and when a leaf was the size of a squirrel's ear, they knew it was the right time to plant. Maybe we should plant blueberry and currant bushes where the old house was right away, and our 'Three Sisters' at home, so you and I can tend them and watch them grow."

The End

A LETTER FROM JO PERRY

When the editor-in-chief of Mysterious Press asked me to write something to accompany a letter Thomas wrote to you, I found myself in a jam. What could I say when our family's grief is so fresh and when Thomas was so well-known?

Then I remembered that love doesn't die—ours for him and his for us—especially when love is deep and long—and that each love is its own story.

Thomas and I fell in love and married forty-five years ago. He died a few weeks before we planned to celebrate the forty-sixth anniversary of our first date with dinner at a favorite old restaurant in Hollywood. Our marriage was happy, but like Jane Whitefield, I struggled with infertility—and this is where my resemblance to Jane begins and ends. Eventually Thomas and I shared the joy of being parents. That he missed the happiness of being a grandfather to his beautiful grandson—one week old as I write this—is heartbreaking. I know that he would have dedicated this book to him.

Thomas was a compassionate and brilliant father and husband. But the private, interior process that is writing was the center of his life, perhaps because writing the way he did required that he use all gifts at once—intelligence, modesty, honesty courage, cleverness, humor, compassion, inventiveness, curiosity and clarity. Through the years he created fictional people so real and interesting that they became part of our family—and perhaps part of your family, too—and changed the way we saw and experienced the world: The Butcher's Boy, Eddie, and Elizabeth Waring; Joe Carver and Kapak; Jack Till; Justine Poole; Chinese Gordon and Dr. Henry Metzger; Jane Whitefield, the specter Harry, Cary, her terrifying enemies, and the desperate people whose lives she transformed and freed—and all other indelible characters with whom Thomas populated his stories.

Thomas enjoyed real people, too. One of the pleasures of writing for him was getting to know his readers in person and through correspondence. Many became friends. So, it feels right that his letter to you concludes *A Tree of Light and Flowers*.

Now that Thomas is gone, if you expected me to reveal something shocking or scandalous about him, I must disappoint you. He was never a hit man, a thief, a mobster or a criminal; he was a good man. And you know everything about him that matters already: The sound of his voice on page, the way he thought, the things he hated and those he loved are in his books, especially in the books about Jane Whitefield whom he admired and cared about so much.

I hope you feel his presence in the book you are about to read. He lives in his pages now.

Jo Perry

November 2, 2025

A LETTER TO THE READER

I'd like to tell you about my new novel to be published in January, 2026. It's the tenth volume of the Jane Whitefield series, *The Tree of Light and Flowers*. I've been writing books about Jane Whitefield since *Vanishing Act*, published thirty years ago. Jane is a Seneca woman who takes people who come to her with convincing reasons to believe they are about to be murdered, guides them to new places, and teaches them to live under new identities. She refers to them as her "runners." Robbing a murderer of his next victim is always dangerous work, and I've tried to keep it as dangerous as I could for Jane.

Since Jane fell in love and married Dr. Carey McKinnon, the surgeon she had met when they were undergraduate students, she has wanted to have a baby. In spite of her unusual courage, intelligence, and willingness to make sacrifices, she wishes for the same things many other women want—a stable, secure life with her husband and a family. The way I kept Jane at work was to deny her wish. Jane and Carey were afflicted with the frustration and heartbreak of unexplained infertility. They endured years of tests and procedures, and shared some times of hope, always followed by disappointment.

Eventually Jane accepted the overwhelming evidence that the baby would never come. As her life went on and she saved more people, her adversaries became more numerous and more frightening. The worst and most powerful of them had realized that the most valuable prize was Jane herself. She knew where her many runners were living, who they were now, and who might pay well to know, too. The lives of those runners depended on Jane's promise that she would die rather than reveal to anyone how to find them. To keep her promise from being a lie, she carried with her an extract of the poison water hemlock plant, her Seneca ancestors' preferred method of suicide.

Jane Whitefield books only happen when two conditions are met. First, I begin to miss her and wonder what she would be doing right now, and second, I realize that I've learned something about her that the reader doesn't know yet.

At the end of the ninth book, I had left Jane realizing she was pregnant. That book was published four years ago, surely a world-record for human pregnancies. It was time to make a decision. I wanted to give her what she'd wanted for so long, but I also felt that Jane would not be the sort of parent who would put a child in jeopardy or risk leaving a baby motherless.

As I was pondering the issue, I remembered something we all learn from living. We are only in charge of what we do, not what happens to us. Most often, people don't go out to find trouble. Trouble finds us. What does a mother do when she and her family are in mortal danger? Whatever she has to, whatever she can. If you'd like to know what Jane can do, I hope you'll read *The Tree of Light and Flowers*.

Sincerely,

Thomas Perry